Murder Most Somerset

The Taunton Tension

Lord Parker

Contents

Chapter 1 Whispers in the Park

In the quaint market town of Taunton, the name Roger Morgan was synonymous with photographic excellence. A true master of his craft, Roger had built a reputation that extended far beyond the boundaries of Somerset, his work celebrated and admired by enthusiasts and professionals alike.

Roger Morgan's home was a testament to his life's work—a sanctuary where the art of photography intertwined with the personal threads of his existence. Nestled on the outskirts of Taunton, the cottage was as much a gallery as it was a dwelling, with walls adorned with the fruits of his labour. Each frame captured a moment of natural splendour, a testament to the years he had dedicated to perfecting his craft.

The early morning light filtered through the bay window, casting a soft glow on the oak desk that served as Roger's creative altar. Here, amidst a meticulously organized chaos of lenses, memory cards, and editing equipment, he laboured over his photographs, each one a piece of his soul rendered in light and shadow. The desk was littered with notes and sketches, a roadmap of a mind that saw the world through a unique perspective.

Roger stood before his latest collection, a series of images that captured the ephemeral dance of dew on petals. These were more than mere entries for the upcoming Flower Show; they were the culmination of a year's worth of patience and passion. He adjusted the lighting, ensuring that each photograph was displayed to its best advantage, his critical eye catching the smallest details.

In the corner of the room, a shelf held an array of photography awards, gleaming under the watchful eye of a single dusty trophy from his days as a landscape architect. It was a silent nod to the path not taken; the life he could have led had the call of the camera not been so insistent.

Roger was so engrossed in his work that he didn't hear Margaret enter the room. She stood silently for a moment, watching him with a mixture of admiration and frustration.

"You're up early," Margaret said, her voice breaking the quiet.

Roger turned, a warm smile spreading across his face. "Good morning, love. I just wanted to get the lighting right for these new shots."

Margaret walked over, her eyes scanning the photographs. "They're beautiful as always. But don't you think you spend too much time in here? We barely see each other anymore."

Roger's smile faltered slightly. "I know, Margaret. But this is important. The Flower Show is just around the corner, and these photos need to be perfect."

Margaret sighed, her frustration evident. "It's always about the Flower Show, Roger. Sometimes I feel like your photography means more to you than our marriage."

Roger reached out, taking her hands in his. "That's not true, Margaret. You know how much I love you. It's just... this is my passion. It's what I'm good at."

Margaret pulled her hands away, her expression hardening. "Passion or obsession? There's a difference. When was the last time we had a proper dinner together? Or even just a quiet evening without you rushing off to your darkroom?"

Roger looked down, guilt washing over him. "I'm sorry, Margaret. I promise after the Flower Show I'll make more time for us. We'll go on that trip you've been wanting."

Margaret shook her head, her eyes glistening with unshed tears. "I've heard that before. Just... don't forget that I'm here too, Roger. I miss you."

Roger felt a pang of regret as he watched her leave the room, her words echoing in his mind. He turned back to his photographs, but the joy he had felt moments before was now tinged with a sadness he couldn't shake.

For years, Roger had been a fixture at the annual Flower Show, his keen eye and artistic sensibility capturing the vibrant hues and delicate beauty of nature's finest blooms. His photographs were more than mere images; they were living, breathing canvases that seemed to transport viewers into the very heart of each flower, allowing them to appreciate the intricate details and subtle nuances that often went unnoticed.

Yet for all his public acclaim, Roger wrestled with private doubts. The solitary hours spent in the darkroom, the relentless pursuit of the perfect shot—these had come at a cost. His marriage, though outwardly stable, bore the silent cracks of neglect, and his friendships within the community were often strained by the competitive undercurrents his success had fostered.

Roger's talent had not gone unrecognized. Time and again, his entries in the show's prestigious photography competition had taken home top honours, earning him a coveted place among the elite ranks of local artists. His winning photographs, masterfully framed and displayed with pride, had become a highlight of the show, drawing crowds of admirers who marvelled at his ability to capture the essence of the natural world.

But the accolades could not silence the nagging voice in his head that whispered of luck and timing rather than skill. Nor could they fill the growing void within—a longing for genuine connection that his lens could not capture. Roger's passion for photography had become both his bridge to the world and his barrier from it.

Beyond his artistic accomplishments, Roger was a beloved figure in the community, known for his warm demeanour and generous spirit. He was a mentor to aspiring photographers, freely sharing his knowledge and techniques, encouraging others to explore the boundless possibilities of the lens. His infectious passion for his craft inspired many to pick up a camera and see the world through a new, more appreciative lens.

Yet even as he taught others, Roger grappled with the fear that his own vision had plateaued. The familiar landscapes and subjects that had once sparked his imagination now seemed to mock him with their constancy. He yearned for a new challenge, a way to reinvent his work, but the comfort of his established niche in Taunton's artistic community was a siren song that was difficult to resist.

As Roger prepared for another Flower Show, he couldn't shake the feeling that he was an imposter in his own life, playing the part of the celebrated photographer while secretly dreading the day his well of inspiration would run dry. It was a fear he kept locked away, a shadow that trailed behind the bright light of his public persona.

Roger Morgan's journey to photographic excellence was a tapestry woven with threads of ambition, loss, and serendipity. As the soft morning light bathed his collection of framed accolades, each one a silent witness to his triumphs, Roger's mind wandered back to the pivotal moments that had led him here.

It was during his tenure as a landscape architect that Roger first felt the pull of the camera. He had a knack for envisioning spaces, for seeing the potential beauty in the undulating curves of the land and the way light played off the surfaces of his creations. Yet he found himself frustrated by the transience of his projects, the way gardens would change and buildings would weather. He wanted to capture their perfection forever, and photography became his tool to do so.

The first photograph that changed everything was an accident—a snapshot of a morning dewdrop clinging precariously to a jade-green leaf, the world reflected in its miniature globe. The image was a revelation, a moment of pure beauty frozen in time. It was then that Roger knew he had found his true calling. He began to carry his camera everywhere, documenting the interplay of nature and the structures he designed, his two passions merging into one.

Roger's transition from architect to photographer was not without its challenges. He spent countless hours learning the craft, studying light, composition, and technique with the dedication of a man possessed. His breakthrough came with a series of photos capturing the ethereal beauty of Somerset's landscapes—a fusion of his architectural eye and his newfound photographic prowess. These images garnered attention, first from local art circles, then from national galleries, and finally international acclaim.

With each passing year, Roger's reputation grew. His work was featured in prestigious exhibitions, and he was invited to judge competitions. The annual Flower Show became a showcase for his talent, his photographs consistently outshining the competition. The awards on his wall were not just metal and glass; they were milestones marking his journey from a man who shaped the land to one who captured its essence.

Despite his success, Roger remained grounded. He remembered the struggle of those early days, the hunger to learn, and the need for guidance. He became a mentor to young photographers, sharing his knowledge generously. His workshops were always full, his lectures well-attended. He took pride in the successes of his protégés, their achievements adding another layer of satisfaction to his own.

As Roger stood in his study, surrounded by the artifacts of his storied career, he couldn't help but feel a twinge of nostalgia for the days of uncertainty, for the thrill of discovery that had once driven him. Yet he also felt a deep sense of gratitude for the winding path that had brought him to this moment, for the chance encounters and the choices made that had shaped him into the artist he had become.

Roger's gaze drifted to a photograph that stood apart from the rest—a candid shot of a woman laughing, her image slightly blurred as if caught in a moment of pure joy. This was his wife, Margaret, the woman who had supported his dreams even when they meant sacrifice. The photo was a bittersweet reminder of a time when their love was as vibrant as the flowers he so loved to capture.

The scent of coffee wafted from the kitchen, a daily ritual that Margaret upheld with an almost religious fervour. It was one of the many small threads that wove their lives together, a shared moment of normalcy in a life that was anything but ordinary.

The past was a mosaic of moments, each one captured in the click of a shutter, and as Roger prepared to unveil his latest work at the Flower Show, he knew that his journey was far from over. Each photograph was a new beginning, a new opportunity to see the world through his lens and share its hidden wonders with those who sought to look deeper.

Chapter 2 Preparations and Paranoia

As Roger prepared to leave for the Flower Show preparations, he paused at the doorway, taking one last look at his sanctuary. This room was a chronicle of his journey, each photograph a chapter, each award a milestone. But beyond the accolades and the acclaim, it was the unspoken stories, the hidden complexities of his life, that truly defined the man behind the lens.

With a deep breath, Roger stepped out of his home and into the bustle of Taunton, ready to face the world with his art and his secrets tucked close to his heart. The Flower Show awaited, and with it the promise of beauty and the peril of old resentments that lay just beneath the surface of the idyllic town.

The market town, alive with the fervour of the Flower Show preparations, greeted him with a symphony of sights and sounds that had become the backdrop to his life's work.

The cobbled streets, worn smooth by the passage of countless vehicles, wound through the town like a stream of history. They led past ancient timber-framed shops that leaned towards each other in companionable slants, their windows dressed in finery befitting the festive occasion. The air was rich with the scent of fresh-cut flowers from the florists, mingling with the aromatic promise of local bakeries where the warm buttery smell of pastries spilled out onto the street.

Market stalls had sprung up like vibrant mushrooms overnight, each canopy a splash of colour against the stone and brick of the town's architecture. Vendors hawked their wares with the good-natured banter of those who loved their trade—fresh produce piled high in a mosaic of greens, reds, and yellows, while artisans displayed their crafts, the fruits of winter's labour ready for the discerning eyes of locals and tourists alike.

Roger navigated through the throngs of people, a tapestry of faces that reflected the town's anticipation for the Flower Show. There were families with children in tow, their laughter rising above the din, and elderly couples who moved with a leisurely pace that spoke of years spent in each other's company. Young couples meandered hand in hand, stealing kisses as if the world around them had faded into the background.

The first of his encounters was with Mrs. Penelope Ashford, the owner of the local bakery, whose scones were as much a staple of Taunton as the annual show itself. "Morning, Roger!" she called out, her hands dusted with flour. "I expect you'll be taking home another ribbon this year?"

Roger offered a humble smile, the kind that had smoothed over many a competitive edge. "I'll be happy just to share my work, Penny. But your scones are the true prize winners here."

Laughter and the scent of baked goods followed him as he continued, nodding to the townsfolk who greeted him with a mix of reverence and warm familiarity. The local florist tipped his hat, the young couple who ran the bookshop waved, and the children darted around his legs with paper flowers in their hands.

Further along, the majestic presence of Taunton Minster church loomed, its spire reaching towards the heavens. The churchyard was a quiet haven from the market's bustle, where the gravestones stood as silent guardians of the past. The ancient yews whispered secrets on the breeze, and the stained-glass windows captured the sunlight, transforming it into a kaleidoscope of colours that danced upon the stone floor inside.

As Roger navigated the church path, his eyes caught sight of Stephen Smith, the very embodiment of the bitterness that had been simmering beneath the surface of the town's festive spirit. Stephen was hunched over his camera, his focus on capturing the perfect angle of the church's spire, a task that consumed all his attention.

"Stephen," Roger greeted, his voice measured, betraying none of the unease he felt at the impending confrontation.

Stephen's head snapped up, his eyes narrowing as they fixed on Roger. The camera, once a tool of artistry, now felt like a barrier between them. "Morgan," he replied, the word heavy with a resentment that had been festering for years.

Roger cleared his throat, attempting to bridge the chasm of animosity with civility. "The Minster makes for a fine subject, doesn't it? Timeless."

Stephen Smith grew up in a middle-class family in Taunton and developed a passion for photography from a young age. His parents supported his hobby, buying him his first DSLR camera when he was 16.

Stephen showed immense talent and won several youth photography competitions in his teens.

After finishing university, Stephen decided to pursue photography semi-professionally instead of getting an office job. He participated in as many competitions as he could, including the prestigious Taunton Flower Show photography contest. For several years, Stephen was a finalist and even won the competition in 2018.

However, in 2019, Stephen was disqualified from the Taunton contest for a minor rules infraction - he had slightly edited one of his entries using Photoshop, which was against the rules. It was Roger Morgan, one of the judges, who caught this violation. Stephen was devastated, as he had been the favourite to win that year's grand prize.

Since then, Stephen has harboured a deep grudge against Roger Morgan and the competition itself. He feels the rules were petty and his disqualification was unjustly harsh given his talent. Missing out on the potential exposure and a big career boost from winning left Stephen bitter.

Stephen's immense passion and competitiveness about photography drove him to perfectionism, but his arrogance about his skills and accomplishments made him hold grudges, especially against those he felt had wronged him. His obsession with adhering to his own moral code of ethics often put him at odds with others, and he struggled with managing emotions like anger and resentment.

The disqualification stung deeply, and Stephen's resentment towards Roger Morgan had only grown over time. His desire for revenge on the competition for the perceived injustice and his need to prove his moral superiority over those he saw as hypocrites had become a consuming force in his life. He yearned to regain the recognition and career advancement he felt was stolen from him.

Stephen snorted, his lips twisting into a wry smile that didn't reach his eyes. "Timeless indeed. Unlike the fleeting fame of certain photographers."

The air grew thick with unspoken accusations, the tranquillity of the churchyard doing little to soften the edge in Stephen's voice. "I suppose you're here to scout for more subjects to claim as your own?" he asked, the bitterness in his tone sharp as a blade.

Roger felt the sting of the words, a reminder of the disqualification that had driven a wedge between them. "The rules are the rules, Stephen. You know that as well as I do."

Stephen's laugh was hollow, a sound that echoed off the church walls with a mocking resonance. "Rules. Is that what you hide behind when you're not busy playing kingmaker? Tell me, Roger, does it ever get tiring holding the dreams of others in your hands, deciding who gets to shine and who doesn't?"

The accusation hung in the air, a spectre of the past that neither man could escape. Roger's success had come at a price, and Stephen's thwarted ambitions were the currency. "I've always admired your work, Stephen. It was never personal."

"Never personal?" Stephen's voice rose, a crescendo of years of pent-up frustration. "You made it personal when you took my chance away. When you stood there smug and self-righteous while my work was cast aside."

The silence that followed was heavy, laden with the weight of their shared history. The Minster, with its ancient gravestones and whispered prayers, stood as a silent witness to the deep-seated rivalry that had taken root in the fertile ground of their passions.

Roger, feeling the futility of further words, gave a slight nod and began to withdraw, the framed photographs under his arm a reminder of the exhibition that awaited. "Good luck with the competition, Stephen," he said, though the words felt hollow even to his own ears.

Stephen watched Roger's retreating figure, his expression a complex tapestry of anger, envy, and a begrudging respect for the man who had become the unwitting architect of his discontent. As the distance grew between them, so too did the resolve within Stephen—a resolve to reclaim the recognition he felt was rightfully his, no matter the cost.

Roger Morgan's passage through the streets of Taunton was a journey marked by the familiar faces of a community intertwined with his own legacy. The morning air was crisp, the kind that heralded the arrival of the Flower Show, an event that painted the town with a brush of excitement and camaraderie.

As he strolled down Hammet Street, he could see the Market House, its grand facade a sentinel watching over the town centre. Roger felt the pulse of the market's heart. The building had stood for centuries, a witness to the ebb and flow of Taunton's life, and now it served as a hub for the day's activities. The chatter of bargaining, the clink of coins, and the rustle of paper bags filled the air with a music that was the lifeblood of the town.

As Roger stood in front of the Market House, the atmosphere subtly shifted. The friendly banter of the market vendors was tinged with an undercurrent of anticipation, and the smiles of the townsfolk were laced with a hint of competition. The Flower Show was not just a display of beauty; it was a battleground for local artists, each yearning for recognition.

At the entrance to the Market House, Roger's path crossed with that of Clara Bennett, a fellow photographer whose work in macro flower photography had begun to gain attention. "Roger, always a pleasure to see you," Clara said, her voice carrying a note of genuine respect tempered with a competitive edge.

"And you, Clara. Your work has been quite the talk of the town. I'm looking forward to seeing your exhibit," Roger replied, his words both a compliment and an acknowledgment of the rising talent around him.

Their exchange was brief, a dance of mutual respect between rivals, before Clara moved on, her camera bag slung over her shoulder, her mind already focused on the day ahead.

Behind the Market House, vendors were setting up their stalls and displays, the air thick with the smell of fresh flowers and the sound of hushed conversations about the day's prospects.

It was here that Roger encountered David Walker, his presence like a storm cloud over the sunny day. Their greeting was a mere formality, the civility of their words doing little to mask the tension that crackled between them.

David Walker had been a working photographer in Taunton for over 25 years. He started out doing portrait photography for families and weddings but gradually transitioned into landscape and architectural photography as his passion and talent grew.

In the early 2000s, David began entering and winning awards in local photography competitions, including the prestigious Taunton Flower Show contest. His moody, evocative shots of historic buildings and countryside scenes brought him acclaim.

However, David always felt he never quite got the recognition he deserved from his peers. He believed his work was frequently overlooked in favour of photographers with more conventional styles. This bred resentment in David towards the Taunton photography community over the years.

The final straw came in 2019 when David took an exceptional nighttime photograph of the Castle Hotel that he was immensely proud of. Months later, he discovered Roger Morgan, a rival photographer, had been using that same image without credit in promotional materials. When David confronted Roger, he was simply brushed off.

This incident made David feel that his work was being openly stolen and disrespected by the very people who were supposed to be his community. He became obsessed with proving his talents were being suppressed by the corrupt insiders running the Taunton photography scene.

David's arrogance about his photography skills and artistic vision was matched only by his deep-seated insecurities and yearning for validation from his peers. He held grudges easily when he felt disrespected and became obsessive about protecting his work and legacy. Increasingly paranoid about perceived slights and conspiracies, David's motivations were driven by a desire to expose what he saw as a corrupt system suppressing true talent and to cement his legacy as one of the great Taunton photographers.

"Roger," David acknowledged, his tone cool and measured.

"David," Roger returned the greeting, his eyes briefly taking in the photographs that David was arranging with meticulous care.

Their conversation was a chess match of veiled barbs and half-concealed animosity, a reflection of the history that lay between them. It was well-known that David harboured resentment towards Roger, believing his own work to be overshadowed by what he perceived as Roger's undue influence within the community.

As Roger excused himself, the air seemed to relax around them, the tension dissipating as he moved away from David's orbit. The encounters that followed were a blend of polite exchanges and subtle jockeying for position, a reminder that beneath the surface of the Flower Show's beauty lay the thorns of ambition and rivalry.

Chapter 3 Floral Festivities and Fractures

Roger's journey took him finally to the gates of Vivary Park, the verdant jewel of Taunton. The park was a canvas awaiting the final brushstrokes of the Flower Show, with volunteers adding splashes of colour to the landscape. The grand Victorian fountain, soon to be the centrepiece of the show, stood silent for now, its waters still as if in anticipation of the crowds that would come to marvel at its splendour.

Entering the park, Roger felt the collective anticipation for the Flower Show, the town's excitement almost tangible. Amidst the natural beauty and community spirit, he found a sense of home, his photographs serving as a bridge between his unique perspective and the eager eyes of the show's visitors.

Finding a secluded bench beneath the outstretched arms of an ancient oak, Roger set down his framed photographs with care, their glass surfaces reflecting the dappled sunlight. He sat, his hands clasped together, fingers entwined as if to hold together the fraying edges of his composure.

The park around him was a palette of vibrant colours and the hum of eager anticipation, but to Roger it all seemed muted, distant. The encounters with David and Stephen had opened old wounds, revealing the festering resentment that lay beneath the surface of his success.

Roger closed his eyes, allowing himself a moment of vulnerability, shielded from the eyes of the world. He pondered the path that had led him here, to this bench, to this moment of introspection. His rise to prominence in the world of photography had not been without its sacrifices—friendships strained, rivalries born, and the ever-present question of whether his passion for his art was worth the cost.

He thought of David's scathing words, the accusation of theft that had never truly been resolved, and Stephen's raw anger over a disqualification that had cut deep. Roger had always prided himself on his integrity, on upholding the standards of the competitions he judged. But in the pursuit of fairness, had he been blind to the personal toll his decisions had taken on others?

The weight of their animosity was a heavy burden, and Roger couldn't help but wonder if the accolades hanging on his walls were a fair trade for the enmity he had earned. Was the recognition of his peers and the public worth the isolation that now seemed to envelop him?

A soft breeze stirred the leaves above, and Roger opened his eyes to the play of light and shadow on the path before him. He had always sought to capture the beauty of the world through his lens, to share the moments of wonder that so often went unnoticed. Yet in doing so, had he become blind to the beauty of human connection, to the need for empathy and understanding?

With a sigh, Roger stood, his resolve returning. He knew that he could not undo the past, nor could he control the feelings of those who saw him as an adversary. But he could control how he moved forward, how he interacted with the world and those who shared his passion for photography.

Picking up his photographs, Roger continued on his way to the competition tent, the weight of introspection now balanced with a renewed sense of purpose. He would face the competition with grace, offer his work to the judgment of others, and perhaps find a way to mend the bridges that had been burned along the way.

The path ahead was uncertain, the outcome of the day's events unknowable. But Roger Morgan, renowned photographer and unwitting catalyst of rivalry, would meet it all with the quiet strength that had brought him this far. The price of his success was high, but the value of self-awareness and the possibility of reconciliation were worth any cost.

The evening had settled over Taunton like a soft blanket, the last vestiges of twilight fading into the deep blue of a clear night sky. Roger Morgan sat in the quiet solitude of his study, the only sounds the gentle ticking of the grandfather clock and the occasional rustle of leaves outside his window. The day's encounters had left him with a lingering sense of unease, the shadows of discord with David and Stephen casting a pall over his thoughts.

As he reviewed his photographs for the umpteenth time, seeking solace in the familiar contours and colours of his work, the ping of his computer broke the silence. A new email had arrived, its subject line blank and the sender's address unfamiliar. Roger's first instinct was to dismiss it as spam, but something compelled him to open the message.

The words on the screen were terse, the tone unmistakably ominous: "Meet me at 2 am by the clubhouse in Vivary Park. You'll want to hear what I have to say about your future in photography."

Roger's brow furrowed, his heart rate quickening. The message was void of any signature; its origin as mysterious as its intent. A rational part of his mind screamed at the absurdity of the situation—the late hour, the anonymity, the veiled threat to his career. Yet curiosity gnawed at him, a persistent whisper that this could be something crucial, something that might affect the very foundation of his life's work.

He glanced at the clock, the hands inching ever closer to the appointed hour. The idea of venturing out into the night to meet a faceless stranger was madness, and yet the seed of concern for his reputation had been planted. The recent animosity from his peers, the whispered accusations, and the undercurrent of jealousy—it all swirled together into a vortex that threatened to swallow his achievements whole.

Roger stood, pacing the length of the room as he weighed his options. To ignore the message could mean allowing whatever machinations were at work to proceed unchecked. To attend the meeting was to step into the unknown, to potentially confront an adversary or a situation he was ill-prepared to face.

The photographs on the wall seemed to watch him, the blooms captured in still life a stark contrast to the turmoil within. He thought of Margaret, of the life they had built together, and the tranquillity that had always been his anchor. Could he risk it all on a mysterious summons?

Yet as the minutes ticked by, Roger's resolve hardened. His reputation, his art, his very identity as a photographer—they were the essence of who he was. If someone sought to threaten that, he had to know, had to face it head-on, regardless of the risk.

With a deep breath, Roger retrieved his coat and camera, the latter an extension of himself, a source of comfort and confidence. He left a note for Margaret, vague enough not to worry her but ensuring she knew where to find him should the need arise.

The night air was cool as he stepped outside, the full moon casting the world in a silvery glow. Vivary Park was a different realm in the darkness, the trees whispering secrets and the shadows stretching long across the grass. Roger's footsteps were quiet on the path, his senses heightened as he made his way toward the clubhouse, the silhouette of which loomed ahead like a sentinel.

As he approached the designated meeting spot, the clubhouse's windows dark and unwelcoming, Roger's grip on his camera tightened. The park was eerily silent, the usual nocturnal chorus muted as if in anticipation of what was to come.

He checked his watch—1:58 am. The full moon casting a serene glow over the landscape. The park, a daytime haven of natural beauty and communal joy, now lay shrouded in an eerie quietude, its familiar contours transformed by the play of light and shadow.

The moment was upon him, the midnight summons about to unfold. Roger Morgan, renowned photographer and unwitting participant in a game of shadows, waited in the stillness, ready to confront whatever—or whoever—had called him to this place at this ungodly hour.

Roger's footsteps on the gravel path were soft but deliberate, each step taking him closer to the unknown. The clubhouse loomed ahead, its facade bathed in the silvery luminescence of the moon, the windows dark, reflecting the night sky and the solitary figure approaching.

He paused for a moment at the edge of the clearing, taking in the scene. The moon hung heavy in the sky, a silent sentinel presiding over the night. Its light filtered through the leaves of the surrounding trees, casting a latticework of shadows that danced upon the ground with the gentle breeze.

Roger's breath formed small clouds of vapor in the cool air, a rhythmic accompaniment to the pounding of his heart. He was no stranger to the nerves that came with a new exhibit or the rush of a photography competition, but this was different. This was a summons cloaked in mystery and veiled threats, a far cry from the world of art and accolades he was accustomed to.

As he approached the clubhouse, a shadowy figure detached itself from the trees, moving towards him with a purposeful gait. Roger's pulse quickened, his senses alert. He could feel the weight of his camera slung over his shoulder, a comforting presence in the unsettling tableau.

"What do you want?" Roger asked, his voice steady despite the undercurrent of apprehension. "It's the middle of the night, can't this wait?"

The figure stopped a few paces away, the details of their face obscured by the darkness. Roger could make out little more than a silhouette, a darker shape against the night. The figure held something in their hand, an object that seemed incongruous with the tranquil setting—a dark, stick-shaped silhouette against the pale light.

Roger's instincts, honed by years of capturing the unseen and the unguarded, screamed that something was amiss. Yet his commitment to his craft, to the reputation he had built, anchored him to the spot. He needed to know if his work, his legacy, was under threat.

The figure raised a long, narrow object, the motion deliberate, and Roger's eyes widened as the moonlight glinted off its surface. Time seemed to slow, the details of the moment etching themselves into his consciousness with the clarity of a photograph snapped at the perfect instant.

But this was no photograph, and there would be no opportunity to develop the image, to see it framed and hung with pride. As the object thrust forward, Roger's world narrowed to a point of sharp, piercing pain—a final, brutal punctuation to the chapter of his life that had been dedicated to capturing the beauty of the world around him.

The clubhouse, the park, and the moon above stood as silent witnesses to the dark tableau; the serenity of the night shattered by a single, violent act. And as Roger fell, the secrets he carried with him seemed to dissolve into the night, leaving behind a mystery as deep and as dark as the shadows that had crept over Vivary Park.

Chapter 4 A Shadow at Vivary Park

The morning sun cast a warm golden glow over Vivary Park, bathing the lush greenery in radiant light that seemed to make every colour more vibrant. The air was thick with the intoxicating fragrance of a thousand blooms, each vying for attention in a kaleidoscope of hues that dazzled the senses.

Meticulously manicured flowerbeds lined the winding paths, bursting with a riot of roses, peonies, and dahlias, their petals unfurled in a breathtaking display of nature's artistry. Towering oak trees provided dappled shade, their branches swaying gently in the summer breeze as if welcoming the arrival of the annual Flower Show.

At the heart of the park, the grand Victorian fountain stood as a magnificent centrepiece, its cascading waters sparkling like diamonds in the morning light. The melodic sound of the falling water created a soothing symphony, complementing the cheerful chirping of birds that flitted from branch to branch, adding their own joyful chorus to the scene.

Everywhere one looked, the park was alive with activity as volunteers and organizers bustled about, putting the final touches on the various exhibits and displays. Colourful tents and marquees dotted the landscape, each one promising a new delight for the eager show visitors who would soon arrive.

In one corner, the aroma of freshly brewed coffee and warm pastries wafted through the air, beckoning early risers to the quaint café that had been set up for the occasion. Nearby, a group of artists gathered, their easels and palettes at the ready, eager to capture the park's beauty on canvas.

As the morning wore on, the park transformed into a vibrant celebration of nature's splendour, a true feast for the senses. The annual Flower Show had arrived, and Vivary Park stood ready to welcome the world to its idyllic embrace.

The morning dew still clung to the blades of grass, glistening like diamonds in the gentle rays of the rising sun. Lily, a young woman in her mid-twenties, strolled leisurely along the winding paths of Vivary Park, her faithful companion Buddy, a chocolate Labrador, trotting happily by her side.

The park was a serene oasis, a verdant escape from the hustle and bustle of the town. Lily inhaled deeply, savouring the sweet fragrance of the blooming flowers that lined the walkways, their vibrant petals unfurled in a kaleidoscope of colours. The melodic chirping of birds and the distant quacking of ducks on the pond created a soothing symphony, a perfect accompaniment to the tranquil morning.

Buddy, ever the adventurous soul, bounded ahead, his tail wagging excitedly as he explored the familiar sights and scents of the park. Lily smiled, content to let him roam within the safety of the well-tended grounds, his boundless energy a constant source of amusement.

As they approached the grand Victorian fountain, its cascading waters sparkling in the morning light, Buddy's demeanour suddenly shifted. His ears perked up and a low growl rumbled from deep within his chest. Lily's brow furrowed in concern as the usually friendly canine began barking insistently, tugging at his leash and leading her towards the fountain.

Perplexed, Lily followed Buddy's urgent prompting, her innate curiosity piqued by his uncharacteristic behaviour. She had always possessed an insatiable inquisitiveness, an inability to simply walk away from potential mysteries or trouble. As a child, her inquisitive nature had often led her down precarious rabbit holes, much to the chagrin of her parents and teachers who constantly had to rein her in.

While Lily had learned to temper that curiosity as an adult, it still bubbled up in situations like this. When Buddy started barking and pulling toward the fountain, her instincts kicked in. She couldn't help but be drawn to investigate what had piqued his interest. As a responsible dog owner highly attuned to Buddy's needs and behaviours, Lily knew he wouldn't be acting so intently without good reason. She decided to trust his instincts and see what had him so riled up, even if it meant potentially stumbling upon something she shouldn't.

Her decision was also influenced by the stillness and peace of the early morning in the park. The quaint setting lulled her into a false sense of security that whatever was happening couldn't be too dangerous or untoward in such a picturesque place. Little did she know, the tranquil scene was about to be shattered by a grisly discovery that would plunge her into the heart of a twisted mystery.

As Lily rounded the corner of the fountain, her heart stopped. There, partially submerged in the water, lay the lifeless body of Roger Morgan, a man whose passion for photography had made him a beloved figure in the community.

A monopod protruded obscenely from his chest. Lily's hands flew to her mouth to stifle a scream as waves of nausea and disbelief washed over her. Her legs trembled, threatening to give way beneath her as the full horror of the scene sank in.

Roger's face, usually alight with enthusiasm and creativity, was now frozen in a ghastly expression of pain and terror. His eyes, once vibrant and observant, stared lifelessly into the distance, their spark extinguished by the cruel hand of violence.

But it was the sight of the monopod, that essential tool of a photographer's trade, that sent a chill down Lily's spine. The sleek metal pole protruded grotesquely from Roger's chest, a crimson stain spreading across his shirt like a macabre bloom. The very instrument he had used to capture beauty had become the instrument of his demise, a twisted irony that defied comprehension.

As if the brutal act itself wasn't horrific enough, the killer had added a chilling touch – one of Roger's prized photographs, a stunning image that had won him accolades at the previous year's show, had been stapled to his forehead. The vibrant colours and intricate details that had once captivated viewers were now marred by the dark stain of his blood, a perverse desecration of art and life.

Scrawled across the photograph in what appeared to be thick black marker was a sinister message: "The first of many." The words seemed to taunt not only Roger's memory but also the very essence of the festival, a celebration of beauty and creativity now tainted by the spectre of violence and malice.

Lily's hand trembled as she fought the urge to retch, her mind struggling to comprehend the depravity of the act before her. The once-serene park, a sanctuary of nature's splendour, had become a macabre crime scene, and the beloved photographer's lifeless form lay at its centre, a grim reminder that even in the midst of beauty, darkness can lurk, waiting to strike with ruthless precision.

Chapter 5 Behind the Lens

The tranquil morning was shattered by the shrill wail of sirens, piercing the air and breaking the idyllic calm that had blanketed Vivary Park. Within minutes, a sleek police cruiser screeched to a halt near the fountain, and two figures emerged, their contrasting demeanours reflecting the yin and yang of the investigative process.

Detective Inspector Harriet "Harry" Lambert was the first to stride purposefully towards the crime scene, her sharp eyes already scanning the surroundings for clues. Harry grew up in a working-class family in Bristol. From a young age, she displayed an insatiable curiosity about understanding what motivated people's behaviour - why they did the things they did, both good and bad. This curiosity initially manifested as being a bit of a neighbourhood busybody, always trying to get to the bottom of local gossip and drama.

However, Harry's sharp intuition and ability to read people caught the attention of a school counsellor, who encouraged her to consider criminal psychology. Harry took those words to heart, pursuing studies in psychology and criminology before joining the police force.

Over her 18 years rising through the ranks, Harry has developed an impressive track record for solving complex cases by getting inside the minds of criminals. Her empathetic nature allows her to keenly analyse evidence through the lens of the perpetrator's psyche and motivations.

This same empathy has also been Harry's Achilles heel at times. She has struggled with becoming too emotionally invested in cases, blurring the lines between understanding the criminal and excusing their actions. This has put her at odds with superiors who view her as having "gone native" and compromised her objectivity.

Close on her heels was Detective Sergeant Thomas "Tom" Reed, his methodical gaze sweeping over the scene with meticulous precision. Tom was born and raised in the quiet town of Bridgwater, Somerset. From a young age, he displayed an innate sense of order, rules, and doing things "by the book." This carried through to his education, where he excelled academically by being a diligent, methodical student who dotted every "i" and crossed every "t."

After university, Tom was drawn to law enforcement to apply his logical, procedural mindset to investigating crimes and maintaining public safety. He steadily rose through the ranks due to his keen eye for detail, unflappable demeanour, and adherence to protocol.

While Tom's traditional approach has made him an outstanding detective, it has also caused friction with colleagues who view his rigid methods as inflexible or lacking creativity.

His reliance on hard facts and attention to detail had proven invaluable time and again, complementing Harry's intuition and creating a formidable investigative team.

As they approached the fountain, the grisly sight of the victim's body sent a ripple of unease through even their experienced ranks. Harry's brow furrowed, her mind already whirring with possibilities, while Tom's eyes narrowed, his focus zeroing in on the smallest details that could unravel the mystery.

"What have we got, Tom?" Harry asked, her voice steady despite the macabre scene before them.

Harry's gaze was drawn to the victim's body, partially submerged in the shallow waters of the fountain. Roger Morgan's face was frozen in a ghastly expression, his eyes wide with terror and his mouth agape as if he had tried to cry out in his final moments. The monopod protruding from his chest was a chilling sight, the sleek metal pole now an instrument of death.

Tom crouched beside the body, his brow furrowed as he studied the positioning of Roger's limbs. "There are no obvious signs of defensive wounds," he murmured, his voice tinged with grim professionalism. "The attack was likely swift and unexpected."

Harry nodded absently, her sharp gaze lingering on the photograph pinned to Roger's forehead. The scrawled message seemed to burn into her mind: "The first of many." She could feel it in her gut - this wasn't a random act. As the crime scene technicians swarmed around them, dusting for prints and bagging evidence, Harry slowly circled the fountain.

Her eyes narrowed as she noticed a scattering of pebbles near the base, some stained with what appeared to be blood spatter. "Tom, over here," she called out. "Looks like there might have been a struggle."

Tom rose fluidly and joined her, his methodical gaze sweeping over the area she indicated. "Good eye. We'll need to get samples for analysis." He turned his attention to the photograph once more. "As for this, it could simply be the killer's way of taking credit. A sick, depraved message to the victim."

Harry shook her head, her instincts rebelling against Tom's clinical assessment. "I don't think so. This feels...personal. Whoever did this knew Roger, had a vendetta against him specifically." She could feel the hairs on her neck prickling with a sense of dread. "And if that message is to be believed, they're not going to stop with just one victim."

Tom's jaw tightened, a flicker of apprehension crossing his features before his professional mask reasserted itself. "Let's not jump to conclusions, Harry. For now, we need to focus on processing this scene, identifying the victim's movements and contacts over the past few days. We build the case from facts, not gut feelings."

As their eyes met, the tension was palpable - two opposing methodologies colliding in that fragile space between instinct and evidence. Harry knew Tom's way had merit, but her mind was already leaping ahead, putting itself in the mind of an obsessed killer who had turned the idyllic park into a grotesque canvas.

Tom nodded grimly, his eyes scanning the surrounding area for any other potential clues. "We'll need to canvass the area, see if anyone saw or heard anything suspicious," he said, his methodical approach kicking into high gear.

As the sun rose higher in the sky, casting its warm glow over the once-serene park, Harry and Tom knew that time was of the essence. The killer was still out there, and with the ominous promise of more victims to come, they would need to work quickly and efficiently to unravel the twisted motives behind this brutal act before the Taunton Flower Show descended into a nightmare of fear and violence.

Harry exchanged a grave look with Tom, their determination solidifying. They had to move quickly to identify the killer before more innocent lives were claimed – all while navigating the treacherous undercurrents of ambition, rivalry, and the darkest depths of human nature that lurked beneath the surface of Taunton's beloved flower show.

As the crime scene team swarmed around them, meticulously documenting every detail, Harry and Tom stood side by side, their contrasting approaches poised to unravel the twisted motives behind this brutal act. The investigation had begun, and the race was on to catch the perpetrator before they could strike again, casting a dark shadow over the vibrant festivities of the Taunton Flower Show.

The grand marquee stood tall, its pristine white canvas billowing gently in the morning breeze. Inside, the air was thick with anticipation and the faint aroma of freshly brewed coffee as the photography community gathered before the crowds arrived. Harry and Tom entered, their eyes sweeping over the assembled group - a motley collection of passionate artists, dedicated organizers, and supportive family members. Each face held a story, a motive waiting to be unravelled.

In one corner, Margaret Morgan sat ramrod straight, her hands clasped tightly in her lap. The Kentucky Derby hat she wore did little to conceal the storm of emotions raging behind her reddened eyes.

Across the way, Stephen Smith paced like a caged lion, his camera bag slung over his shoulder. His eyes burned with an intensity that hinted at obsession and the bitter sting of past disappointments. When his gaze met Harry's, his lip curled ever so slightly in a sneer of recognition.

Scattered about were the other competitors - a diverse array of personalities united by their shared passion for capturing beauty through the lens. Some chatted amiably, while others nursed their nerves with trembling hands wrapped around Styrofoam cups.

The organizers, a small cluster of well-meaning volunteers, busied themselves with last-minute preparations. Their forced smiles and hushed tones betrayed the weight of the tragedy that had befallen their beloved event.

As Harry and Tom approached the group, a hush fell over the marquee. All eyes turned towards them, a kaleidoscope of emotions flickering across upturned faces - fear, curiosity, defiance. The investigation had begun in earnest, and no one was above suspicion.

With a steadying breath, Harry stepped forward, her voice cutting through the tension like a knife. "I know this is a difficult time, but we need to uncover the truth about what happened to Roger. I'll be asking each of you some questions, and I expect full cooperation." Her gaze swept the room, daring anyone to challenge her resolve.

The game was afoot, and in this arena of artistic expression, jealousy and resentment could prove as deadly as any weapon. Harry and Tom would need to tread carefully, for beneath the surface of creative passion lurked darker currents that had already claimed one life.

In the center of the marquee stood Margaret Morgan, the wife of Roger Morgan, her face a stoic mask as she fielded condolences from well-wishers.

Margaret grew up in a small village outside of Taunton. She came from a working-class family and dreamed of a comfortable middle-class life. At 22, she met Roger Morgan, a young amateur photographer with grand ambitions. They fell in love quickly and married within a year.

Margaret supported Roger's photography passion, working as a secretary to pay the bills while he pursued his art. However, as the years went by and Roger's success remained modest, resentment began to build. Margaret had given up her own dreams of having a career to support Roger's endeavours.

When Roger started gaining recognition and some financial success from winning local photography competitions like the Taunton Flower Show, Margaret was proud at first. But she grew increasingly jealous of the time and attention Roger devoted to his craft over their marriage. The final straw was discovering Roger's affair with a younger glamour model he had been photographing.

As Harry and Tom approached, Margaret's eyes narrowed imperceptibly. "Detectives. I suppose you'll want to ask me some questions."

"My condolences for your loss, Mrs. Morgan," Harry said gently. "This must be incredibly difficult, with the festival and all."

Margaret waved a hand dismissively. "Roger lived for this event. He'd want it to go on." Her lips tightened. "Though I can't imagine who could have done such a horrible thing."

Tom cleared his throat. "Do you know if your husband had some...rivalries within the photography community? Tensions can run high during competitions like this."

"Rivalries?" Margaret let out a bitter laugh. "That's putting it mildly. Roger was obsessed with winning, with being the best. He'd stop at nothing to ensure his pictures came out on top, even if it meant sabotaging others."

Harry raised an eyebrow. "That's quite an accusation. Did he have any specific feuds with fellow photographers?"

"Take your pick." Margaret's gaze drifted to a nearby display, her eyes hardening. "Stephen Smith, for one, that's him over there in the corner. Roger got him disqualified a few years back over some ridiculous rule infraction. Stephen's never forgiven him for it."

Tom made a note. "We'll look into that. What about on a more...personal level? Any romantic entanglements that may have sparked jealousy?"

A muscle ticked in Margaret's jaw as she turned back to the detectives. "You mean like that tart he was running around with? The model?"

"I see you were aware of his indiscretions," Harry said carefully.

"Aware?" Margaret barked out a harsh laugh. "I'm his bloody wife, for god's sake. Of course I knew. Though Roger tried to hide it at first, like his photography meant more to him than my feelings."

Tom's brow furrowed. "So, there was a rift in your marriage? Resentment, perhaps, over his dedication to his work?"

Margaret's eyes flashed dangerously. "You don't know the half of what I sacrificed so that man could chase his grand ambitions. I gave up everything for his dreams, and how did he repay me? By flaunting his affairs in my face, making me the laughingstock of the town."

As her voice rose, other photographers turned to look over curiously. Harry put a calming hand on the woman's arm. "We understand this is immensely painful, Margaret. Just one more question - did you happen to see or hear anything out of the ordinary last night?"

Margaret stared at her for a long moment before shaking her head tightly. "No. I was at home, alone, like I am most nights thanks to Roger's 'dedication'." She laughed bitterly. "But I'm sure you'll find plenty of others here with motives against my husband. He made enemies like other people make friends."

With that parting shot, Margaret turned on her heel and disappeared into the crowd, leaving Harry and Tom to digest the revelations about the victim's secret life and bitter marital struggles.

In the corner indicated by Margaret stood Stephen Smith.

Harry and Tom approached Stephen, who was busy studying a large print with an intense scowl.

"Stephen Smith?" Harry said, flashing her badge. "I'm Detective Inspector Lambert, this is DS Reed. We'd like to ask you a few questions about Roger Morgan."

Stephen's eyes narrowed as he turned to face them. "What about him?"

"We understand you had a bit of a history with Mr. Morgan from previous competitions," Tom stated, his tone neutral but probing.

A muscle twitched in Stephen's jaw. "You could say that. That arrogant prick got me disqualified in 2019 over a stupid technicality."

"He was just enforcing the rules as a judge," Harry pointed out. "Surely you can respect that as a professional."

Stephen barked out a harsh laugh. "Professional? Morgan was a self-important blowhard who thought he was Ansel Adams reincarnated. He relished using those 'rules' as an excuse to take petty shots at anyone he saw as competition."

"So, you held a grudge against him over being disqualified?" Tom pressed.

"Wouldn't you?" Stephen shot back. "That disqualification cost me a major career opportunity. But of course, a talentless hack like Morgan wouldn't understand what it's like to have your dreams crushed over nothing."

Harry studied Stephen carefully. "This seems like more than just professional rivalry. Did something else happen between you two?"

Stephen's eyes flashed with barely concealed rage. "Morgan was a hypocrite who preached about ethics while cheating and stealing from real artists like me and David Walker. He got what he deserved."

"Mr. Smith, you mentioned David Walker. What can you tell me about your relationship with him and the issues you had with Mr. Morgan?" asked Harry.

"David was a true artist, but Morgan always looked down on him. He used his position on the committee to keep David from getting the recognition he deserved. You'll find David at the other end of the marquee, go and ask him all about it," he replied.

"And you felt the same way? That Mr. Morgan had wronged you both in some manner?" Harry continued to push.

"Wronged us? That's putting it mildly, Detective. Roger Morgan didn't just wrong us - he robbed me of something I had earned through years of hard work and dedication to my craft and robbed David by stealing his photograph and posing it as his own. He played gatekeeper and decided my talents weren't worthy in his eyes. Well, I have my own moral code that I live by, and I won't let hypocrites like him deny me what is rightfully mine any longer. Mark my words, Detective, Roger Morgan got what was coming to him, and I have no regrets over it."

As a hush fell over the marquee, Harry and Tom exchanged a loaded glance. Stephen Smith's resentment and jealousy had clearly run much deeper than a simple competitive grudge. The investigation was only just beginning.

Harry and Tom weaved through the large collection of presentation boards, their eyes scanning the exhibits until they landed on David Walker, who was fussing over the precise placement of his framed photographs. As they approached, David looked up, his expression a mix of arrogance and disdain.

"Well, if it isn't the detectives come to admire the real artists," he sneered. "I'd offer to let you bask in the brilliance of my work, but I wouldn't want you to be blinded by its radiance."

Tom frowned at the man's bravado, but Harry simply arched an eyebrow. "We're actually here about an incident last year, Mr. Walker. The one involving Roger Morgan using your photo without permission?"

David's face flushed with anger. "Ah yes, that bloody thief. He had the audacity to pass off my

Castle Hotel masterpiece as his own! Can you believe the disrespect?"

"I understand you confronted him about it," Harry pressed. "How did he respond?"

"Brushed me off like a bloody amateur!" David spat. "Told me not to get so worked up over it. As if he's the authority on what's proper in this incestuous little photography club."

Tom made a note in his pad. "So, it's fair to say you weren't pleased with how the committee handled your complaint against Mr. Morgan?"

"Pleased?" David barked a harsh laugh. "Those pompous fools did nothing! All because Morgan's one of their golden boys who can do no wrong."

His hands clenched into fists as years of resentment bubbled to the surface. "They're a corrupt bunch, stifling true talent like mine while promoting mediocre hacks like Roger Morgan. Well, this year's exhibition will show them all. My work will blow that drivel away."

A sly smile crossed Harry's lips. "We'll be sure to have a look. Maybe the judges will finally give your...brilliance...the recognition it deserves."

David's eyes narrowed, sensing her veiled barb. Before he could retort, Margaret Morgan appeared at his side, placing a calming hand on his arm.

"David darling, the judges are coming 'round. Are you ready?"

With a huff, David straightened his shoulders. "Of course I'm ready. Unlike some money-grubbing sellouts, I don't need to resort to cheap gimmicks. My photographs will speak for themselves."

As he stalked away, Tom leaned in close to Harry. "You think he's got a point about there being favourites? Could explain his obsession with proving himself."

Harry watched David's retreating form, her instincts picking up on the seething resentment just beneath the surface.

"I think Mr. Walker's bitterness runs much deeper than a few slights. We'd better keep an eye on that vengeful ego of his."

The seeds of jealousy and obsession had taken root long ago in the fertile soil of the Taunton photography scene. And Harry couldn't shake the feeling that David Walker's twisted pursuit of validation was about to bear rotten, deadly fruit.

The warm August sun was just beginning to dip below the horizon, casting long shadows across the park's pristine grounds. Harry and Tom had spent the entire day canvassing the area, interviewing potential witnesses, and scouring every inch of Vivary Park for any shred of evidence that could lead them to the twisted individual responsible for Roger Morgan's brutal murder.

As they made their way back towards the fountain, the scene of the crime, Harry couldn't shake the uneasy feeling that had settled in the pit of her stomach. Something about this case felt different, more sinister than the typical crimes they investigated. The killer's taunting message, promising more victims to come, weighed heavily on her mind.

Chapter 6 Suspicions and Secrets

The mid-afternoon sun was high in the sky, the summer heat was quite noticeable when Harry and Tom arrived at the nondescript building housing the Taunton coroner's office. A sombre pall hung in the air, a stark contrast to the vibrancy and celebration that had filled Vivary Park earlier that morning.

As they stepped through the double doors into the sterile lobby, the harsh fluorescent lights seemed to strip away any lingering traces of the warmth from outside. The air carried a faint, antiseptic smell that caused Tom's nose to crinkle ever so slightly. To Harry, however, it was a regrettably familiar scent - the unmistakable aroma of death and the clinical procedures used to examine it.

They signed in with the bored-looking clerk, then made their way down a dimly lit corridor. Harry felt the weight of the case pressing down on her with each step. Roger Morgan's horrific murder had sent shockwaves through the community, shattering the illusion of safety that had cloaked the picturesque town. Now it was up to her and Tom to provide the answers, to pursue justice no matter how dark the path might be.

The corridor opened into a large, tiled room with harsh overheads bathing everything in a bluish-white glow. Several gurneys lined the walls, covered in shapeless lumps beneath crisp white sheets. In the centre of the room, the coroner, Dr. Eliza Hawthorne, stood hunched over a stainless-steel table upon which lay the broken body of Roger Morgan.

Tom cleared his throat, and Dr. Hawthorne looked up, her face impassive. "Detectives," she greeted with a curt nod. "I was just going over the preliminary findings on our victim." She waved them closer with a latex-gloved hand.

As they approached, Harry felt her breath catch in her throat. Despite having witnessed countless autopsies over her career, the sight of a life reduced to a battered husk never failed to rekindle her sense of determination to seek justice for the dead.

"As you can see, the victim suffered a single puncture wound to the chest from that monopod. Based on the lividity patterns and body temperature, I'd estimate the time of death between midnight and 1 a.m.", Eliza began.

"So, he was killed in the early morning hours when the park was deserted. Any sense of the attack itself,

Eliza? Could this have been a crime of passion or opportunity?" Harry asked.

Eliza pointed to the entry wound, "The angle and force of the wound track suggests this was no heat-of-passion crime. Whoever did this meant business. They would have had to grip that monopod firmly and employ a significant thrust to penetrate so deeply."

Harry rubbed her chin, "So a strong attacker then. Any way to tell if we're looking for a male or female?"

"It's difficult to say for certain without more evidence. However, the strength required makes a male perpetrator more likely in my opinion. Of course, we can't rule out a very strong female or the element of surprise." explained Eliza.

Harry Noted, "What about defensive wounds? Did the victim put up any struggle?"

Eliza shook her head, "None that I could find. The attack seems to have been quick and efficient. No signs of a prolonged struggle."

Harry frowned, "Damn. I was hoping he might have left some DNA evidence from his attacker under his nails or something. This killer was methodical."

"Indeed. I'll have more details for you once I can get the body back to the mortuary for a full examination. Let me know if you need anything else."

"You've been a help as always, Eliza. I'll loop back with you once we gather more evidence from the scene."

The heavy double doors of the coroner's office swung shut behind Harry and Tom with a hollow thud, cutting off the sterile scent of disinfectant and death. They emerged into the harsh midday sun, squinting against the bright rays that seemed to mock the darkness they had just witnessed.

A grim silence hung between them as they crossed the cracked pavement of the parking lot, the soles of their shoes crunching over loose gravel. Tom's jaw was tightly clenched, his eyes focused straight ahead with that intense professionalism that was his trademark. But Harry could see the slight furrow in his brow, a barely perceptible crack in his stoic exterior - the gruesome crime scene had rattled even her stalwart partner.

As they approached the sleek black Avon and Somerset police sedan, Harry's hand instinctively went for the door handle, but she paused. Turning to face Tom, she searched his eyes, seeing the same questions and doubts swirling there that plagued her own mind.

Harry flipped through the coroner's report "Eliza's findings are...disturbing, to say the least. The angle of the monopod entry wound, the lack of defensive marks - it all points to this being a carefully calculated attack."

Tom nodded grimly, "An up-close and personal killing. The killer wanted to look into Roger's eyes as he died. It's a signature of sorts, a twisted need for intimacy with the victim."

"And then there's the matter of the photograph.", said Harry, shaking her head slowly, "Pinning his own work to his forehead like a sick trophy? This is the act of someone with a very specific grudge against Roger."

Tom was busy making notes, "We'll need to take a closer look at any personal or professional rivalries he may have had. In a competitive circle like this photography community, jealousy can fester and turn toxic."

Harry frowned, "There's one other detail that's really sticking with me. The lack of blood at the main crime scene. If the fatal blow was struck at the fountain, there should have been more evidence of a struggle, more spatter..."

"You think he was killed elsewhere and then moved to the fountain as a staged scene?", asked Tom.

Harry nodded grimly, "it's just a hunch, but my gut is telling me this park location was chosen deliberately by the killer to make a statement. They wanted Roger found at the heart of the place that celebrated his passion and success."

"Which opens up a whole new line of inquiry into where the actual murder took place. Whether it was a crime of opportunity or...", Tom puzzled.

"Or the killer lured Roger somewhere under false pretences. Either way, it's clear this was not a random act of violence. We're dealing with a dangerously calculating individual consumed with hatred for Roger Morgan.", said Harry meeting Tom's gaze.

"Off the record, what's your gut telling you?" Harry asked Tom, her voice was low, the words meant only for him.

Tom considered her for a long moment before exhaling slowly. "That poor bastard never saw it coming." He shook his head grimly. "Whoever did this was unhinged. Completely depraved."

Harry nodded, her expression hardening with grim determination as she pulled open the car door.

"Then we don't stop until we find the sick fuck and put them away for good."

The heavy thud of the car doors slamming shut seemed to punctuate the weight of their shared mission. As the engine turned over and they peeled out of the parking lot, Harry and Tom were unified in their grim purpose - to shine a light into the twisted, obsessive depths that had spawned such depravity, and make sure no more innocent lives were claimed by the darkness.

The sleek police sedan pulled into the carpark behind the Taunton police station, the tires crunching on the gravel. Harry and Tom emerged, both weary from their long day investigating the demise of Roger Morgan.

As they entered through the rear entrance, the bustle of the station washed over them - ringing phones, the clack of computer keys, and the murmured conversations of officers and detectives hard at work. The familiar smells of stale coffee and decades-old file cabinets filled Harry's nostrils, providing an odd sense of comfort after the jarring scenes at Vivary Park.

They made their way down the corridor towards the CID office, nodding at the occasional greeting from a passing colleague. Harry could feel the weight of the investigation pressing down on her shoulders with each step. So many threads to untangle, so many fractured psyches to examine.

The CID office was a flurry of activity, desks cluttered with case files and half-eaten takeaway containers. Tom immediately settled in at his workstation, the model of procedural efficiency as he began transferring his handwritten notes to the computer database.

Harry, on the other hand, allowed herself a moment to pause and absorb the organized chaos surrounding her. Her gaze drifted to the evidence board that had been hastily assembled, Roger Morgan's haunting crime scene photo taking center stage. She could feel the gears in her mind beginning to turn, piecing together the disjointed fragments of their interviews into a cohesive psychological profile of the killer.

With a steadying breath, she crossed over to the board, plucking a dry-erase marker from the tray. The rhythmic squeak of felt on laminate filled the air as she began connecting the threads, scribbling notes and circling key details. This was her process, her way of giving form to the half-formed hunches that danced at the edges of her consciousness.

Tom glanced up from his terminal, his brow furrowing slightly at Harry's unorthodox methods. But he knew better than to interrupt her when the spark of insight was kindling. They were partners, yes, but their approaches could be as different as night and day.

Harry stared intently at her work on the board, her brow furrowed as she tried to make sense of the tangled web before her. Beside her, Tom pored over the witness statements, his methodical eyes scanning each line for any inconsistencies or potential leads.

"I'm telling you, Tom, this whole thing reeks of obsession," Harry said, tapping a finger against the photo of David Walker. "That man is a powder keg of resentment just waiting to blow."

Tom shook his head, unmoved. "We can't go convicting people based on personality flaws. We need concrete evidence linking him to the crime."

"Like what? A signed confession?" Harry scoffed. "Killers like this don't leave tidy little trails of breadcrumbs. We have to read between the lines, get inside their heads."

Tom set the statements down, fixing Harry with a level stare. "And that's exactly why we follow procedure. So we don't get lost in unsubstantiated theories and let personal biases cloud our judgment."

Before Harry could retort, their supervisor, DCI Roberts, entered the room, his presence immediately commanding attention. "What have we got so far?"

Harry jumped in first. "I think we need to take a closer look at David Walker and Stephen Smith. Both have clear motives stemming from long-standing grudges against Roger and the photography community."

Tom cleared his throat. "With all due respect, sir, those are just potential motives at this point. We have no physical evidence linking either man to the crime scene."

DCI Roberts held up a hand, stemming the rising tension. "Then we pursue all angles until something solid surfaces. Lambert, you focus your efforts on exploring those personal vendettas. Reed, I want you to go back over Roger Morgan's life with a fine-toothed comb - business dealings, relationships, anything that could point to other potential conflicts."

The pair exchanged a loaded glance, a silent acknowledgment of the diverging paths they were being asked to take. Harry gave a curt nod, her jaw set in determination.

As the room cleared out, leaving just Harry and Tom alone with the case board, she turned to her partner. "You know I'm right about this, don't you? This killer didn't choose Roger at random."

Tom sighed, refusing to be baited into another debate. "I know you have your methods, Harry. Just...don't let your instincts lead you too far down the rabbit hole, alright?"

With a wry smile, Harry gestured to the board. "You know me, Tom. I'll follow the evidence wherever it takes me."

As their eyes met, the unspoken challenge hung in the air. The hunt was on, and each would pursue their quarry by whatever means necessary, united in their pursuit of justice, yet divided by the fundamental philosophies that made them such an inseparable, explosive partnership.

The evening sun cast a warm glow over the charming cottage nestled on the outskirts of Taunton. From the outside, Roger Morgan's home exuded an air of tranquil domesticity, with its neatly trimmed hedges and flower boxes overflowing with vibrant blooms. But as Harry and Tom approached the front door, a sense of unease settled over them, a premonition that the quaint facade concealed far more sinister secrets.

The door opened, and Margaret Morgan stood before them, her eyes rimmed with dark circles from sleepless nights. "Detectives," she greeted them, her voice strained. "I wasn't expecting you so soon."

"My apologies for the early hour, Mrs. Morgan," Harry said gently. "But we would like to take a look around, see if there's anything that might shed light on your husband's... activities."

Margaret's brow furrowed, but she stepped aside, ushering them into the cozy living room. "I don't know what else you expect to find. Roger was a simple man, devoted to his photography."

Tom's gaze swept over the room, taking in the framed photographs adorning the walls – all masterful compositions of natural scenery, devoid of any human subjects. "It seems your husband preferred capturing the beauty of nature over people."

A flicker of something indecipherable passed over Margaret's features. "Yes, well, people can be...complicated."

Harry watched the other woman closely, her instincts picking up on the undercurrent of tension. "Mrs. Morgan, we understand this is an incredibly difficult time, but it's imperative that we have a clear picture of who your husband was, his relationships and any...proclivities that may have put him at risk."

Margaret's lips pressed into a thin line. "If you're asking about that Tart of a model he was hanging around, I knew all about that those goings-on."

"Even so, we'll need to take a look around," Tom interjected. "Is there perhaps a study or workspace where he spent most of his time?"

With a resigned sigh, Margaret led them down the hallway to a small room lined with bookshelves and a sturdy oak desk. "This was Roger's sanctuary. He could spend hours in here, editing his photos, lost in his own world."

As Harry and Tom began their methodical search, Margaret hovered in the doorway, her arms wrapped protectively around herself. Tom's eyes were immediately drawn to the immaculate organisation of the space, every item in its precise place.

"He certainly seemed to value order," Tom remarked, running his fingers along the edge of the desk, undisturbed by even a speck of dust.

Harry, meanwhile, was focused on the bookshelves, scanning the titles ranging from technical photography manuals to volumes on the history of art and aesthetics. Her gaze snagged on a thick leather-bound album tucked haphazardly between two larger books, its edges worn from frequent handling.

Pulling it free, she opened the cover, and her breath caught in her throat. "Tom, you might want to take a look at this."

The album was filled with glossy photographs, each one more revealing than the last – a veritable shrine dedicated to a young, beautiful woman with cascading blonde hair and a coy, seductive smile. Newspaper clippings and handwritten notes detailing the woman's movements and habits were interspersed between the images, painting a disturbing portrait of obsession.

"Bloody hell," Tom muttered, his brow furrowing as he flipped through the pages. "You don't think..."

Before he could finish the thought, a muffled thump from the corner of the room caught their attention.

"What was that?"

Margaret 's eyes widened, her complexion ashen. "I... I don't know. It came from over there."

Exchanging a weighted glance, Harry and Tom proceeded cautiously towards the source of the sound – a large, antique wardrobe tucked into the corner. With a steadying breath, Harry grasped the handles and pulled, revealing a small, hidden door set into the wall behind.

The detectives stared in stunned silence at the dimly lit space beyond – a veritable shrine dedicated to the same woman from the album. Photographs, some candid, others more explicit, with the model reclining on a bed, wearing only stockings and suspenders, surrounded by a selection of adult toys, her large breasts glinting with oil in the harsh lamplight. The photographs covered every inch of the walls, accompanied by scraps of paper with scribbled notes and mementos like pressed flowers and ribbons.

In the centre of the room, a life-sized mannequin commanded attention, its form adorned with a sheer negligee that clung to its curves like a whispered secret. The delicate fabric, almost ethereal in its transparency, left little to the imagination, hinting at the provocative silhouette beneath. The mannequin's legs were sheathed in silky stockings held in place by garters, the suspenders a stark contrast to the softness of its skin-like surface.

A peep-hole bra encased the mannequin's chest, the bold design framing its assets with an audacity that was both brazen and alluring. The bra's cut-out circles offered a teasing glimpse, a promise of hidden delights. Below, a G-string traced the slender lines of its hips, a daring piece that completed the ensemble with a risqué flourish.

The mannequin's face, devoid of expression, nonetheless conveyed an invitation, its posture and attire a silent siren call. The blank visage was a canvas for desire, its stillness belied by the charged atmosphere of the room, each article of clothing a deliberate choice in this tableau of seduction.

Harry felt the bile rise in her throat as the full, horrifying implications of Roger Morgan's secret life came crashing down around them. This was no mere indiscretion or fleeting infatuation – it was the twisted, all-consuming obsession of a deeply disturbed mind.

Turning slowly, she met Tom's gaze, a silent understanding passing between them. Whatever dark secrets lay at the heart of this case, they were only just beginning to unravel the tangled web of depravity and madness that had ultimately led to Roger Morgan's brutal demise.

As for Margaret, the woman stood frozen in the doorway, her hand covering her mouth in a mask of abject horror and disbelief, she was aware of the affair, but this... this was something unexpected to say the least. The life she thought she knew had been shattered, replaced by a nightmare from which there was no waking.

The quaint cottage on the outskirts of Taunton had given up its secrets, but at what cost? Harry could only wonder what other horrors awaited them as they ventured deeper into the darkness that had consumed Roger Morgan's soul.

Chapter 7 The First Red Thread

Dawn Menzies' silhouette cut a striking figure against the sprawling canvas of Longrun Meadow. The late afternoon sun, descending towards the horizon, bathed her in a soft, golden light that seemed to dance around her, igniting the auburn highlights in her flowing chestnut hair. As a glamour model, Dawn's beauty was her currency, and even in the solitude of nature, she possessed an effortless grace that could command the attention of any lens.

Her high cheekbones, a testament to her natural elegance, were accentuated by the contemplative expression that played across her face. Her eyes, a vivid shade of emerald, reflected a tapestry of emotions as they scanned the familiar landscape. They were the windows to a soul that had seen both the shimmering highs of a public life and the shadowy lows of private turmoil.

Dawn's full, rose-tinted lips were set in a pensive line, a stark contrast to the radiant smile that graced billboards and magazine covers. Today, there was no camera crew, no flashing lights, no directive to portray a character or sell a fantasy. Here, amidst the rustling reeds and the gentle babble of the River Tone, she was simply Dawn—unadorned and unobserved.

Dawn's journey to the heart of Somerset's photography scene was as unexpected as it was meteoric. Born to a family of modest means in the outskirts of Taunton, Dawn's childhood was one of simple pleasures and unspoken aspirations. Her parents, though supportive, were often preoccupied with making ends meet, leaving Dawn to find solace in the pages of glossy magazines and the dreams they inspired.

As a teenager, Dawn's natural beauty became apparent, but it was her poise and confidence that truly set her apart. She possessed an allure that was both refined and raw, a duality that caught the eye of a local photographer during a school event. The photos from that day captured a young woman on the cusp of discovery, her potential as evident as the lens flare that haloed her figure.

Word of Dawn's photogenic grace spread quickly, and it wasn't long before she was navigating the burgeoning Somerset glamour scene. Her ascent was a whirlwind of local fashion shows, car boot calendar shoots, and the occasional regional magazine spread. Dawn's look—a blend of classic English rose and modern allure—resonated with audiences, and her reputation grew.

It was during a charity event that Dawn's path crossed with Roger Morgan, the esteemed photographer whose name was whispered with reverence in artistic circles. Roger, with his keen eye for talent and beauty, saw in Dawn a muse who could transcend the typical glamour shots. He offered to mentor her, to refine her raw edges and elevate her from a local beauty to a model of national interest.

Under Roger's tutelage, Dawn's portfolio flourished. His guidance transformed her understanding of the camera, teaching her to convey emotion with a glance and tell stories with her posture. Their professional relationship deepened into a complex tapestry of respect, ambition, and a shared desire to create art that would endure.

Yet, as their collaboration bore fruit, so too did a more intimate connection. The lines between mentor and muse blurred, giving way to stolen moments and whispered promises. Their affair was a secret symphony, composed of longing looks and the silent click of the shutter, capturing a passion that existed in the space between light and shadow.

Despite the intensity of their connection, Dawn remained acutely aware of the precariousness of their situation. Roger, though separated from his wife in all but name, was still a married man, and the potential scandal of their affair loomed over them like a gathering storm. Dawn wrestled with guilt, torn between her feelings for Roger and the fear of the consequences should their secret be exposed.

As Dawn's career reached new heights, so too did the stakes of their clandestine relationship. Each photoshoot, each public appearance, was a dance on the edge of revelation. And as she walked through Longrun Meadow on that fateful afternoon, the weight of her hidden world pressed upon her, a burden she bore with the elegance of a woman who had learned to find beauty in the tension of the unresolved.

The meadow was her refuge, a place where she could shed the expectations of her profession and breathe in the tranquillity of the natural world. The tall grasses swayed in the breeze, whispering secrets to which only she was privy. The path beneath her feet, a winding ribbon of dirt and gravel, led her away from the complexities of her life and towards a horizon lined with the promise of peace.

As she walked, the heels of her boots sank softly into the earth, each step a deliberate act of communion with the land that had become her silent confidant. The river flowed alongside her, a constant companion on her journey through the meadow, its waters glinting like sapphires under the watchful eye of the sun.

Dawn's fitted blouse and jeans hugged her form, a casual ensemble chosen for comfort rather than the allure of the spotlight. Yet, even in this state of undress, her presence was magnetic, a force of nature unto itself. The meadow, with its undulating waves of green and bursts of wildflower colour, served as the perfect backdrop to her introspection.

The serenity of the scene was a balm to her soul, a much-needed respite from the whispers and rumours that clung to her like shadows. Here, in the embrace of Longrun Meadow, Dawn allowed herself the luxury of solitude, the freedom to confront the tangled web of her own thoughts without the fear of judgment or consequence.

As the sun dipped lower, casting elongated shadows across the landscape, Dawn's walk was a dance with the fading light, a quiet celebration of the day's last moments of warmth. She was unaware of the tragedy that had unfolded, of the darkness that had claimed a life and would soon cast its pall over her own.

But for now, Dawn was alone with the meadow and the river, her beauty a mere footnote to the story of the earth's enduring splendour. The soft rustle of the grass underfoot served as a soothing symphony to the inner discord that plagued her. Each step she took was an effort to distance herself from the tangled web of her life—a life that had become a delicate balance between the public image of a successful glamour model and the private reality of a woman caught in the throes of an illicit love affair.

As she moved through the meadow, the light breeze caressed her skin, a tender touch that stood in stark contrast to the harsh truth she harboured. The affair with Roger Morgan, her mentor and confidant, was a secret melody that played sweetly yet sorrowfully in the hidden chambers of her soul. It was a relationship that had started under the guise of artistic collaboration, but the chemistry between them had ignited a passion that neither could deny.

The natural beauty of the meadow, with its wildflowers nodding in the wind and the birdsong that filled the air, was a reminder of the simplicity and honesty that Dawn yearned for in her own life. She longed to be free of the deceit, to live openly and without the fear of judgment or the pain of betrayal. Yet, the thought of a life without Roger, without the intensity of their stolen moments, was a future painted in shades of grey.

Dawn paused by the riverbank, watching as the water flowed over pebbles and through reeds, its journey seemingly unending and untroubled. She envied the river's purpose and its clarity, qualities that her life desperately lacked. The reflection of the sun on the water's surface sparkled like so many camera flashes, a reminder of the world she inhabited—one where appearances were everything, and the truth was often obscured by the lens.

The meadow, with its serene beauty, was a bittersweet sanctuary. It offered a temporary escape, a place where she could pretend that the only roles, she played were those of her choosing. But as the sun began its descent, casting long shadows across the landscape, Dawn knew that the peace she found here was fleeting. The reality of her situation loomed as large as the setting sun, and the meadow's whisper was a quiet admonition of the inevitable choices she would have to face.

With a heavy heart, Dawn turned to leave the meadow, the grass swaying gently behind her as if to say goodbye. The turmoil inside her remained, a stark contrast to the peace of the natural world around her, and the path back to her life—a life entwined with Roger's—seemed more daunting with each step she took.

The meandering path through Longrun Meadow was a place of convergence for those who sought the quietude of nature, and on this particular afternoon, it brought together two souls, each immersed in the world of photography, yet each walking a distinct journey within it.

Larry Stubbs was a familiar figure in the local photography community, known for his landscape shots that seemed to capture the very breath of Somerset. His work was characterized by a patience that allowed him to wait for the perfect interplay of light and shadow, a skill that earned him quiet respect among his peers. His demeanour was as steady as his tripod; his presence, like his photography, was unobtrusive yet undeniable.

As he made his way along the river, his camera bag slung over his shoulder, Larry's eyes were always searching, not just for the next great shot, but for the stories behind the faces he encountered. His curiosity about the lives of his peers was genuine, driven by a belief that understanding the person behind the camera could reveal the soul behind the lens.

It was this curiosity that flickered in his eyes as he recognized Dawn Menzies ahead of him on the path. He knew of her, of course; her reputation as a glamour model was well-established, and her recent forays into photography had not gone unnoticed. Larry had always admired the way she seemed to bring a different perspective to her work, perhaps a remnant of her time spent in front of the camera.

"Dawn, a pleasure to see you here," Larry greeted her, his voice carrying the ease of a man comfortable in his own skin and in the presence of another's artistry. "Not often we get to see the world through the same viewfinder, is it?"

Dawn looked up; her contemplative solitude interrupted by the familiar face. She offered a small, appreciative smile, recognizing the friendly overture for what it was—an olive branch extended in the sometimes-competitive thicket of their industry.

"Hello, Larry," she replied, her voice tinged with the remnants of her earlier introspection. "It's a rare day when I'm not on the other side of the camera, but sometimes it's nice to just... be a part of the scenery."

Larry nodded, understanding the sentiment. "The meadow has a way of making us all feel like part of a larger canvas," he said, his gaze sweeping over the expanse of green and the gentle flow of the river. "It's a good place to find balance."

They walked together for a while, the silence between them comfortable, filled with the ambient sounds of the meadow. Larry's steps were measured, his eyes occasionally scanning the environment, always the photographer looking for the unseen angle, the hidden beauty.

"So, what brings you out here today, Dawn? Inspiration? Escape?" Larry asked after a time, his tone light but perceptive. He had a knack for asking questions that opened doors, inviting others to share their world with him.

Dawn hesitated, caught off guard by the question that seemed to probe gently at the edges of her private thoughts. She wasn't sure how much to reveal, how much of her turmoil to expose to this man who was both a colleague and a near stranger.

"Just needed some air, I suppose," she said, her answer a half-truth that danced around the deeper currents of her heart.

Larry offered a nod, accepting her response while giving her the space she needed. He was well-versed in the language of the unspoken, the subtle cues that spoke volumes more than words ever could.

Their walk continued, the photographer and the model, the observer and the observed, their paths intersecting in the quiet sanctuary of Longrun Meadow, where the only witness to their meeting was the timeless flow of the River Tone.

Larry, ever the observer, noticed the faraway look in Dawn's eyes, the subtle furrow of her brow that hinted at an inner struggle. He respected her privacy, yet his concern was palpable. They had reached a small clearing, a favourite spot for local photographers to capture the interplay of light and shadow, when he decided to breach the silence with news that had shaken the community to its core.

"Dawn, have you heard about Roger Morgan?" Larry asked, his tone sombre, eyes searching her face for a reaction. He expected surprise, perhaps sadness—Roger was well-known and respected, after all—but he was wholly unprepared for the torrent of emotions his words would unleash.

Dawn stopped in her tracks, her heart seeming to skip a beat. "Roger? What about him?" she managed, her voice barely a whisper, dread seeping into the edges of her words.

Larry's expression softened with sympathy as he delivered the news, unaware of the intimate bond between Dawn and the deceased. "He was found dead this morning. It's... it's a murder investigation now. I thought you might have known him, with the photography circles overlapping and all."

The world around Dawn seemed to tilt on its axis, the colours of the meadow dulling as if a cloud had passed over the sun. Her knees weakened, and she reached out to a nearby oak for support. Roger, her mentor, her secret lover, gone? It couldn't be. This had to be some cruel joke, a mistake.

"Murdered?" she echoed, her voice a mix of confusion and rising panic. "But... how? When?" The questions tumbled out, each one a plea for Larry to retract his statement, to tell her it was all a misunderstanding.

Larry's face was a mask of concern as he watched Dawn grapple with the news. "I'm so sorry, Dawn. They found him in the fountain in Vivary Park with a monopod thrust through his chest. It seems to have happened sometime last night."

Dawn's mind raced, images of Roger—alive, vibrant, laughing—clashing violently with the reality that he was now just a memory. Her breaths came in short gasps as the shock gave way to a profound grief that enveloped her like a shroud. Tears welled in her eyes, spilling over and tracing paths down her cheeks.

She turned away from Larry, her body wracked with sobs that she couldn't suppress. The meadow, once a place of solace, now felt like a vast, empty space echoing with her cries. Roger was gone, and with him, a piece of her heart, a secret chapter of her life that no one else had known.

Larry reached out tentatively, placing a hand on her shoulder. "Dawn, I had no idea you were close to Roger. I'm so sorry to be the one to tell you this."

Through her tears, Dawn looked up at Larry, her eyes revealing the depth of her pain. "We were... it was complicated. I..." She hesitated, the truth on the tip of her tongue. In this moment of raw agony, the need to share her burden was overwhelming.

Larry, taken aback by the intensity of Dawn's reaction, stood by her side, his initial surprise melting into a deep sense of empathy. He had not expected this revelation, this window into the private life of a woman he knew only through the lens of professional respect. As a photographer, he was accustomed to capturing the surface of things, but now he was peering into the depths of a human soul laid bare by tragedy.

"I... I was seeing Roger," Dawn confessed between sobs, her words spilling out amidst the torrent of her grief. "It was a secret, something... something just for us."

Larry's eyes widened as the pieces fell into place, the implications of her words casting a long shadow over the already dark news. He understood now why the meadow, a place of solace, had become a crucible for her pain. Dawn and Roger's hidden affair was not just a personal matter; it was a thread in a larger tapestry that could unravel into a motive for murder.

"Oh, Dawn," Larry said, his voice soft and laden with concern. "I had no idea. This must be so hard for you." He hesitated, unsure of how to comfort her, how to ease the pain that was so palpable in her every breath.

Dawn looked up at him, her eyes red and swollen from crying, searching his face for a sign of judgment, but finding none. In Larry's expression, she saw only kindness, a willingness to listen, to offer solace in the midst of her storm.

"I don't know what to do," she admitted, her voice a fragile whisper. "He was... he was everything. And now he's gone, and I can't even mourn him openly. I can't claim my grief."

Larry reached out, his hand gently touching her arm, grounding her. "You can mourn him, Dawn. You can mourn him with me. I won't pretend to understand everything you're going through, but I'm here for you."

As they stood together, the meadow bore witness to a moment of profound vulnerability. Dawn, a woman whose image had been crafted for public consumption, was now sharing a piece of her true self with Larry, a man who had captured countless scenes but was now tasked with holding space for a reality far more complex than any photograph could convey.

The weight of the secret they now shared seemed to anchor them to the spot, two figures amidst the vastness of the meadow, connected by the invisible threads of empathy and human connection. Larry's role had shifted from that of a fellow photographer to a confidant, a keeper of Dawn's most guarded truth.

As the sun began to dip lower in the sky, casting a golden hue over the landscape, the reality of the situation settled over them. Dawn's affair with Roger was not just a matter of the heart; it was a piece of a puzzle that would draw the attention of those seeking to solve the mystery of his death.

For now, though, Larry offered Dawn the comfort of his presence, a silent promise to be there for her as the investigation unfolded and the meadow slowly reclaimed its peace in the encroaching twilight.

The sun had begun its descent, casting a soft, melancholic light over Longrun Meadow. The River Tone flowed quietly, indifferent to the human drama unfolding on its banks. Dawn Menzies stood beside Larry Stubbs, her revelation hanging between them like a delicate mist, threatening to settle and obscure the path ahead.

Dawn's confession to Larry had been impulsive, a desperate grasp for solace in the face of overwhelming grief. But as the initial shock of sharing her secret began to fade, a new wave of anxiety took hold. The implications of her admission were far-reaching, and the tranquillity of the meadow now seemed a cruel mockery of the turmoil within her.

She looked at Larry, his face etched with empathy and concern, and realized that her clandestine affair with Roger Morgan was a secret no longer. The protective veil she had carefully constructed around her private life had been torn away, leaving her exposed and vulnerable.

"What have I done?" she whispered, more to herself than to Larry. The weight of her words settled heavily on her shoulders, a burden that threatened to crush her.

Larry's eyes met hers, and in them, she saw not only kindness but also the dawning realization of the gravity of the situation. "Dawn, I want you to know that you can trust me," he said softly. "But you need to be careful. This... this changes things."

Dawn nodded, her mind racing with the potential fallout from her disclosure. She was no stranger to the public eye, but the scrutiny that came with a murder investigation was a different beast entirely. Her relationship with Roger, once a private affair of the heart, could now paint her as a suspect in the eyes of the police.

The meadow, once a place of escape, now felt like an open plain where she was all too visible. The gentle rustling of the grass and the distant calls of the birds were a stark contrast to the silent scream of panic that echoed in her head.

As the last rays of the sun dipped below the horizon, the meadow was bathed in twilight, the day's warmth retreating before the encroaching chill of evening. Dawn shivered, a physical response to the cold realization that her life was about to be scrutinized in a way she had never imagined.

Larry, sensing her distress, offered a reassuring presence. "Whatever happens, you're not alone," he said, his voice a steady anchor in the shifting sands of her reality.

But as they parted ways, the solace of his words was quickly swallowed by the growing sense of foreboding that enveloped her. Dawn's steps were heavy as she made her way out of the meadow, each one echoing with the fear that her secret affair, now revealed, had irrevocably entwined her fate with the tragic end of Roger Morgan.

Chapter 8 Revelations at the Fountain

As the first rays of morning light filtered through the blinds of the Taunton police station, the CID office was already abuzz with activity. The murder of Roger Morgan had sent shockwaves through the community, and the pressure was on to find the killer before the beloved Flower Show was irreparably tainted by tragedy.

In the centre of the room, a large whiteboard had been erected, its surface already crowded with crime scene photos, witness statements, and hastily scrawled theories. Harry and Tom stood before it, their faces illuminated by the harsh fluorescent lights overhead.

Harry's eyes were fixed on the photograph of the hidden shrine discovered in Roger's study - a disturbing collage of candid shots featuring Dawn Menzies, the glamour model whose presence had electrified the photography competition. Red string connected the photos like a twisted spider's web, hinting at an obsession that had spiralled out of control.

"This proves it," Harry said, her voice tight with conviction. "Roger was fixated on Dawn. The affair, the secrecy... it all points to a motive for murder."

Tom frowned, his gaze methodically scanning the other evidence pinned to the board. "We can't jump to conclusions based on a few photographs. For all we know, this could be part of his artistic process. We need to dig deeper, look at the facts."

Harry spun to face him; frustration etched into her features. "The facts? The fact is, we have a dead man with a monopod through his chest and a message promising more victims. We don't have time to play by the book, Tom."

Tom's jaw tightened, but he kept his voice level. "And what if we're wrong? What if we focus all our attention on this one angle and let the real killer slip through our fingers? We need to be thorough, follow every lead."

The tension between them was palpable, a crackling energy that threatened to ignite at any moment. Around them, the other detectives and officers studiously avoided eye contact, busying themselves with paperwork and hushed phone conversations.

Harry took a deep breath, forcing herself to step back from the brink. She knew Tom's approach had merit, even if it chafed against her instincts. "Fine. We'll run down every lead, dot every i and cross every t. But we can't ignore the significance of this shrine. It's a window into Roger's mind, and it could be the key to unlocking this whole case."

Tom nodded, a flicker of understanding passing between them. They were two sides of the same coin, their differing methods ultimately working towards the same goal. "Agreed. Let's start by interviewing Dawn Menzies herself. If there was an affair, she might have insight into Roger's state of mind leading up to the murder."

As they gathered their notes and prepared to head out, the weight of the investigation seemed to press down on them from all sides. The Flower Show was in full swing, a vibrant celebration of life and beauty, but beneath the surface lurked a darkness that threatened to consume them all.

Harry and Tom exchanged a look of grim determination, silently vowing to see this through to the end. They would peel back the layers of secrets and lies, no matter how ugly the truth might be. For the sake of the victims, for the sake of justice, they would not rest until the killer was brought to light.

Vivary Park was a kaleidoscope of activity, the annual Flower Show in full swing on its inaugural day. Visitors streamed through the avenues lined with tents, each one a treasure trove of delights. The air was filled with the mingled scents of exotic blooms, artisanal foods, and the excited chatter of the crowd.

In a small arena nestled amidst the vibrant displays, a bird of prey exhibition was underway. A crescent of tents formed a backdrop to the spectacle, their canvas walls fluttering gently in the breeze. Within the arena, majestic raptors soared and dove, their powerful wings slicing through the air as they demonstrated their natural prowess. The audience watched, transfixed, as the falconers guided their feathered charges through a series of breathtaking manoeuvres.

Beyond the arena, the park was a hive of commerce and curiosity. Tents of every hue stretched along the pathways, each one offering a unique selection of wares. At one stall, the pungent aroma of chilli spreads filled the air, the vibrant reds and oranges of the jars a visual feast. Next door, a display of Panama hats in every style and shade beckoned to passers-by, promising a touch of tropical elegance.

Amidst this lively scene, Harry and Tom navigated the crowds, their focus on the task at hand. They approached Stephen Smith, a figure who stood out from the throng, his camera clutched tightly in his hands and a scowl etched upon his face.

Harry approached Stephen, who was scowling at his photo display. "Mr. Smith, do you have a moment? We'd like to ask you a few more questions about Roger Morgan."

Stephen turned, his eyes flashing with barely concealed anger. "What more is there to say? The man was a hypocrite and a cheat."

Tom raised an eyebrow. "Those are strong accusations. Can you elaborate on that?"

A harsh laugh escaped Stephen's lips. "Gladly. Last year, I had captured the most stunning shot of the Weston-Super-Mare pier at sunset. It was a masterpiece, Detective. The light, the colours - sheer perfection."

Harry nodded, encouraging him to continue. "And what happened with this photograph?"

Stephen's jaw clenched. "Roger bloody Morgan is what happened! He went to the competition committee and accused me of using artificial intelligence to enhance the image. Said it gave me an unfair advantage."

"And did you?" Tom asked, his tone neutral.

"Of course not!" Stephen snapped. "I'm a purist. I would never stoop to such tactics. But Morgan, he couldn't stand the thought of being upstaged. So he fabricated this story to get me disqualified."

Harry frowned. "That's a serious allegation, Mr. Smith. Do you have any proof of this sabotage?"

Stephen scoffed. "Proof? The proof is that my masterpiece was removed from the competition, while Morgan's derivative drivel took home the top prize. He manipulated the system to serve his own ego."

Tom made a note in his pad. "And how did the committee respond to these accusations against you?"

"They bought his lies, hook, line, and sinker," Stephen seethed. "Disqualified me on the spot, without so much as a proper investigation. All because precious Roger Morgan could do no wrong in their eyes."

Harry studied Stephen carefully. "That must have been quite a blow, to have your work dismissed like that."

Stephen's hands clenched into fists. "It was a travesty. That photograph was my ticket to recognition, to establishing myself in the art world. And Morgan ripped it away from me, all because he couldn't handle a little competition."

Tom leaned forward. "Mr. Smith, I have to ask - given the depth of your resentment towards Mr. Morgan, where were you on the night of his murder?"

Stephen's eyes widened. "You think I -? No. No, I had nothing to do with that. As much as I despised the man, I wouldn't resort to murder."

Harry held his gaze. "But you can understand our need to ask, given the circumstances."

A tense silence stretched between them before Stephen spoke again, his voice low and bitter. "Roger Morgan destroyed my dreams, Detectives. He took something precious from me, something I can never get back. So yes, I hated him. But his death? That's on his own head, not mine."

As Harry and Tom walked away, the weight of Stephen's revelations hung heavy in the air. The tangled web of rivalry and resentment within the photography community was growing more complex by the minute, and the path to justice was anything but clear.

Harry and Tom made their way through the bustling marquee, the aroma of fresh coffee guiding them towards a mobile catering van parked at the edge of the festivities. The barista, a cheerful young woman with a pixie cut, greeted them with a warm smile as she handed over two steaming cups of rich, dark roast.

They found a quiet spot near a vibrant display of exotic orchids, the delicate blooms providing a stark contrast to the weight of their conversation. Harry took a sip of her coffee, savouring the warmth that spread through her as she collected her thoughts.

"Stephen seemed to have a real axe to grind with Morgan," Tom mused, his brow furrowed. "That bit about being disqualified over a technicality? It clearly left a mark."

Harry nodded; her eyes distant as she processed the information. "And the way he spoke about David Walker... there's definitely more to that story. We need to dig deeper into the history between those three."

"Agreed," Tom said, draining the last of his coffee. "But let's tread carefully. These artistic types, they're a passionate bunch. We don't want to stir up more trouble than we solve."

As they discarded their empty cups and made their way deeper into the exhibition gardens, Harry couldn't shake the feeling that they were wading into a quagmire of long-held grudges and simmering resentments. The beauty of the flowers around them seemed to mock the ugliness of human nature that had led to Roger's untimely demise.

The sound of laughter drew their attention to a nearby display, where a small group had gathered around a towering arrangement of sunflowers and dahlias. At the centre of the group stood a distinguished older gentleman in a tailored suit, his silver hair gleaming in the sunlight. Beside him, engaged in animated conversation, was a familiar face - David Walker.

Harry and Tom exchanged a glance, the opportunity to question their next suspect presenting itself with serendipitous timing. As they approached, snippets of the conversation drifted towards them - talk of the upcoming mayoral election and the importance of the arts in Taunton's community.

Harry and Tom approached David Walker, as the mayor was swallowed up by a thrum of local media. David turned around as they neared, a flicker of annoyance crossing his features.

"Hello again Mr Walker, we'd like to ask you a few more questions about Roger Morgan.", Harry said with a wry smile on her face.

David sighed dramatically. "I suppose it was only a matter of time before you came sniffing around. What do you want to know?"

Tom fixed him with a steady gaze. "We understand there was some bad blood between you and Mr. Morgan. Care to elaborate?"

"Bad blood?" David scoffed. "More like professional rivalry. Roger always had to be the star, couldn't stand anyone else getting attention."

Harry raised an eyebrow. "And that rivalry, it never escalated beyond a little healthy competition?"

David shifted uncomfortably. "Look, I may have made some threats in the heat of the moment. Called him a hack, said he'd get what was coming to him. But it was just bluster, nothing serious."

"Threats like that can be quite serious, Mr. Walker," Tom pressed. "Especially when the subject ends up dead."

"You think I killed him?" David's eyes widened. "That's absurd! I envied his success, sure, but I'm not a murderer."

Harry leaned in, her voice low. "Then perhaps you can point us in the direction of someone who had a more...personal grudge against Mr. Morgan."

David hesitated, glancing around furtively. "You didn't hear it from me, but you might want to take a closer look at Margaret."

"His wife?" Tom frowned. "What makes you say that?"

"Let's just say, Roger's dedication to his craft didn't exactly make for a happy home life." David lowered his voice conspiratorially. "I've heard them arguing more than once, and the resentment in Margaret's voice...it was palpable."

Harry exchanged a glance with Tom. "Interesting. And you think this resentment could have boiled over into something more sinister?"

David shrugged. "All I know is, behind every successful man is a woman who's been pushed to the brink. Margaret had sacrificed a lot for Roger's ambitions. Maybe she finally snapped."

"We'll take that under advisement," Tom said, jotting down a note. "If you think of anything else, be sure to let us know."

As they turned to leave, David called out, "Detectives? For what it's worth, I hope you catch the bastard. Roger may have been a thorn in my side, but he didn't deserve this."

Harry nodded grimly. "That's what we're here to ensure, Mr. Walker. That justice is served, no matter where the evidence leads us."

With that, they melted back into the crowd, their minds churning with this new information. The tangled web of rivalries and resentments was slowly unravelling, but the final picture remained frustratingly out of focus. Only by pulling on each thread, no matter how uncomfortable, would they uncover the dark truth behind Roger Morgan's untimely demise.

Tom guided the car through the winding streets, the late afternoon sun glinting off the windshield. He glanced over at Harry, who was staring out the passenger window, her brow furrowed in thought.

"So, what's your read on David Walker?" Tom asked, breaking the contemplative silence. "The man certainly has an ego on him."

Harry snorted. "That's putting it mildly. Did you see the way he sneered at the mere mention of Roger's name? That was pure, unadulterated loathing."

Tom nodded. "No love lost there, that's for sure. But bad blood alone doesn't make him a killer."

"Agreed," said Harry. "But Walker's resentment runs deep. He truly believes Roger wronged him by stealing that photograph and passing it off as his own."

"You think that's enough to push him over the edge? To commit murder as some form of twisted retribution?"

Harry shrugged. "Obsession can make people do unthinkable things. In Walker's mind, maybe killing Roger was the only way to finally prove his superiority, to show the world he's the true artist."

Tom considered this for a moment. "It's a compelling motive, I'll give you that. But we can't discount the other photographers. They all seemed to have some kind of axe to grind with Roger."

"True," Harry conceded. "But there was something about the intensity in Walker's eyes, the barely concealed rage simmering just beneath the surface. I've seen that look before in killers consumed by a single, destructive obsession."

Tom sighed as he turned the car onto Margaret's street. "Well, let's hope Margaret can shed some more light on her husband's rivalries. If Walker is our guy, we're going to need more than hunches and gut feelings to nail him."

Harry met Tom's gaze, her eyes alight with grim determination. "Then we keep digging until we unearth the truth, no matter how deep it's buried. Roger deserves justice, and I won't rest until we give it to him."

As the car pulled to a stop outside the Morgan residence, the detectives steeled themselves for the difficult conversation ahead, both keenly aware that the key to unravelling this twisted case may lie hidden in the tangled web of jealousies and resentments that seemed to permeate the Taunton photography community.

The mid-morning sun cast a warm glow over the quaint cottage on the outskirts of Taunton. As Harry and Tom pulled up in their unmarked police car, the tranquil scene was disrupted by the sight of thick, dark smoke billowing from the front garden. The acrid smell of burning fabric assaulted their nostrils as they stepped out of the vehicle, exchanging a puzzled glance.

Rounding the corner of the neatly trimmed hedge, they found Margaret Morgan standing before a raging bonfire, her face set in grim determination as she tossed armful after armful of men's clothing onto the flames. The fire crackled and hissed, greedily consuming the once-cherished garments of her late husband.

"Mrs. Morgan, what's going on here? Why are you burning your husband's clothes?", asked Harry.

Margaret turned to face them, her eyes red-rimmed and her jaw set.

"I want every trace of that man gone from my life. Every stitch, every thread that touched his lying, cheating skin."

Tom informed Margaret, "I understand you're upset, but destroying evidence is a serious matter. We need to examine his belongings for any clues related to the investigation."

Margaret laughed bitterly.

"Clues? What more do you need than that sick shrine he had hidden away? The one devoted to his mistress, filled with those explicit photos and mementos of their sordid affair?"

"Finding that must have been quite a shock. I can only imagine how betrayed you must feel." Harry replied.

"Betrayed doesn't begin to cover it. I knew about the affair, you see. I thought it was just a fling, a middle-aged crisis. But that room... it was something else entirely."

She shook her head, fresh tears spilling down her cheeks.

"That wasn't just an affair. It was an obsession. A twisted fixation that consumed him. And there I was, the dutiful wife, supporting his "photography" all those years. What a fool I was."

"Mrs. Morgan, I know this is difficult, but we need to understand the full scope of your husband's...activities. Can you tell us more about this mistress? Did you know her name?", Tom questioned.

Margaret's expression changed from woe to anger, "I've already explained this to you once, it was Dawn. Dawn Menzies. She was some young, blonde thing, barely old enough to be our daughter. Roger met her at a photography workshop or some such nonsense."

"And you had no idea the affair had progressed to such a disturbing level? The stalking, the secret shrine?", asked Harry.

"Of course not! I thought she was just a bit of fluff on the side. I never imagined Roger capable of something so depraved. But that room...it was like looking into the mind of a madman."

She turned back to the flaming bin, tossing in another armful of clothes.

"So yes, I'm burning every trace of him. I want to purge the stain of his presence from my life. Let the police sift through the ashes. I'm done being the loyal wife of Roger bloody Morgan."

Harry exchanged a glance with Tom before turning back to Margaret. "Be that as it may, we still have some questions that need answering. We were hoping you could come down to the station with us, help us fill in a few blanks."

Margaret stared at the detectives for a long moment, the flames casting eerie shadows across her face. Finally, she nodded curtly. "Fine. Just let me finish up here."

As she turned back to the bonfire, tossing the last few items of clothing onto the hungry flames, Harry and Tom retreated to the car, the weight of the investigation heavy on their shoulders.

Minutes later, Margaret emerged from the house, her face an inscrutable mask. She climbed into the back of the police car without a word, her gaze fixed straight ahead as they pulled away from the smouldering remains of her old life.

The drive back to the station was tense and silent, the only sound the hum of the engine as they navigated the winding roads of Taunton. Harry couldn't shake the feeling that they were on the cusp of a major breakthrough, that the secrets hidden within the ashes of Roger Morgan's past held the key to unlocking the mystery of his brutal murder.

As they pulled into the station parking lot, Margaret's voice cut through the stillness. "I hope you find who did this," she said quietly, her eyes meeting Harry's in the rearview mirror. "And when you do, I hope they rot in hell for what they've done."

With those chilling words hanging in the air, the detectives led Margaret inside, ready to delve deeper into the tangled web of lies and obsession that had ultimately led to Roger Morgan's demise.

The fluorescent lights hummed overhead, casting a harsh glow on the drab, grey walls of the interview room. The space was sparse, furnished with only a metal table and a few uncomfortable chairs, their legs scraping against the scuffed linoleum floor. A one-way mirror dominated one wall, reflecting the room's occupants like a murky pool of secrets.

Margaret Morgan sat at the table, her hands clasped tightly in her lap, her knuckles white with tension. She looked small and fragile in the unforgiving light, her eyes rimmed with dark circles that spoke of sleepless nights and unrelenting grief. Her once immaculate appearance was now dishevelled, her hair hanging limply around her face, her clothes rumpled and careworn.

The door opened with a soft click, and Detective Harry Lambert entered, followed closely by her partner, Tom Reed. Harry's sharp gaze immediately fell upon Margaret, her eyes searching the widow's face for any flicker of emotion that might betray the truth hidden beneath the surface. Tom, in contrast, hung back, his presence a silent, steady support as he observed the room with a practiced eye.

As Harry and Tom took their seats across from Margaret, the air in the room seemed to thicken with the weight of unspoken questions and barely concealed suspicions. The detectives' files lay open on the table, the pages rustling softly in the stillness, a reminder of the evidence that had led them to this moment.

Margaret's gaze darted nervously between the two detectives, her breath coming in shallow, uneven gasps. The walls seemed to close in around her, the room suddenly too small, too suffocating. She could feel the pressure building in her chest, the truth clawing at her throat, desperate to be heard.

Harry leaned forward, her elbows resting on the table, her eyes locked on Margaret's. The silence stretched between them, a fragile thread waiting to be snapped. And then, with a voice that was both gentle and unyielding, Harry began the interview, the first question hanging in the air like a looming storm, ready to break over the room and wash away the façade of normalcy that had for so long concealed the dark secrets lurking beneath the surface.

"Mrs. Morgan, we've uncovered some information that your husband Roger may have been involved with another woman, a photographer named Dawn Menzies. Did you know anything about this?"

Margaret scoffed bitterly, "Of course I knew. That bastard didn't even try to hide it. Always running off to "collaborate" with her on some project or another."

"So, you were aware of their affair?", Tom questioned her again.

"Affair? Is that what we're calling it? More like a sordid little fling he just couldn't resist rubbing in my face. Dawn Menzies, with her youthful looks and "raw talent". It made me sick watching him fawn over her work, praising her genius."

"It sounds like there was a lot of resentment there. The disrespect must have been very painful for you." Harry asked with a look of curiosity.

"You have no idea what that man put me through. I gave up everything for him, supported his precious photography career. And how does he repay me? By chasing after some starry-eyed ingenue."

"Do you think Ms. Menzies returned his affections? Was the relationship serious in your view?", asked Tom.

"Serious?" Margaret laughed harshly, "Roger wasn't capable of a serious relationship, even with his own wife. But I've no doubt that little tart strung him along, used his influence to get ahead. She knew exactly what she was doing, batting her lashes and cooing over his brilliance."

Harry pressed further, "Did you ever confront Roger or Dawn about their involvement? Any arguments or ultimatums to put an end to it?"

Margaret's voice raised, "You think I just sat back and took it? I told Roger he was making a fool of himself, that everyone could see what was going on. Put an end to it? I wanted to put an end to her, to watch the great Dawn Menzies crumble without Roger to prop her up."

"Margaret... Did you ever take steps to do that? To sabotage Dawn in some way?", questioned Tom.

Margaret's demeanour became defensive "What exactly are you implying? I may have hated the girl, wanted to wipe that smug smile off her face, but I'm not a murderer."

Harry reassured her, "No one is accusing you of anything. We're just trying to understand the dynamics at play. Roger's affair clearly wounded you deeply."

"Wounded doesn't begin to describe it. That girl destroyed my marriage, my life. And now... Now she gets to live on while Roger rots in the ground. There's no justice in that.".

"Thank you for your honesty, Mrs. Morgan. I know this isn't easy. We'll do everything we can to get justice for Roger." Harry said with a reassuring smile.

"Justice? I stopped believing in that long ago, Detective. But you do what you have to do. I've nothing left to lose."

"I think we've taken up enough of Mrs. Morgan's time for now," Harry said, her tone gentle but firm. She could sense the widow's growing distress, the toll that this ordeal was taking on her already fractured psyche.

Tom nodded in agreement, his own features softening with a touch of sympathy. "Thank you for your cooperation, Mrs. Morgan. We understand how difficult this must be."

Margaret stood abruptly, her chair scraping against the floor with a jarring sound. "If that's all, I really must be going. I have...arrangements to make." Her voice wavered, the unspoken implications of her words hanging heavy in the air.

Harry exchanged a glance with Tom before turning back to Margaret. "Of course. Please, allow us to give you a lift home. It's the least we can do."

The widow hesitated for a moment, her pride warring with the exhaustion that seemed to seep from her very pores. In the end, practicality won out, and she nodded her assent.

As they exited the marquee, the bustle of the Flower Show preparations seemed to fade into the background, the vibrant colours and excited chatter a stark contrast to the sombre mood that clung to the trio like a shroud.

The journey to Margaret's home was marked by a heavy silence, broken only by the occasional direction given in a voice barely above a whisper. When they arrived at the quaint cottage, Harry insisted on walking Margaret to the door, a small gesture of support in the face of unimaginable grief.

"If you think of anything else, anything at all, please don't hesitate to contact us," Harry said, pressing her card into Margaret's hand.

The widow nodded, her fingers curling around the small rectangle of paper as if it were a lifeline. "Thank you, Detective. I will."

As Harry watched Margaret disappear into the house, the door closing with a soft click, she couldn't shake the feeling that there was more to this case than met the eye. The secrets that lay behind the façade of the Morgan's seemingly perfect life were only just beginning to unravel, and she knew that the path ahead would be fraught with twists and turns.

With a sigh, Harry turned back to the car where Tom waited, ready to plunge once more into the tangled web of lies and obsession that had claimed Roger Morgan's life. The Flower Show, with all its beauty and promise, would have to wait. Justice, like the blooms that graced the event, demanded careful cultivation and unwavering dedication.

Harry stared at the murder board, her brow furrowed in concentration as she tried to piece together the tangled web of motives and alibis surrounding Roger Morgan's brutal murder. The fluorescent lights of the CID room cast a harsh glare on the photographs and scribbled notes, each one a fragmented piece of the puzzle that refused to fit neatly together.

Beside her, Tom paced restlessly, his frustration palpable in the tense set of his shoulders. "We need to bring Margaret back in for questioning," he insisted, jabbing a finger at her photograph. "She knew about the affair, and we still don't have a solid alibi for her on the night of the murder."

Harry shook her head, unconvinced. "Margaret's not our killer, Tom. She's a victim in all of this, too. Her world's been turned upside down."

"Betrayal is a powerful motive, Harry. You of all people should know that." Tom's words hung heavy in the air, a reminder of the personal demons that haunted Harry's past.

She bristled, her eyes flashing with a mix of anger and pain. "Don't make this about me, Tom. We need to stay focused on the facts."

"The facts are that Margaret had opportunity and motive. We can't ignore that just because you sympathise with her."

Harry turned to face him fully, her voice low and intense. "And what about Dawn? The woman at the center of this whole sordid affair? We still don't know anything about her or her relationship with Roger."

Tom scoffed. "What's there to know? She was a pretty young thing, and Roger couldn't keep it in his pants. It's the oldest story in the book."

"No, there's more to it than that. You saw that hidden room, the obsession bordering on madness. That's not just a casual fling." Harry tapped her finger against Dawn's photograph, her mind whirring with possibilities. "We need to understand what drew Roger to her, what hold she had over him. That's the key to unravelling this whole mess."

Tom sighed, running a hand through his hair in exasperation. "Fine. We'll track down Dawn, see what she has to say. But I still think we need to keep the pressure on Margaret. She knows more than she's letting on."

Harry nodded, a flicker of determination sparking in her eyes. "Agreed. We'll work both angles, leave no stone unturned."

As they turned back to the murder board, the weight of the investigation settled heavily on their shoulders. The secrets and lies that had torn apart Roger Morgan's life had created a labyrinth of suspicion and doubt, one that would test the limits of their partnership and their own convictions.

But Harry knew one thing for certain - the truth, no matter how ugly or painful, had to be brought to light. For Roger, for Margaret, and for the shattered lives left in the wake of this twisted obsession. Justice demanded nothing less.

As the bustling energy of the Taunton Flower Show swirled around them, Detective Inspector Harriet "Harry" Lambert and Detective Sergeant Thomas "Tom" Reed found themselves nestled in a quaint local café, seeking a moment of respite amidst the chaos of their investigation. The aroma of freshly brewed coffee and homemade pastries enveloped them, a stark contrast to the grim reality of the case that consumed their thoughts.

Harry absently stirred her tea, her mind whirring with the pieces of the puzzle that refused to fit together seamlessly. Tom, ever the methodical one, pored over the case notes, his brow furrowed in concentration as he searched for any detail they might have overlooked.

Their quiet contemplation was interrupted by the approach of a man with a friendly, if somewhat curious, expression. He appeared to be in his early 40s, with a mop of unruly brown hair and a well-worn camera bag slung over his shoulder. The man extended his hand in greeting, his eyes flickering with recognition.

"Detective Inspector Lambert and Detective Sergeant Reed, I presume?" he said, his voice carrying a hint of excitement. "I'm Larry Stubbs, a local photographer. I saw you both at the fountain yesterday, where poor Roger was found."

Harry and Tom exchanged a glance, their guard instantly up. They had hoped to keep a low profile, but it seemed their presence had not gone unnoticed. Harry stood, shaking Larry's hand with a polite, if somewhat guarded, smile.

"Mr. Stubbs," she acknowledged, her tone even. "I'm afraid we can't discuss the details of an ongoing investigation, but we appreciate your concern."

Larry nodded, his expression turning sombre. "Of course, I understand. It's just such a shock, you know? Roger was a fixture in the photography community here. I can't imagine who would want to harm him."

Tom leaned forward; his interest piqued. "You knew the victim well, then?"

Larry shrugged, sliding into the empty seat at their table with a familiarity that suggested he was used to inserting himself into conversations. "As well as anyone, I suppose. We've crossed paths at various events and competitions over the years. He was a brilliant photographer, but he could be...difficult at times."

Harry's eyebrow arched, her instincts telling her that Larry might have more to offer than mere condolences. "Difficult how, exactly?"

Larry hesitated, as if weighing his words carefully. "Let's just say that Roger was fiercely competitive and not always the most gracious winner. He had a way of getting under people's skin, you know?"

As Larry continued to regale them with anecdotes about Roger's tumultuous relationships within the photography community, Harry and Tom listened intently, their minds working in tandem to sift through the information for any potential leads.

The café bustled around them, the laughter and chatter of the flower show attendees a jarring juxtaposition to the dark undercurrents of the case they were navigating. Harry and Tom knew that every interaction, every piece of gossip, could hold the key to unravelling the mystery of Roger's murder.

It was then that Larry mentioned having had a conversation with Dawn while they were out walking in Longrun Meadow. Harry and Tom looked at each other with excitement, the piece of the puzzle that was missing had just been found.

Larry wrapped his hands around a steaming mug of coffee that had just been placed before him by a friendly waitress. He nodded his thanks, his mind still reeling from the encounter he'd had with Dawn. "She seemed lost in thought when I first saw her," he began, his voice soft. "I almost didn't want to disturb her, but I felt she needed to know about Roger."

Tom leaned forward, his elbows resting on the table. "How did she react when you told her?"

Larry's brow furrowed, the memory clearly painful. "It was like watching a light go out. She just... crumpled. I've never seen grief hit someone so hard, so fast. It was as if her world had shattered in an instant."

Tom's pen hovered over his notebook; his eyes locked on Larry. "Did she say anything? Anything that might give us a clue about her relationship with Roger?"

Larry hesitated, his loyalty to Dawn warring with his desire to help. "She said they were seeing each other. That it was a secret, something just for them." He sighed, shaking his head. "I got the sense it was complicated, that there were layers to their relationship I couldn't even begin to understand."

The detectives exchanged a glance, the pieces of the puzzle really were starting to fall into place. Tom's voice was gentle as he asked, "Did she mention anything else? Any fears or concerns?"

Larry's grip tightened on his cup, his knuckles turning white. "She was devastated. Kept saying she didn't know what to do, that she couldn't even mourn him openly. It was like she was trapped in her own pain, with no way out."

Harry's heart ached for Dawn, even as his mind raced with the implications of her secret affair. "Thank you, Larry. I know this can't be easy for you, but your information could be crucial to our investigation."

As Larry finally took his leave, promising to be available should they have any further questions, Harry and Tom were left with a new thread to follow, a new avenue to explore in their quest for justice. The Taunton Flower Show may have been a celebration of beauty and creativity, but beneath its vibrant surface lurked a tangled web of rivalries, resentments, and secrets waiting to be uncovered.

As they prepared to leave the café, the weight of Dawn's grief seemed to hang in the air, a tangible presence that followed them out into the bustling streets of Taunton. The knowledge of her relationship with Roger added a new layer of complexity to the case, one that would require all their skills and intuition to unravel.

As Harry and Tom stepped out of the cosy confines of the café, the bustling streets of Taunton enveloped them in a cacophony of sights and sounds. Pedestrians hurried past, their faces a blur of preoccupation and purpose, while the distant hum of traffic and the occasional honk of a car horn provided a constant backdrop to the urban symphony.

Harry paused for a moment, her keen eyes scanning the surroundings with the instincts honed by years of police work. It was then that she noticed a figure standing across the street, partially obscured by the shadow of a shop awning. The person wore a dark, hooded sweatshirt, their face hidden from view, but there was something about their posture that set off alarm bells in Harry's mind.

As if sensing her gaze, the figure shifted slightly, their head turning in Harry's direction. A chill ran down her spine as she realised the person was watching them intently, their stance almost predatory in its intensity.

Without a second thought, Harry sprinted forward, weaving through the startled pedestrians as she crossed the street with single-minded determination. Tom called out after her, his voice laced with confusion and concern, but Harry's focus was solely on the mysterious observer.

The hooded figure turned abruptly and began to move away, their pace quickening as they melted into the crowded sidewalk. Harry gave chase, her heart pounding in her ears as she dodged and darted around the oblivious shoppers and businesspeople going about their daily routines.

The pursuit led her down a narrow side street, the buildings looming overhead and casting long shadows across the pavement. Harry's footsteps echoed off the cobblestones as she scanned the area for any sign of the elusive figure, but they had vanished as suddenly as they had appeared.

Breathing heavily, Harry stood alone in the alleyway, a sense of unease settling over her like a shroud. The encounter had lasted only moments, but it left her with a profound sense of disquiet. Who was this mysterious person, and why were they watching her and Tom so intently?

As she made her way back along the alley, her mind raced with possibilities. Could this be connected to the brutal murder of Roger Morgan? Was someone trying to intimidate them, to throw them off the scent of the real killer?

Tom's concerned face came into view as she retreated up alley, his brow furrowed with worry. "What happened? Are you alright?"

Harry shook her head, trying to clear the cobwebs of apprehension. "I'm fine. It's just... there was someone watching us. I tried to catch up to them, but they disappeared."

"Damn it!" Harry cursed, slamming her palm against the grimy brick wall. "We almost had them!"

Tom, his usually impeccable suit now dishevelled, shook his head in frustration. "Whoever they are, they know these streets like the back of their hand. We need to regroup, figure out our next move."

Harry's mind raced, piecing together the fragments of the case. "This can't be a coincidence, Tom. The hooded figure showing up just as we're about to question Dawn? They're connected, I can feel it."

Tom's brow furrowed, his analytical mind processing the implications. "If you're right, then Dawn could be in serious danger. We need to find her, and fast."

"Agreed," Harry said, her voice laced with urgency. "Let's head back to the station and see if we can track her down. Every minute counts."

Tom's expression grew serious, his eyes scanning the surrounding area with renewed vigilance. "We'll need to be careful. If someone's trying to interfere with the investigation, we can't let them rattle us."

Harry nodded; her jaw set with determination. The encounter had only strengthened her resolve to uncover the truth behind Roger Morgan's murder and bring the killer to justice. No matter who was watching from the shadows, she would not be deterred.

As they made their way out of the alley, and into the High Street, the weight of the case bore down on them like a suffocating fog. The killer was always one step ahead, toying with them, leaving a trail of bodies and broken lives in their wake. But Harry and Tom were determined to see this through, to bring justice to the victims and closure to the shattered community of Taunton.

Dawn Menzies held the key to unravelling this twisted web of obsession and murder, and they would stop at nothing to ensure her safety and uncover the truth lurking in the shadows of the once-idyllic town.

Chapter 9 Dawn's Descent

The afternoon sun cast a warm glow over the tranquil canal, its gentle waters reflecting the vibrant hues of the surrounding buildings. Dawn Menzies sat on her balcony, her eyes fixed on the shimmering surface, as if seeking solace in the rhythmic flow of the current. The distant sounds of the Taunton Flower Show drifted on the breeze, a stark contrast to the turmoil that gripped her heart.

Inside her flat, the silence was broken only by the soft ticking of a clock, each second a reminder of the void left by Roger's absence. Dawn's thoughts were a tangled web of grief, confusion, and fear, the weight of her secret affair bearing down upon her like a suffocating blanket.

Dawn's mind drifted to stolen moments with Roger, memories now tinged with a bittersweet ache. She recalled the day they snuck away to an old barn on the outskirts of town, a photographer and his muse seeking a rustic backdrop. The air had been heavy with the scent of sun-warmed straw and aged wood, dust motes dancing in the slanted beams of light that pierced the slatted walls.

In that cocoon of golden light and shadow, surrounded by bales of hay and the distant lowing of cattle, they had come together in a passionate embrace. The prickle of straw against bare skin, the taste of sweat and desire, the muffled laughter as they tumbled into an itchy pile of hay - fragments of sensations, forbidden and thrilling.

Other rendezvous played through her mind like a bittersweet montage. Moonlit walks in Vivary Park, hands clasped, hearts pounding at the risk of discovery. The muted hush of the park at night enveloped them as they strolled along winding paths, moonlight dappling the leaves overhead and crickets singing a discreet chorus. Stolen kisses by the fountain, the splash of water and the cool mist a sensual counterpoint to the heat building between them.

Each meeting place was seared into her memory - the abandoned greenhouse where the earthy scent of tomato vines cloaked their clandestine coupling; the banks of the River Tone where the babble of the water over stones drowned out gasps and sighs of pleasure; the darkroom where the intoxicating aroma of developing chemicals mingled with the musk of desire and the only light was the dim red glow that turned their entwined bodies into a study of shadows...

As the memories washed over Dawn, the ghost of Roger's touch against her skin, his scent, his deep voice whispering her name, the pain of his loss cut ever deeper, staining each treasured, secret moment with the indelible knowledge that there would never again be another. The settings remained - the barn, the park, the river - but now stood as mere haunted scenery, backdrops to a love story cut tragically short.

Suddenly noise from the front door snapped her back to the present. Dawn's heart raced as she rose from her seat, her footsteps tentative as she approached the source of the disturbance. A glance through the peephole revealed an empty hallway, but as she opened the door, her eyes were drawn to a small, white envelope lying on the floor.

With trembling hands, Dawn retrieved the mysterious message, her name scrawled across the front in a familiar hand. She tore open the envelope, her breath catching in her throat as she read the contents:

Dawn,

I have news about Roger. Meet me at the children's playground in Vivary Park at 10 pm. Come alone.

Larry Stubbs

The note was brief, its words cryptic and unsettling. Dawn's mind raced with questions, her heart torn between the desire for answers and the fear of what those answers might bring. Larry Stubbs, Roger's closest friend and confidant, had always been a peripheral figure in their lives, but now he held the key to a mystery that consumed her every waking thought.

As the afternoon light began to fade, Dawn found herself drawn back to the balcony, the note clutched tightly in her hand. The canal below seemed to whisper secrets, its waters holding the promise of revelation and the threat of darkness in equal measure. The decision lay before her, a crossroads that would determine the path of her future.

With a heavy heart and a mind filled with trepidation, Dawn knew she had no choice but to follow the trail laid out before her. The playground in Vivary Park, a place of innocence and joy, now loomed as a destination of uncertainty and dread. As the clock ticked ever closer to the appointed hour, Dawn steeled herself for the journey ahead, knowing that the truth, no matter how painful, was the only way forward.

Dawn walked along the canal path, her mind a whirlwind of emotions. The news of Roger's murder had shaken her to the core, and the weight of her confession to Larry about their affair hung heavy on her heart. Despite her hesitation, she had decided to go to the meeting, hoping to find some clarity or comfort in the midst of the chaos.

The night was clear, with a full moon casting an eerie glow over the water. The distant hooting of owls added to the unsettling atmosphere, their calls echoing through the stillness. As Dawn made her way along the path, she noticed how empty it was, with overgrown bushes creeping out over the walkway in places. The shadows seemed to dance and shift in the moonlight, playing tricks on her already frayed nerves.

Suddenly, a rustling in the bushes startled Dawn, causing her to turn around with a start. Her heart raced as she peered into the darkness, trying to discern the source of the sound. To her relief, she spotted a large rabbit emerging from the foliage, its nose twitching as it searched for a snack. Dawn let out a shaky laugh, chiding herself for being so jumpy.

Continuing her journey through the town, Dawn passed the cricket ground. The large floodlights cast long shadows across the pitch, the moonlight transforming the usually lively space into a ghostly landscape. The eerie stillness was broken only by the occasional gust of wind, which whispered through the trees and sent a chill down Dawn's spine.

As she walked up the high street, Dawn encountered a group of people spilling out of the pub, their laughter and chatter a stark contrast to the sombre mood that enveloped her. She quickened her pace, not wanting to draw attention to herself. Further along, she noticed a couple of homeless people huddled in sleeping bags, their makeshift shelter surrounded by a fortress of alcohol cans. The pungent smell of urine assaulted her nostrils as she passed the Crown Walk, a reminder of the harsh realities that existed just beneath the surface of the town's quaint facade.

Finally, Dawn reached the gates of the park, which were now locked for the evening. She stood outside, staring at the imposing iron bars that separated her from the meeting place. The darkness beyond seemed to beckon her, promising answers to the questions that plagued her mind. Yet, the thought of scaling the gates and venturing into the unknown filled her with trepidation.

Dawn took a deep breath, trying to gather her courage. She knew that whatever awaited her in the park could change the course of her life forever. The weight of her secrets, the pain of Roger's loss, and the uncertainty of the future all converged in this moment. With a final glance at the moon above, Dawn reached out and grasped the cold metal of the gate, ready to confront the shadows that lurked within.

As Dawn gracefully leaps down from the ornate iron gates of Vivary Park, her feet land softly on the well-trodden path that winds its way towards the serene lake. The early evening air is crisp and cool, carrying with it the faint scent of freshly cut grass and the delicate perfume of the newly planted flower beds that line her route.

The path to her right is bathed in the warm glow of the setting sun, casting elongated shadows across the manicured lawns. As she passes the war memorial, a solemn granite obelisk standing sentinel over the tranquil grounds, Dawn's mind is filled with a sense of reverence for those who sacrificed their lives for the greater good.

The flower beds, meticulously prepared for the upcoming Flower Show, are a riot of colour and texture. The vibrant hues of the blooms seem to dance in the gentle breeze, their petals brushing against Dawn's legs as she walks by. The air is heavy with their fragrance, a heady mix of sweetness and earthiness that fills her lungs and soothes her troubled mind.

As the lake comes into view on her right, Dawn's gaze is drawn to the ducks gathered on the banks, their heads tucked snugly into their wings as they settle in for the night. The water's surface is like a mirror, reflecting the orange and pink hues of the sky above, a perfect picture of serenity.

Passing the bowling club, memories of a passionate encounter with Roger flood Dawn's mind. She can almost feel the soft grass beneath her bare skin, the thrill of their forbidden tryst heightened by the risk of discovery. The sudden illumination of the lights, the frantic scramble for clothes, and Roger's ungraceful leap over the fence into the stream—a moment of pure adrenaline and laughter amidst the secrecy of their affair.

Further along the path, Dawn notices a wooden hut on her left, its weathered exterior a testament to the passage of time. A homeless person, wrapped in a tattered blanket, has made the shelter their temporary home. A supermarket carrier bag, stuffed with meagre possessions, serves as a makeshift pillow. The sight is a poignant reminder of the harsh realities that exist beyond the manicured beauty of the park.

As Dawn finally reaches the playground, the emptiness of the space is a stark contrast to the usual laughter and joy that fills the air during the day. The swings sway gently in the breeze, their chains creaking softly, while the merry-go-round stands motionless, waiting for the next child's hand to set it spinning.

Pulling out her phone, Dawn begins to scroll through the images stored within, each one a frozen moment in time. The photos of her and Roger together, stolen snapshots of a love that could never be fully realized, bring a bittersweet smile to her face. As she loses herself in the memories, the minutes tick by, and the lengthening shadows of the playground equipment stretch across the ground, reaching out to her like ghostly fingers.

In the stillness of the deserted playground, Dawn waits for Larry, unaware that the events about to unfold will shatter the fragile peace of this moonlit rendezvous and change the course of her life forever.

The night was still, the silence broken only by the distant hooting of an owl and the gentle rustling of leaves in the breeze. The moonlight cast an eerie glow over the deserted playground, the shadows of the equipment stretching long and distorted across the ground.

Dawn stood alone; her attention focused on the glowing screen of her phone as she scrolled through the images that held so many memories. The soft light from the device illuminated her face, highlighting the mix of emotions that played across her delicate features - nostalgia, longing, and a hint of sadness.

Unbeknownst to Dawn, a figure emerged from the shadows of the old tea rooms nearby. The building loomed in the darkness, its windows boarded up and its walls covered in a tangle of ivy. The figure moved with a purposeful stealth; their footsteps muffled by the soft grass as they crept closer to the unsuspecting woman.

As the figure drew nearer, the moonlight glinted off the object gripped tightly in their hand - a cricket bat, its smooth surface worn from use. The figure's knuckles were white with the intensity of their grip, betraying the tension and anticipation that coursed through their body.

The air seemed to grow colder as the figure approached, a sense of menace emanating from their presence. Dawn, lost in her thoughts and memories, remained oblivious to the danger that lurked just steps away. The figure raised the bat, their muscles coiled and ready to strike, as they closed the distance between themselves and their unsuspecting target.

In that moment, the tranquillity of the night was shattered, the sinister intentions of the shadowy figure made manifest in the stillness of the playground. Dawn, caught unawares, was about to find herself at the center of a twisted plot, her fate hanging in the balance as the cricket bat cast its ominous shadow across the moonlit scene.

As Dawn stood in the moonlit playground, her attention focused on the glowing screen of her phone. Lost in thought, scrolling through images of happier times with Roger, she failed to notice the shadowy figure emerging from the darkness behind her.

The assailant moved a few final steps with a chilling, practiced stealth, their footsteps muffled by the soft grass. Gripping the cricket bat tightly, knuckles white with tension, they closed the distance to their unsuspecting victim. The moon's pale light glinted off the polished wood, a cold and unfeeling witness to the impending brutality.

Just as Dawn sensed a presence, a prickling unease that caused her to look up from her phone, the figure struck. With a powerful, merciless swing, the bat connected with the back of Dawn's head, the sickening crack of impact echoing through the empty playground. The force of the blow was devastating, the trauma immediate and irreversible.

In that fraction of a second, Dawn's world went black, her body crumpling to the ground like a marionette with its strings cut. Her phone slipped from her grasp, the screen shattering as it hit the pavement, a cruel metaphor for the fragility of life. The images of her and Roger, frozen in time, became a macabre backdrop to the scene of her demise.

As the assailant dragged Dawn's lifeless body through the moonlit playground, the once joyful atmosphere took on a sinister, nightmarish quality. The colourful play equipment cast eerie shadows across the ground, their shapes distorted and menacing in the silvery light. The only sound was the soft rustling of leaves in the gentle breeze and the laboured breathing of the killer as they hauled their grim burden towards the miniature railway.

The railway, a charming feature that brought delight to countless children on sunny Sunday afternoons, now seemed to take on a darker purpose. The tracks gleamed coldly in the moonlight, a stark contrast to the vibrant, cheerful colours of the tiny locomotives that usually traversed their loops, carrying giggling youngsters for a mere £1 per ride.

With a final, unceremonious heave, the assailant positioned Dawn's body across the raised tracks, her limbs splayed at unnatural angles, her once lively eyes now staring blankly at the indifferent night sky. The killer stepped back, their chest heaving from the exertion, and surveyed their handiwork with a detached, almost clinical gaze.

The mystery assailant removed Dawn's skirt, stockings and suspenders, her shirt, and her bra before taking out a lipstick and writing the message across Dawn's bare breasts.

"More will follow."

In a final act of desecration of Dawn's body, the assailant took one of Dawn's stockings and tied it tightly around her neck to conceal the nature of the murder.

In the silence of the night, the playground took on an air of macabre anticipation, as though waiting for the moment when the first unsuspecting parkgoer would stumble upon the grisly scene. The miniature railway, once a source of innocent joy, now served as a stage for a twisted display of violence and obsession, its cheerful facade forever tainted by the horror that had unfolded upon its tracks.

As quickly as they had appeared, the assailant melted back into the shadows, leaving Dawn's lifeless form lying in the ghostly glow of the moonlight. The playground, once a place of childhood laughter and joy, had become a silent, eerie tableau of death, the only movement the gentle swaying of the swings in the night breeze.

Chapter 10 Blood on the Rails

The fluorescent lights of the CID office buzzed and flickered, casting harsh shadows across the cluttered desks as the night wore on. Harry and Tom sat hunched over the scattered case files, empty coffee cups and takeaway containers littering the space between them. The once lively chatter of the bullpen had long since faded, leaving only the hum of computer fans and the occasional creak of a chair to break the heavy silence.

Harry rubbed her bleary eyes, the words on the page before her blurring together. She glanced up at Tom, noting the deep furrow of his brow as he pored over witness statements for the umpteenth time. The air between them was thick with unspoken tension, the weight of the case bearing down on them both.

"It has to be Walker," Harry said suddenly, her voice cutting through the stillness. "His obsession with Roger, the history of animosity between them... it all fits."

Tom sighed, leaning back in his chair. "We can't just go on gut instinct, Harry. We need solid evidence linking him to the crime."

"Evidence?" Harry scoffed. "The man practically confessed his hatred for Roger to anyone who would listen. He had motive, opportunity-"

"But no physical proof placing him at the scene," Tom countered, his own frustration bubbling to the surface. "We can't just go arresting people based on hunches and hearsay."

Harry slammed her hand down on the desk, sending papers fluttering. "Damn it, Tom! While we sit here debating semantics, the real killer is out there, probably planning his next move. We must act before someone else gets hurt!"

Tom opened his mouth to retort but was cut off by the shrill ring of the telephone. They both froze, eyes locked on the offensive device as it continued its insistent clamour. With a muttered curse, Harry snatched up the receiver.

"DI Lambert," she barked, her free hand clenching into a fist.

Tom watched as the colour drained from her face, her eyes widening with each passing second. A sense of dread settled in the pit of his stomach.

"Where?" Harry demanded, already reaching for a pen to jot down the address. "We're on our way."

She slammed the phone back into its cradle, her movements sharp and jerky as she gathered up her jacket. Tom was on his feet in an instant, the argument forgotten in the face of this new development.

"What is it? What's happened?" he asked, dreading the answer even as the words left his lips.

Harry met his gaze, her expression grim. "There's been another murder. This one is worse than Roger Morgan. Phil saw it and lost his breakfast!"

Tom felt the breath leave his lungs in a rush, the implications hitting him like a physical blow. The killer had struck again, leaving another life shattered in their wake.

As they raced out of the office, the harsh fluorescent lights flickering overhead, Tom couldn't shake the feeling that they were running out of time. The shadow of the killer loomed larger with each passing moment, and the weight of the case seemed to press down on them with suffocating force.

They had to find a break, and fast, before more innocent blood was spilled. The game was on, and the stakes had never been higher.

As the police cars screamed past Jellalabad barracks, their sirens piercing the night air, Harry and Tom's pulses raced with a sense of urgency. They navigated the winding roads of Taunton, their destination clear in their minds: the children's playground at the back of Vivary Park, nestled beside the Taunton Deane Cricket Club and the Taunton Deane Shooting Association.

The tires screeched as they turned into the park entrance, gravel spraying beneath the wheels. The once peaceful grounds were now awash in the flashing blue and red lights of the police vehicles, casting an eerie glow across the manicured lawns and carefully tended flower beds.

As they raced towards the playground, the detectives couldn't shake the feeling that they were on the cusp of a grim discovery. The secluded location, hidden away from the main thoroughfares of the park, seemed to hold an ominous secret waiting to be uncovered.

With each passing moment, the tension mounted, the weight of the unknown pressing down upon them. The playground, a place once filled with the laughter and joy of children, now loomed ahead, a silent witness to the horrors that had unfolded within its boundaries.

Harry and Tom leapt from the car, the gravel crunching beneath their feet as they hurried towards the playground, guided by the bobbing beams of their torches. The once cheerful play area now seemed sinister in the gloom, the brightly coloured equipment casting long, distorted shadows across the damp earth.

A small cluster of uniformed officers stood huddled near the swings, their hushed whispers carrying an undercurrent of shock and revulsion. As the detectives approached, the group parted, revealing the grisly tableau that had shattered the tranquillity of the early morning.

The moonlight cast an ethereal glow over Dawn's exposed flesh, highlighting the curves and planes of her lifeless form. Her alabaster skin seemed to shimmer under the celestial spotlight, a macabre display of beauty in the face of tragedy.

As the first hints of dawn began to paint the horizon, the soft light gradually illuminated the grisly scene, revealing the dark message scrawled across her breasts in vivid red lipstick: "More will follow". But it was her face that drew their horrified gazes - frozen in a rictus of terror, her wide, glassy eyes seemed to stare directly into their souls.

Harry swallowed hard, fighting back the wave of nausea that threatened to overwhelm her. Beside her, Tom's jaw clenched, his knuckles turning white as he gripped his torch with a force that belied his outward composure.

Harry and Tom exchanged a look of grim determination. The Flower Show, once a beacon of beauty and community, had now been irrevocably tainted by the spectre of death.

Harry crouched down, her eyes scanning Dawn's body with a mixture of sorrow and clinical detachment. "No obvious signs of a struggle," she murmured, her gloved hand gently brushing a strand of hair from Dawn's face. "But the stocking around her neck... that's not accidental."

Tom nodded grimly; his gaze fixed on the ligature mark that marred Dawn's throat. "Looks like it was used to strangle her. The killer wanted to make sure she was dead."

"And the message," Harry said, her voice tight with disgust as she gestured to the words scrawled across Dawn's bare breasts. "'More will follow.' This isn't just a murder, Tom. It's a threat."

Tom's jaw clenched, his eyes hardening with determination. "Whoever did this, they're not done. We need to find them before they strike again."

Harry stood, her gaze sweeping over the macabre scene once more. "No skirt, no underwear... the killer undressed her, staged her body like this for a reason. It's a display of power, of control."

"Just like with Roger," Tom mused, his mind racing with the implications. "The monopod through the chest, the careful positioning... it's the same killer, Harry. It has to be."

Harry nodded, a sense of dread settling in the pit of her stomach. "Two victims, both connected to the photography world, both brutally murdered and left for us to find. What's the endgame here, Tom? What message are they trying to send?"

Tom shook his head, frustration etched into his features. "I don't know. But we need to find out, and fast. Before anyone else ends up like Dawn."

Harry and Tom approached Dr. Eliza Hawthorne was crouched beside Dawn's body, her latex gloves stained with the grim remnants of the examination.

Harry asked, "What have we got, Eliza?"

Eliza stood, her face grim. "Single blow to the head, likely with a blunt object. The damage was immediate and irreversible."

Tom questioned, "What do you mean? The scene suggested strangulation as the cause of death."

Eliza shook her head. "That was my first thought as well, given the ligature marks on her neck. However, the facial colouring is inconsistent with asphyxiation."

Tom leaned in, studying Dawn's pale, lifeless features. "How so?"

"In a typical strangulation case, you'd expect to see a distinctive reddish-purple discoloration due to the blood pooling in the face," Eliza explained, gently tilting Dawn's head to the side. "But as you can see, her complexion is remarkably pallid."

Eliza pointed to the stocking tied around Dawn's neck. "This was used to conceal the nature of the murder. The killer knew what they were doing."

Harry: "So, we're looking at someone with a plan, someone strong enough to take her out with a single blow."

Tom frowned. "Could be a man or a woman, but the strength required suggests a male perpetrator."

Harry sighed. "Methodical, efficient, and strong. Not much to go on, but it's a start."

Eliza: "I'll have more for you once I get her back to the lab. The sooner we catch this bastard, the better."

Harry and Tom approached the visibly shaken security guard, his nametag identifying him as "Bill". The man's face was ashen, his eyes wide with a mixture of shock and disbelief. His hands trembled slightly as he gripped the fabric of his uniform, as if trying to anchor himself to reality.

The detectives exchanged a knowing glance before Harry stepped forward, her voice gentle but firm. "Good morning, Bill. I'm DI Lambert and this is DS Reed. We understand you were the one who discovered the body. Can you walk us through what happened?".

Bill nodded solemnly, "I was doing my usual rounds just after 3 am. As I approached the miniature railway, I noticed something draped over the tracks. At first, I thought it might be a discarded costume or prop, but as I got closer... he shudders, his face paling at the memory ...I realized it was a woman's body. She was completely naked and wasn't moving. I immediately called for backup and secured the scene."

"Did you notice anything unusual or out of place before you found the body? Any suspicious activity or individuals in the park?", asked Tom.

Bill shook his head "No, it was a quiet night. The park had been closed for hours, and I didn't see anyone else around. Although..." he pauses, frowning slightly.

Harry leant in "Although what, Bill? Any detail, no matter how small, could be important."

"Well, I did notice a strange smell near the body. It was sweet, almost like flowers, but with a sickly undertone. I didn't think much of it at the time, given the nature of the Flower Show, but now...", continued Bill.

Tom exchanged a glance with Harry "That's very helpful, Bill. Can you describe the smell in more detail? Did it remind you of any specific flower or scent?"

Bill closed his eyes, trying to recall, "It was cloying, like rotting fruit mixed with the sweetness of roses. I've never smelled anything quite like it before. I'm sorry I can't be more specific."

"No, that's great, Bill. Your information could prove invaluable. Just a few more questions - did you happen to see or hear any vehicles leaving the park around the time you discovered the body?", asked Harry.

Bill paused for a moment "Now that you mention it, I did hear a car engine starting up somewhere near the retirement home, but I didn't see the vehicle itself. It was maybe 10 or 15 minutes before I found the body."

Tom jotted down notes, "Thank you, Bill. You've been a great help. If you remember anything else, no matter how insignificant it may seem, please don't hesitate to contact us."

"Of course. I just hope you catch whoever did this. It's a tragedy, and the poor girl deserves justice." Remarked Bill.

Harry placed a reassuring hand on Bill's shoulder "We'll do everything in our power to make sure that happens, Bill. Thank you again for your assistance."

Harry and Tom stood at the edge of the crime scene, the flashing lights of the police cars casting an eerie glow over the once tranquil park. The naked body of Dawn Menzies lay before them, her lifeless eyes staring up at the starless sky. The silk stocking was wrapped tightly around her slender throat, the fabric biting into her pale flesh.

Harry crouched down, her keen eyes scanning the scene for any clues the killer might have left behind. "This is no coincidence," she muttered, her voice low and grim. "First Roger, now Dawn. There's a connection here, a pattern we're not seeing."

Tom nodded; his brow furrowed in thought. "The staging of the bodies, the personal nature of the kills... This isn't some random psycho. This is someone with a very specific agenda."

"And that stocking," Harry added, rising to her feet. "It's a message, a calling card. The killer wants us to know that these murders are linked."

Tom's gaze drifted to the flower show tents in the park. "Roger and Dawn were both connected to the photography community, to the Flower Show. Could be someone with a grudge, a rival with an axe to grind."

Harry's lips pressed into a thin line, her mind whirring with possibilities. "Or maybe it's more personal than that. Roger's obsession with Dawn, the affair... Could be a lover's quarrel turned deadly."

"Margaret did seem awfully quick to point the finger," Tom mused. "Hell, hath no fury and all that."

Harry shook her head, unsatisfied. "No, there's more to it than a simple love triangle. This killer, whoever they are, they're methodical, calculating. They're not just lashing out in a fit of passion. This is a carefully orchestrated plan."

As the crime scene techs bustled around them, collecting evidence and snapping photos, Harry and Tom stood in silent contemplation, the weight of the case bearing down on them. Two lives snuffed out, a community gripped by fear, and a killer still on the loose.

"We need to dig deeper," Harry said at last, her voice steeled with determination. "Every secret, every grudge, every twisted motive. We'll turn over every rock in this town until we find the truth."

Tom met her gaze, his own resolve mirroring hers. "And we won't stop until justice is served. For Roger, for Dawn, and for everyone else this bastard has hurt."

As they turned back to the grim tableau before them, Harry and Tom knew that the hunt was only just beginning. In the shadows of Taunton, a killer lurked, their dark obsessions threatening to tear the very fabric of the community apart. And it would be up to them to unravel the twisted threads before another life was claimed.

Chapter 11 The Forensic Truth

The mid-morning sun cast a harsh glare across the windshield as Harry manoeuvred the unmarked police car through the bustling streets of Taunton. Beside her, Tom sat in pensive silence, his eyes fixed on the passing storefronts and pedestrians, yet his mind clearly elsewhere, undoubtedly grappling with the grim task that lay ahead.

The news of Dawn Menzies' murder had hit them like a punch to the gut, a brutal reminder of the stakes they faced in their pursuit of the killer. Harry's knuckles whitened as she gripped the steering wheel, her jaw clenched with a mixture of anger and determination. She had seen her fair share of senseless violence throughout her career, but there was something about this case, about the calculated cruelty of the crimes, which chilled her to the bone.

As they approached the nondescript brick building housing the medical examiner's office, Harry felt a weight settle in her chest. She knew all too well the grim tableau that awaited them inside - the sterile, fluorescent-lit hallways, the acrid tang of disinfectant mingling with the unmistakable odour of death. It was a world apart from the vibrant beauty of the Taunton Flower Show, a stark reminder of the fragility of life and the depths of human depravity.

Tom stirred, breaking the heavy silence that had enveloped the car. "You know, no matter how many times we do this, it never gets any easier." His voice was low, tinged with a weariness that belied his years on the force.

Harry nodded, her eyes never leaving the road. "It's not supposed to be easy, Tom. The day it is, that's when we need to hang up our badges."

As she pulled the car into the parking lot, the gravel crunching beneath the tires, Harry steeled herself for the task ahead. She knew that the answers they sought lay within those walls, etched into the lifeless flesh of Dawn Menzies. It was their job to read the story written there, to piece together the clues that would lead them to her killer.

With a shared look of grim resolve, Harry and Tom exited the car and made their way towards the entrance, the weight of their duty heavy on their shoulders. The mid-morning sun continued to beat down, an incongruous backdrop to the darkness they were about to confront. But they pressed on, driven by the knowledge that every step, no matter how painful, brought them closer to the truth and, perhaps, to the justice that Dawn and the other victims so desperately deserved.

As Harry and Tom entered the sterile confines of the autopsy suite, the harsh fluorescent lights cast an eerie glow over the lifeless form of Dawn Menzies. Dr. Eliza Hawthorne stood beside the stainless-steel table; her expression grim as she prepared to walk the detectives through her findings.

"Detectives," Eliza began, her voice clinical yet tinged with a note of solemnity. "As you can see, the victim suffered a catastrophic head injury. The skull has been fractured in multiple places, with extensive damage to the underlying brain tissue."

Harry leaned in closer, her keen eyes taking in the gruesome details. Dawn's once-beautiful face was now a mess of mottled bruises and lacerations, her features distorted by the force of the blows that had ended her life. Clumps of her blonde hair were matted with dried blood; the golden strands now stained a rusty brown.

"The pattern of the fractures suggests the killer used a large, blunt object with a flat surface," Eliza continued, pointing to a particularly deep indentation on the left side of Dawn's skull. "I found traces of wood embedded in the wound, likely transferred from the murder weapon upon impact."

Tom frowned, his mind racing with the implications. "So, we're looking for something like a wooden board or a baseball bat?"

Eliza nodded. "Possibly. The killer would have needed significant strength to inflict this level of damage. The stocking around her neck appears to be a deliberate attempt to mislead investigators, as the ligature marks are superficial and post-mortem."

As Eliza gently lifted the sheet covering Dawn's torso, Harry's breath caught in her throat. There, scrawled across the model's ample breasts in garish red lipstick, was the chilling message: "More will follow." The words seemed to mock them, a taunting reminder of the killer's twisted agenda.

"There's more," Eliza said quietly, her gloved fingers tracing a 3-inch, precise incision beneath each breast. "It appears the killer removed her breast implants. I found traces of silicone residue in the wounds."

Harry and Tom exchanged a troubled glance, the implications of this revelation weighing heavily upon them. This was no ordinary murder - it was a calculated, ritualistic act, carried out by someone with a deeply disturbed mind.

As they thanked Eliza and made their way out of the morgue, Harry couldn't shake the image of Dawn's mutilated body from her thoughts. The once-vibrant model, whose beauty had captivated the crowds at the Flower Show, now lay cold and lifeless, a tragic testament to the depths of human cruelty.

With renewed determination, Harry and Tom stepped out into the sunlight, their resolve hardened by the knowledge that a dangerous predator stalked the streets of Taunton. They would not rest until they had unravelled the twisted web of secrets and lies surrounding Dawn's murder and brought her killer to justice.

Harry and Tom exited the medical centre, the weight of the new murder hanging heavily on their shoulders. As Tom slid into the driver's seat, Harry leaned against the car, her eyes distant and troubled. "This changes everything, Tom. We can't ignore the connection between Roger's murder and this new victim."

Tom nodded; his jaw clenched tight. "Agreed. But what's the link? Why target two seemingly unrelated men?"

Harry shook her head, frustration evident in her voice. "I don't know. But I have a feeling Margaret

Morgan might be able to shed some light on the situation."

"You think she knows more than she's letting on?" Tom asked, raising an eyebrow.

"Call it a hunch," Harry replied, "But there's something about her, Tom. Something that doesn't quite add up."

Tom sighed, running a hand through his hair. "Alright, let's pay her another visit. See if we can rattle some information loose."

As they pulled out of the parking lot, the flashing lights of the ambulance and police cars fading in the rearview mirror, Harry couldn't shake the feeling that they were on the precipice of something much larger than a couple of murders. The threads of the case were beginning to intertwine, forming a tapestry of secrets and lies that threatened to unravel at any moment.

"We need to tread carefully, Tom," she said, her voice low and serious. "Whoever's behind this, they're not going to go down without a fight."

Tom glanced over at his partner, a flicker of concern in his eyes. "We'll get them, Harry. We always do."

But as they sped through the darkening streets of Taunton, the weight of the investigation bearing down on them, both detectives knew that this case would test them in ways they had never been tested before. The hunt was on, and the stakes had never been higher.

As Harry and Tom approached the Morgan residence once more, the air seemed to crackle with tension. The revelation of Dawn Menzies' identity and her sordid affair with Roger had cast a new light on the investigation, and the detectives were determined to uncover the truth, no matter how painful it might be.

Margaret greeted them at the door, her eyes red-rimmed and her face drawn. The events of the past few days had clearly taken their toll, and Harry felt a pang of sympathy for the woman whose world had been shattered by her husband's betrayal.

"Mrs. Morgan," Harry began gently, "we need to ask you some more questions about Dawn Menzies and her relationship with your husband."

Margaret's jaw tightened, and for a moment, Harry thought she might refuse. But then, with a sigh of resignation, she stepped aside and ushered them into the living room.

The detectives settled onto the sofa, Tom leaned forward, his elbows resting on his knees. "We understand that this is difficult, but it's important that we have all the facts. Can you tell us more about when you first learned of the affair?"

Margaret's hands twisted in her lap, her knuckles white with tension. "It was about six months ago," she began, her voice barely above a whisper. "I found a text message on Roger's phone, something about meeting up at a hotel. I confronted him, and he admitted it."

Harry nodded; her pen poised over her notebook. "And how did you react?"

A bitter laugh escaped Margaret's lips. "How do you think? I was devastated, furious. I wanted to confront her, to make her pay for what she'd done to my marriage."

Tom exchanged a glance with Harry before pressing on. "And did you? Confront her, I mean?"

Margaret shook her head, her eyes distant. "No. Roger begged me not to, said he'd end things with her. I believed him, like a fool."

Harry leaned forward, her voice gentle but firm. "Mrs. Morgan, I know this is hard, but we need to know the truth. Did you have anything to do with Dawn Menzies' disappearance?"

Margaret's head snapped up, her eyes wide with shock. "What? No! I had no idea she was even missing until you told me. I may have hated her for what she did, but I would never hurt anyone."

"Margaret," Harry began softly, "I'm afraid I have some more tragic news. We've discovered another body - Dawn Menzies, the model your husband was... involved with."

Margaret's eyes widened, a flicker of shock and perhaps something else, something darker, flashing across her features before she composed herself. "Dawn? But how... where...?"

Harry sighed heavily. "Her body was found early this morning, in the children's playground at the park."

Margaret's hand flew to her mouth, stifling a gasp. "Oh my God. That's horrible. Who would do such a thing?"

"That's what we intend to find out," Harry replied, her voice hardening with resolve. "Dawn's murder, coming so soon after Roger's, cannot be a coincidence. Whoever did this has a vendetta, a twisted obsession that's spiralled out of control."

She fixed Margaret with a probing stare. "I know this is difficult, but I need you to be completely honest with me. Is there anyone you can think of who might have wanted to harm Dawn or your husband? Anyone with a grudge or a motive for revenge?"

Margaret shook her head, her eyes welling with tears. "No, I... I don't know. Roger had his flaws, his indiscretions, but I can't imagine anyone hating him enough to do this."

As Harry and Tom continued their questioning, the pieces of the puzzle began to fall into place. Margaret's alibi for the night of Roger's murder checked out, and her genuine surprise at the news of Dawn's disappearance seemed to rule her out as a suspect.

But as they left the Morgan residence, Harry couldn't shake the feeling that they were still missing something crucial. The secrets and lies that had torn apart Roger and Margaret's marriage had created a tangled web of motives and opportunities and untangling it would require all of their skills and intuition.

As they climbed into the car, Tom turned to Harry, his brow furrowed. "So, if it wasn't Margaret, who else had motive and opportunity?"

Harry tapped her pen against her notebook, her mind whirring with possibilities. "We need to dig deeper into Dawn Menzies' life, find out who else she might have been involved with. And we need to take a closer look at those other photographers, the ones who were jealous of Roger's success."

Tom nodded, his expression grim. "It's not going to be easy, but we'll get to the truth. For Roger's sake, and for Dawn's."

As they pulled away from the curb, the weight of the investigation settled heavily on their shoulders. The Taunton Flower Show, with all its beauty and promise, seemed a distant memory now, overshadowed by the dark secrets and twisted obsessions that had claimed two lives.

But Harry and Tom were determined to see justice done, no matter the cost. They would follow the evidence wherever it led, pulling on each thread until the truth was finally revealed. It was their duty, their calling, and they would not rest until the killer was brought to light.

The harsh fluorescent lights of the CID room cast an eerie glow on the crime scene board as Harry and Tom stood before it, their faces etched with grim determination. The once sparse board was now a chaotic collage of photographs, witness statements, and hastily scrawled notes, a visual representation of the tangled web they found themselves ensnared in.

In the center of the board, two images dominated the space: the lifeless bodies of Roger Morgan and Dawn Menzies, their unseeing eyes staring out from the glossy prints. Harry's gaze lingered on Dawn's picture; her heart heavy with the weight of another life cut brutally short.

Beside the photographs, a new addition to the macabre display: the message left on Dawn's body, scrawled in vivid red marker. "More will follow." The words seemed to pulse with malevolent intent, a chilling promise of further bloodshed.

Tom stepped forward, his fingers tracing the lines of connection between the victims. "Two murders, both linked to the photography competition," he murmured, his voice low and pensive. "The staging of the bodies, the messages... it's clear we're dealing with someone who has a point to make."

Harry nodded, her mind whirring with the implications. "And they're not finished. The killer is taunting us, daring us to stop them before they claim another victim."

The room seemed to close in around them, the weight of the responsibility bearing down on their shoulders. The once vibrant and joyful Taunton Flower Show had become a hunting ground for a twisted mind, and they were the only ones who could put an end to the carnage.

Harry's eyes drifted to the hastily scribbled timeline of events, the dates and times of the murders standing out in stark relief. "We're running out of time," she said, her voice tight with urgency. "The longer this goes on, the more danger everyone at the festival is in."

Tom's jaw clenched, his determination mirroring her own. "Then we keep digging. We go over every scrap of evidence, every witness statement, until we find something that leads us to the killer."

"Harry, about that hooded figure you chased earlier... any new insights or theories on who they might be and how they're connected to the case?", Tom asked.

Harry shook her head, frustration evident in her voice "Not yet. Whoever they are, they know how to disappear without a trace. It's like they're always one step ahead of us."

"Do you think they could be our killer? Stalking us to keep tabs on the investigation?", Tom said.

"It's possible, but something doesn't quite add up. If they're the murderer, why risk exposing themselves like that? Why not just lay low?", replied Harry.

Tom rubbed his chin thoughtfully, "Unless they're trying to send a message. Intimidate us, throw us off balance."

"Or maybe they're not the killer at all. Could be someone else with a vested interest in the case. A witness, an accomplice...," said Harry.

"...or a victim. Someone who's afraid to come forward directly.", added Tom.

Harry nodded grimly "Exactly. We need to find out who they are and what they know. They could hold the key to cracking this whole thing wide open."

"Agreed. Let's review the witness statements again, see if there's any mention of a hooded figure lurking around the crime scenes.", said Tom.

"Good idea. And let's keep our eyes peeled. If they're bold enough to stalk us in broad daylight, chances are we haven't seen the last of them.", said Harry.

As they turned back to the board, their eyes scanning the sea of information before them, a sense of purpose settled over the room. They would not rest until they had unravelled the twisted strands of this case and brought the killer to justice. For the sake of the victims, for the people of Taunton, they would not fail.

The CID room had become their battleground, the crime scene board their map to navigating the treacherous waters of this investigation. With each passing moment, the urgency grew, the knowledge that a ruthless killer still lurked in the shadows, poised to strike again. Harry and Tom exchanged a look of silent understanding, a promise to stand together against the darkness that threatened to engulf the once-peaceful town of Taunton.

Chapter 12 Fragments of Obsession

The CID room felt oppressive, the walls seeming to close in as Harry and Tom pored over the case files and evidence once more. The harsh fluorescent lights cast an unflattering pall over the cluttered desks and whiteboards covered in scribbled notes and crime scene photos.

Harry pinched the bridge of her nose, trying to alleviate the dull throbbing behind her eyes. They had been over every shred of evidence a dozen times, but the killer's trail remained maddeningly cold. She glanced over at Tom, taking in the deep furrow of his brow as he pored over witness statements for the umpteenth time. The air between them was thick with unspoken tension, the weight of the case bearing down on them both.

"It has to be Walker," Harry said suddenly, her voice cutting through the stillness. "His obsession with Roger, the history of animosity between them... it all fits."

Tom sighed, leaning back in his chair. "We can't just go on gut instinct, Harry. We need solid evidence linking him to the crime."

"Evidence?" Harry scoffed. "The man practically confessed his hatred for Roger to anyone who would listen. He had motive, opportunity-"

"But no physical proof placing him at the scene," Tom countered, his own frustration bubbling to the surface. "We can't just go arresting people based on hunches and hearsay."

Harry slammed her hand down on the desk, sending papers fluttering. "Damn it, Tom! While we sit here debating semantics, the real killer is out there, probably planning his next move. We must act before someone else gets hurt!"

Tom ran a weary hand over his face. "I know it's frustrating, but we can't afford to get reckless or make assumptions. We have to stay focused on the evidence."

"The evidence isn't getting us anywhere!" Harry exclaimed. "We're missing something, some key piece that will crack this whole case wide open."

Tom regarded her calmly. "Then we go over it again, from the beginning if we have to. We can't let the killer's taunts and mind games rattle us."

Harry sighed heavily. "You're right, you're right. It's just...the thought of this sicko still being out there, poised to strike again. It makes my skin crawl."

"Mine too," Tom admitted. "But that's why we have to keep at it, follow every thread until we unravel the truth. The victims deserve justice."

A determined look settled over Harry's features. "You're damn right they do. Alright, let's go through the case files again, fresh eyes. We'll find that missing link, I know it."

As they turned back to the evidence board, the weight of the case bearing down heavily, Harry and Tom steeled themselves for the long hours ahead. Though frustration and dead ends loomed, they would not give up until they brought the Taunton killer to justice, no matter how deep into the darkness they had to venture.

The evidence board loomed before them, a tangled web of photographs, timelines, and scribbled notes that threatened to overwhelm. Harry stood before it, arms crossed, her brow furrowed in concentration as she studied the intricate tapestry they had woven.

"I don't think Margaret had anything to do with Roger's murder," she said at last, her voice cutting through the weighted silence that had settled over the room. "The grief in her eyes, the way she spoke of him...it felt genuine."

Tom leaned back against the desk, running a hand over his stubbled jaw. "I'm inclined to agree. As much as she may have resented his obsession with photography, I didn't get the sense she was capable of such violence." His gaze drifted to the crime scene photos, the brutal imagery at odds with the idyllic cottage surroundings. "No, this was the work of someone else. Someone with a much darker motive."

Harry nodded slowly, her eyes narrowing as she studied the scant leads they had assembled thus far. "David Walker and Stephen Smith are still our strongest potential suspects. Both had long-standing feuds with Roger, jealousy over his success in the photography world." She tapped a finger against Walker's rap sheet, the pages thick with a history of aggression and instability.

"Don't forget about Dawn Menzies," Tom interjected, gesturing to the striking image of the young model that had been hastily pinned to the board. "Her connection to Roger is still a mystery, but you don't get a secret room like that built without some serious obsession."

Harry tapped her finger against the photo of David Walker pinned to the evidence board. "I'm telling you, Tom, this guy reeks of someone with a massive grudge against Roger. Just listen to how he talks about him - calling him a 'hack' and saying he doesn't deserve his success."

Tom furrowed his brow as he studied the witness statement from Walker. "He certainly seems bitter, but is that enough to make him a murderer? We've seen professional rivalries get heated before without it devolving into violence."

"But this goes beyond just a rivalry," Harry insisted. "Walker is obsessed with proving himself, with getting the recognition he thinks he deserves. Add in his claims that the photography club was corruptly favouring Roger, and you have all the ingredients for a dangerous grudge."

Tom considered this for a moment. "You might be onto something. The statements from the other members do paint a picture of Walker as the outcast, the one always overlooked while Roger was put on a pedestal." He made a note on his pad. "We should look closer at any history of confrontations or threats between the two men."

Harry nodded, her eyes drifting to the crime scene photos. "And let's not forget the staged aspect of Roger's body with that monopod through his chest. It could have been Walker's sick way of mocking Roger's profession, a final 'screw you' from the rival he thought was so undeserving."

"Definitely an angle worth pursuing," Tom agreed grimly. "I'll have forensics go over Walker's home and studio again, see if they can find any fibres or trace evidence to link him to the crime scene."

"What about Larry Stubbs?" Harry said, tapping her finger against the photographer's name. "He admitted to having a confrontation with Roger over the competition results."

Tom shook his head. "A heated argument doesn't make him a killer. We'd need something more concrete to bring him in for questioning."

Harry's brow furrowed as she studied the board intently. "I'm not so sure. Look at his statement - he was one of the last people to see Roger alive at the fountain that night. And he had means and opportunity as a photographer at the show."

"But no clear motive beyond professional rivalry," Tom countered. "That's pretty thin, even for you."

A tense silence stretched between them, the weight of the case bearing down. Finally, Harry sighed. "You're right. We can't rule him out entirely, but we'd be going out on a limb pursuing Stubbs as a prime suspect right now."

Tom nodded; his expression grim. "For now, we need to focus on the players with more substantive ties to Roger - Margaret, Dawn, the photography club members with long-standing grudges."

A heavy silence fell between them, the weight of the case pressing down with suffocating force. Harry's gaze drifted back to the board; her mind whirring as she sought to untangle the twisted threads before them.

"We're missing something," she murmured, more to herself than to Tom. "Some crucial piece of the puzzle that ties all of this together." Her fingers danced over the assembled evidence, searching for the elusive pattern that would bring clarity from the chaos.

"Stephen Smith is looking more and more like our primary suspect," Harry said, tapping her finger against the man's mug shot. "His vendetta against Roger goes back years from what we've uncovered."

Tom nodded grimly. "The guy has clearly got a massive chip on his shoulder about being an outsider in the local photography scene. Obsessed with proving his talents were being overlooked."

"Which fits the taunting 'hidden in plain sight' message left with Roger's body," Harry pointed out. "This could have been his way to shove his supposed genius in everyone's faces while getting revenge."

She traced the red string connecting Smith to Dawn Menzies' photo. "And let's not forget his rumoured infatuation with Dawn. Maybe he saw Roger's affair as the ultimate insult - the pretty model picking the 'mediocre hack' over a true visionary like himself."

Tom frowned as he reviewed the case notes. "The timelines do seem suspicious. Smith was unaccounted for during the estimated times of death for both victims so far." He looked up at his partner. "You really think he's capable of such brutal murders just to get back at Roger and his clique?"

Harry's expression was grim. "Obsession can push people to do unspeakable things, Tom. We've seen it before." Her eyes drifted to the crime scene photos, her mind automatically reconstructing the horrific acts of violence.

"Smith is clearly unhinged enough to buy into his own delusions of grandeur. Couple that with years of pent-up resentment..." She shook her head slowly. "It's a powder keg just waiting to go off."

Tom exhaled heavily. "If you're right, we need to move fast before he has a chance to make good on those 'hidden in plain sight' threats. God knows how many more victims he's got planned."

"Then we don't stop until we've got enough evidence to bury the bastard. No more deaths, no more messages." Her jaw set with determination. "It's time to catch ourselves a murderer."

Tom watched her, a flicker of concern in his eyes. He knew that look, had seen it countless times before when a case had ensnared her in its grasp. Harry would not rest until she had unravelled every last secret, no matter how dark the path became.

With a resolute nod, he pushed off from the desk, his expression hardening with renewed determination. "Then we start again from the top. We go over every witness statement, every shred of evidence, until the missing piece reveals itself."

As he moved to join her before the board, their shoulders brushed ever so slightly - a wordless gesture of solidarity in the face of the daunting task ahead. The hunt was on, and they would pursue it relentlessly, united in their pursuit of justice no matter how twisted the trail became.

Chapter 13 Echoes from the Exhibition

The weight of the investigation seemed to press down on Harry and Tom as they sat in the police station, sifting through the evidence once again. The crime scene photos and witness statements were burned into their minds, but still the pieces refused to fall into place.

Harry rubbed her temples, frustration etched across her face. "We're missing something, Tom. Some crucial detail that could crack this case wide open."

Tom nodded grimly, leaning back in his chair. "You're right. We've been going over the same facts again and again, but we're still no closer to finding the killer."

A heavy silence fell between them, the ticking of the clock on the wall seeming to mock their lack of progress. Finally, Harry spoke up, her voice tinged with determination.

"We need to go back to Vivary Park. Re-examine the crime scenes with fresh eyes. Maybe being there in person will jog something loose."

Tom considered her words, then gave a resolute nod. "You're right. A new perspective is exactly what we need right now." He began gathering the case files, his movements brisk and purposeful. "Let's head out. Time to turn over every rock until we find the answers we're looking for."

As they made their way to the parking lot, Harry couldn't shake the feeling that the park held secrets yet to be uncovered. The lush gardens and winding paths had borne witness to unspeakable acts of violence, and she was determined to make them give up their grim truths.

The drive to Vivary Park was shrouded in a heavy silence, the weight of the investigation pressing down upon Harry and Tom like a thick fog. As they navigated the winding streets of Taunton, the lush greenery and quaint storefronts blurred past, a stark contrast to the darkness they were delving into.

Turning onto the familiar path leading into the park, Harry's grip tightened on the door handle, her knuckles whitening with resolve. This was where it had all begun – the brutal murder of Roger Morgan, a twisted act that had shattered the tranquillity of their beloved town.

Little did they know, a hooded figure watched from the shadows, their gaze following the unmarked police car as it wound its way through the park's narrow lanes. Keeping to the treeline, the mysterious observer moved with practiced stealth, their motives as obscured as their face.

As Harry and Tom stepped out of the vehicle, the warm summer breeze carried the faint scent of freshly mown grass and blooming flowers, a cruel juxtaposition to the grim task at hand. The once-idyllic fountain stood before them, its waters now tainted by the memory of Roger's lifeless body, contorted in a final rictus of terror.

Scanning the area with a critical eye, Harry couldn't shake the feeling that they were being watched. A prickle ran down her spine, but when she turned, there was nothing but the gentle sway of branches and the distant laughter of children at play.

Unbeknownst to the detectives, the hooded figure melted deeper into the shadows, their presence as elusive as the truth they seemed determined to conceal.

With a shared look of grim determination, Harry and Tom began their meticulous search, scouring every inch of the crime scene for any clue, any shred of evidence that might have been overlooked. The killer had been one step ahead thus far, but they were determined to turn the tables, no matter how dark the path might become.

As Harry's gaze swept over the grisly scene once more, a prickle ran down her spine - the unmistakable feeling of being watched. Her eyes narrowed as she scanned the tree line bordering the park, searching for any sign of movement amidst the shadows.

That's when she spotted it - a solitary figure, clad in a dark hooded sweatshirt, partially obscured behind the gnarled trunk of an oak tree. Though the face was concealed, Harry could sense the intensity of the person's stare, fixed directly upon her and Tom.

"Tom," she murmured, her voice taut. "We've got company."

Tom followed her line of sight, his body tensing as he too registered the presence of the mysterious observer. For a moment, the world seemed to hold its breath, the only sound the faint crunch of gravel as the hooded figure shifted ever so slightly.

Then, as if sensing it had been detected, the figure turned and melted into the bushes, disappearing from view with unnerving swiftness. Harry felt her heart pounding as she instinctively moved to give chase, but Tom's firm grip on her arm held her back.

Harry's eyes narrowed as she studied the bushes in the distance. "That hooded figure from earlier...I can't shake the feeling they're connected to all this somehow."

Tom nodded slowly. "You could be right. We can't afford to leave any stone unturned at this point." He paused, stroking his chin thoughtfully. "Maybe we should try luring them out again, get a closer look."

A plan began to take shape as Harry considered their options. "Okay, here's what we do. I'll head back towards the cafe, make myself an obvious target. You circle around and wait for them to take the bait."

"You really think they'll show themselves again so brazenly?" Tom asked with a raised eyebrow.

Harry smirked. "If my hunch is right, this person can't resist keeping tabs on our investigation. They'll take the chance to shadow me, and that's when you'll be waiting to box them in."

The determination in her voice brooked no argument from her partner. With a curt nod, Tom grabbed his coat. "Alright then. Let's get this lunatic before anyone else gets hurt."

The sun was dipping low over Vivary Park as Harry strode purposefully along the path, her eyes scanning the treeline for any sign of movement. She allowed herself to become an easy target, pulling her phone from her pocket and speaking into it animatedly as if relaying details of the case to Tom.

Out of the corner of her eye, she spotted it - a flicker of motion amidst the shadows of the trees. The hooded figure emerged cautiously, keeping a safe distance as they trailed behind Harry. She fought to keep her pace casual, her heart hammering in her chest.

Suddenly, Tom appeared further up the path, seemingly coming from the opposite direction. In one fluid motion, he drew his weapon, levelling it at the startled figure. "Police! Don't move!"

The hooded stranger froze, their head whipping back and forth between the two detectives in panic. Realising they were cornered; they turned and broke into a desperate sprint towards the bowling green.

"Don't let them get away!" Harry shouted, giving chase with Tom hot on her heels.

Their quarry raced across the manicured lawn, desperation lending speed to their movements. But there was no escape - Tom angled off to the side, cutting them off from the path with Harry rapidly closing the gap from behind.

Cornered at last, the hooded figure whirled to face their pursuers, chest heaving from exertion. Harry and Tom held their positions, weapons raised as they slowly advanced.

"Show us your face," Harry called out, her voice laced with steely authority. "Whatever your involvement in all this, running will only make it worse for you."

The hooded figure turned; hands raised in surrender. As they stepped into the open area, Harry recognised the young man from their earlier encounter. "You again? What's your name, and why were you watching us?"

For a long, tense moment, the figure remained motionless, seemingly weighing their options. Then, with trembling hands, they reached up and slowly lowered their hood...

The young man swallowed hard, his eyes darting between Harry and Tom. "M-My name is Darcy. I wasn't watching you; I swear! I was just... I saw something the night that man was killed."

Tom stepped forward, his expression a mix of curiosity and scepticism. "You were here that night? What exactly did you see?"

Darcy nodded fervently. "I was sleeping rough in the park when I heard a commotion near the fountain. I peeked out and saw a man standing over that bloke's body. He was fiddling with something on Roger's head before he took off running."

"You seem pretty certain the killer is a man, Darcy. How can you be sure?" asked Tom.

"The sheer force required to shove that pole through the man in the fountain, it had to be a man. A woman would have a very difficult time generating that kind of strength, unless we're talking about an exceptional case." replied Darcy.

"But we can't rule it out entirely. There are always exceptions." said Harry.

"True, but the evidence suggests we're looking for someone with significant physical power. Plus, the removal of the breast implants feels like an act of rage, a symbolic desecration of the female form." Said Tom.

"Almost like the killer was punishing Dawn for her looks, for being a model and having her body artificially enhanced.", he continued.

Harry exchanged a meaningful look with Tom. This was a potential key witness. "Can you describe this man you saw? Any distinguishing features?"

Darcy shook his head regretfully. "It was too dark, and he was wearing a hooded jacket pulled low over his face. But I know it was definitely a man."

"Why didn't you come forward sooner?" Tom pressed; his tone tinged with suspicion.

"I was scared, alright?" Darcy replied defensively. "I didn't want to get involved with a murderer! But then I saw you two poking around and... I don't know, I thought maybe I should say something."

Harry studied the young man intently, her instincts telling her he was being truthful. "Thank you for coming forward, Darcy. I know this is scary, but we really need your help. We'll need to get your full statement down at the station."

Darcy shook his head vehemently. "No way, I can't go to the police station. You don't understand what they'll do to me."

Tom stepped forward. "We're not going to hurt you. We just want to get to the bottom of this murder."

"Easy for you to say," Darcy spat. "You've got a roof over your head, a warm bed to sleep in. I'm just a homeless bloke, nobody cares what happens to me."

Harry crouched down, meeting Darcy's eyes. "That's not true. We care, Darcy. You may have seen something that could help us catch a killer. Isn't that worth taking a chance?"

Darcy wavered, his bravado cracking as he searched Harry's sincere gaze. "You...you promise I'll be safe? That you'll make sure nothing happens to me?"

"You have my word," Harry said solemnly. "We'll protect you, but we need you to be brave and help us first."

After a long moment, Darcy nodded slowly. "Alright. I'll tell you what I saw. But you've got to keep me safe, you hear?"

Tom clapped him on the shoulder. "You've got nothing to worry about, mate. We've got your back. You can have a shower and a decent meal, well as decent as you can get in a police canteen."

As Darcy rose to his feet, Harry felt a surge of pride. It had taken patience and understanding, but they had gained a crucial ally in their fight for justice. With Darcy's help, perhaps they could finally unravel the twisted web of secrets surrounding Roger Morgan's murder.

As they led Darcy away, Tom leaned in close. "You believe his story? For all we know, he could be an accomplice trying to throw us off track."

Harry's expression was pensive. "Call it a gut feeling, but I think he's legit. We need to chase down every lead, no matter how small. This could be the break we've been looking for."

With renewed determination, they headed back towards their car, a sense of cautious optimism taking hold. The hooded figure's identity may still be a mystery, but at least now they had a potential witness to guide them towards the truth.

Chapter 14 Darcy's Witness

The drab interview room felt even more oppressive than usual as Harry and Tom sat across from Darcy, the homeless man's eyes darting nervously around the cramped space. Despite their best efforts to put him at ease, his slight frame seemed to shrink further into the hard plastic chair with every passing moment.

"Darcy, I know this is difficult, but anything you can tell us about what you saw that night could be crucial," Harry said, her voice low and soothing. "We just need you to start from the beginning."

Darcy swallowed hard, his hands wringing the tattered edges of his coat. "I-I was just tryin' to get some sleep, you know? Tucked away in one of them huts near the bandstand."

Tom leaned forward, his expression open and attentive. "Go on."

"Well, I heard this racket, like someone knockin' over some cans or summat. Thought it might be that mangy fox comin' back for the ducks, so I poked my head out to have a look-see." Darcy's eyes grew distant, as if he were transported back to that fateful night. "That's when I saw 'im. This bloke, all dressed in black, with a hoodie pulled up over his head. He was headed towards the clubhouse, carrying' what looked like one of them javelin things."

Harry and Tom exchanged a weighted glance, their interest piqued. "Did you see anyone else?" Harry asked gently.

Darcy nodded, his movements jittery. "There was another fella, standing' by the clubhouse. I couldn't make out his face or nothing', but I heard him say, 'What d'you want? It's the middle of the night, can't this wait?'"

A tremor ran through Darcy's slight frame as he recounted the next part. "Then...then the one with the hoodie, he just...he raised his arms, and he struck that javelin straight through the other bloke's chest. Over and over, like a madman."

Tom's jaw tightened, but he remained silent, allowing Darcy to continue at his own pace.

"The poor sod dropped like a sack of potatoes," Darcy whispered. "But it didn't stop there. The killer, he...he took out this big staple gun looking' thing and..." He swallowed thickly. "I heard it, the staples firing' into the body."

A heavy silence hung in the air, broken only by the sound of Darcy's ragged breathing. Harry reached across the table, her hand hovering just above his in a gesture of reassurance. "You're doing great, Darcy. What happened next?"

Darcy's eyes glistened with unshed tears. "He dragged the body over to the fountain, positioned it just so. Like it were some sort of sick display." He shuddered. "I couldn't watch no more after that. I high tailed it out of there, didn't stop running' 'til I hit the high street."

As the weight of Darcy's words settled over them, Harry and Tom exchanged a heavy look. They now had a crucial eyewitness account, a glimpse into the twisted mind of a killer. But it also meant that Darcy's life could be in grave danger.

The weight of Darcy's revelation hung heavy in the air as Harry studied the haunted look in his eyes. She could see the internal struggle playing out, the fear of trusting the authorities warring with his desire for justice. With a gentle reassurance, she placed her hand on his arm.

"Darcy, you've been incredibly brave," Harry said, her voice thick with gratitude. "But I need to ask one more thing of you. We're going to get you set up somewhere safe, somewhere you can be protected until we bring this monster to justice. Are you okay with that?"

Tom nodded firmly in agreement. "You're a key witness in a murder case. Your safety is our top priority."

Darcy seemed to relax slightly at their words, the tension in his shoulders easing just a fraction. Harry pressed on, "The best way for us to keep you secure is to get you off the streets for now and into safe accommodation."

She pulled out her phone, quickly tapping out a message. "I'm arranging a room for you at a local hotel. You'll have a roof over your head, a warm bed, and we can have officers posted to ensure no harm comes to you."

The gratitude and relief that washed over Darcy's face was palpable. For so long, he had been adrift, a forgotten soul in the underbelly of society. But now, for the first time in years, he felt seen, his voice finally being heard.

The CID room had become their battleground, the crime scene board their map to navigating the treacherous waters of this investigation. With each passing moment, the urgency grew, the knowledge that a ruthless killer still lurked in the shadows, poised to strike again. Harry and Tom exchanged a look of silent understanding, a promise to stand together against the darkness that threatened to engulf the once-peaceful town of Taunton.

Fuelled by a renewed sense of purpose, they turned their attention back to the witness statements, scouring each line for even the faintest hint of the hooded figure's identity or motives. The furrow of Tom's brow deepened as he pored over the accounts, his eyes narrowing at any inconsistencies or potential leads.

"Here, this statement from the groundskeeper at Vivary Park," he said, tapping the paper. "He mentions seeing someone lurking near the fountain around the time of the first murder."

Harry leaned in, her gaze intense. "Did he get a good look at them? Any distinguishing features?"

Tom shook his head grimly. "Just that they were wearing a dark hooded sweatshirt and kept to the shadows. But it corroborates your sighting from earlier."

A heavy silence hung between them as they digested this new piece of the puzzle. The hooded figure was no mere spectre, but a corporeal presence woven into the very fabric of their investigation.

The CID room felt oppressive, the weight of the investigation pressing down on Harry and Tom as they pored over the witness statements once more. The hooded figure spotted by Darcy had become an obsession, a tantalizing thread that could potentially unravel the entire case.

"This has to be connected," Harry muttered, tapping her pen against the stack of papers. "Darcy saw someone fleeing the scene of Roger's murder, and now Dawn has turned up dead in eerily similar circumstances."

Tom nodded grimly; his brow furrowed in concentration. "You're right. It's too much of a coincidence. Whoever this hooded person is, they're either the killer or have crucial information about the murders."

A heavy silence fell over the room as they contemplated the implications. The case had taken a dark turn, the stakes higher than ever before. They were no longer just seeking justice for Roger Morgan, but for Dawn Menzies as well – a woman whose life had been brutally cut short, her secrets forever silenced.

Suddenly, Harry sat up straighter, her eyes alight with determination. "Stephen Smith and David Walker. They were both involved with Dawn in some capacity, right? Maybe one of them saw or heard something that could shed light on this hooded figure."

Tom's expression mirrored her own, a renewed sense of purpose taking hold. "It's worth a shot. We need to chase down every lead, no matter how small."

Without another word, they gathered their notes and headed out of the CID room, the familiar weight of their badges pressing against their chests. The hunt was on, and they would stop at nothing to bring Roger and Dawn's killer to justice.

The streets of Taunton blurred past the windows of the unmarked police car as Harry navigated the winding roads, her knuckles white on the steering wheel as she gripped it tightly. Beside her, Tom's gaze was fixed on the case file, his mind undoubtedly running through every possible scenario, every potential connection.

"Stephen Smith's place is closest," Harry said, her voice cutting through the tense silence. "We'll start with him."

Tom nodded; his jaw set in a grim line. "Let's just hope he's more forthcoming than he was during the initial questioning. Something tells me he's holding back."

Chapter 15 False Leads and Flickers of Truth

The unmarked police car rolled to a stop in front of the nondescript bungalow, its engine ticking as it cooled in the evening air. Harry and Tom exchanged a weighted glance, the case file on Dawn Menzies' murder clutched tightly in Tom's hands.

"You ready for this?" Harry asked, her voice low. Tom gave a grim nod, and they stepped out onto the cracked driveway.

An overgrown garden surrounded the house, weeds creeping up through the broken pavers leading to the front door. Shadows seemed to linger in every corner, adding to the sense of unease prickling at the back of Harry's neck.

Tom rapped his knuckles against the weathered door. "Stephen Smith? Police, open up."

A heavy silence answered them. Harry's eyes narrowed as she peered through a dingy front window, searching for any sign of movement within.

"He's got to be home," Tom muttered. "His car's in the drive."

As if on cue, the sound of approaching footsteps reached their ears. The door swung open, revealing a dishevelled man in his thirties squinting out at them. A pungent odour wafted from the house's interior.

"What's all this, then?" Stephen Smith slurred, his eyes bloodshot.

Harry stepped forward; her badge displayed. "Mr. Smith, remember us, I'm Detective Inspector Lambert, this is Detective Sergeant Reed. We'd like to ask you a few questions about your whereabouts the night Dawn Menzies was murdered."

A flicker of something indecipherable passed over Smith's face before he regained his composure with a sneer. "Figures the filth would come sniffing around, sticking their noses where they don't belong."

The tension ratcheted up a notch as Tom bristled at the insult. "We'll ask you to watch your tone, Mr. Smith. This is an active murder investigation."

"May we come in, Mr. Smith?" Harry asked, her tone polite but firm. "We have some questions regarding the murder of Dawn Menzies."

Stephen's eyes narrowed, but he stepped aside, allowing them entry into his modest home. As they settled into the living room, the walls adorned with framed photographs and awards, Tom wasted no time getting to the point.

"Where were you the night Dawn Menzies was killed?"

Stephen scoffed. "Is that what this is about? You think I had something to do with that tart's murder?"

"We're just trying to establish alibis at this point," Harry interjected. "Any information you can provide would be helpful."

Stephen leaned back in his chair, his expression unreadable. "Well, if you must know, I was here, working on a personal project."

"This personal project wouldn't happen to involve Dawn Menzies, would it?" Tom pressed.

A flicker of surprise crossed Stephen's face before he regained his composure. "As a matter of fact, it did. I've been documenting her...activities for the past few weeks."

Harry's brow furrowed. "What kind of activities?"

Stephen leaned forward, his voice lowering conspiratorially. "Dawn was blackmailing someone. Larry Stubbs, that weasel of a photographer who's always sniffing around the Flower Show circuit."

Tom's eyes widened. "Blackmailing him? Over what?"

"From what I gathered, there was some kind of inappropriate incident at one of Stubbs' photoshoots. Dawn had evidence, and she was using it to bleed him dry." Stephen shook his head in disgust. "I've been secretly photographing their meetings, building a file on the whole sordid affair."

Harry's mind raced, trying to process this new twist. "And you didn't think to come forward with this information before?"

Stephen shrugged, unrepentant. "I was waiting for the right moment, the right leverage. But now, with Dawn dead..." He trailed off, leaving the implication hanging in the air.

Stephen's expression hardened. "If you want proof of Dawn's duplicity, I can show you." He gestured for them to follow. "Come with me to the darkroom. I have evidence of the blackmail."

Harry and Tom exchanged a glance before nodding. "Lead the way, Mr. Smith," Harry said.

Stephen led them through a door at the back of his house into a dimly lit darkroom. The pungent aroma of chemical developing solutions hung heavy in the air. Pushing open the door, Stephen flicked on the lights, revealing a cramped space lined with photography equipment. "In here," he said gruffly.

"I've been following Dawn for weeks," Stephen said, his voice hushed. "Trying to get the perfect shot for a new project I'm working on."

Harry leaned in, studying the images intently. They depicted Dawn in various locations around Taunton - the park, the high street, a quiet residential area. In each one, she appeared deep in thought, her movements furtive.

Tom's brow furrowed as he picked up one of the photos. "What's this?" He pointed to a figure lurking in the background, their features obscured by the shadows.

Stephen swallowed hard. "That's Larry Stubbs."

A tense silence fell over the room as Harry and Tom digested this new revelation. Harry was the first to speak. "Are you telling us that Dawn was meeting with Larry Stubbs? In secret?"

Stephen nodded, his expression grave. "It gets worse." He sorted through the stack until he found the photo he was looking for - an image of Dawn and Larry in a secluded alleyway, their body language tense as Dawn handed over a large brown envelope.

"I don't know what's in that envelope," Stephen continued. "But I know it can't be good. Not with the way they were acting, like two people engaged in something illicit."

Tom ran a hand over his face, the weight of the case seeming to bear down on him. "This changes everything. If Stubbs was involved with Dawn, it puts him squarely in the centre of this whole mess."

Harry's eyes narrowed as she studied the photos once more. "But why? What could possibly link a glamour model to a local photographer in a way that would lead to murder?"

The words hung heavy in the air, their implications sending a chill down Harry's spine. She exchanged a loaded glance with Tom, both of them picking up on the undercurrent of obsession in Stephen's voice.

"You'll want to take these photos into evidence, I assume," Stephen said, already beginning to carefully remove the prints from the trays. "I fear they may make me a target, if the killer truly is fixated on Roger and his circle."

As Harry and Tom collected the precious photographs, handling them with the utmost care, a new layer of complexity was added to the case. Stephen's actions, however well-intentioned, hinted at a dangerous obsession that could have set him on a deadly path.

The questions multiplied with each new revelation. Was Stephen simply an overzealous artist who had taken his passion too far? Or was there something darker lurking beneath the surface, a twisted psyche that could have driven him to unimaginable acts of violence?

Harry shook her head as they walked back to the car, Stephen's defiant words still ringing in her ears. "I don't buy his whole 'innocent bystander' act for a second. There's no way he didn't know what Dawn was up to with Roger."

Tom nodded grimly. "He's definitely hiding something. The way he got defensive when we brought up the blackmail photos..." He trailed off, making a note in his pad. "We can't rule him out as an accomplice, or even the one pulling Dawn's strings."

"Exactly." Harry's eyes narrowed as she considered the possibilities. "Dawn may have been the mastermind behind the scheme, but she could have had help. Stephen was obsessed with her - who's to say he wouldn't do her bidding to get in her good graces?"

They reached the car, and Tom opened the door for her. "You think he was her accomplice in the blackmail plot? Maybe even took things further by killing Roger when he got cold feet?"

Harry paused, one foot inside the vehicle as she mulled it over. "It's a theory. Stephen is unhinged enough, and we know he had a hell of a grudge against Roger. Teaming up with Dawn to take the bastard down could have been his way of getting revenge."

Sliding into the driver's seat, she gripped the steering wheel tightly. "We can't let him off the hook yet. Not until we know exactly what role he played in this whole sordid mess."

Tom's jaw set in a hard line as he buckled his seatbelt. "You got it. Stephen Smith stays on the suspect list as a potential accomplice. We'll tear his life apart if we have to - something tells me this is just the tip of the iceberg."

As the engine roared to life, Harry and Tom exchanged a grim look of determination. The case had taken a dark turn, and they would stop at nothing to uncover the twisted web of lies and obsession that had led to such depravity. No one was off limits - not even those closest to the victims.

The engine hummed as Harry navigated the winding streets towards David Walker's home. In the passenger seat, Tom tapped his pen rhythmically against his notepad, his brow furrowed in thought.

"So what do you make of this Larry Stubbs?" he asked, breaking the silence. "Think he could be our man?"

Harry shrugged, her eyes not leaving the road. "It's possible. He was one of the last people to see Roger alive that night. And he certainly had motive with that confrontation over the competition results."

"But his alibi for the time of the murder seemed solid," Tom countered. "According to his wife, he was home all evening."

"Wives can be convinced to lie," Harry said darkly. "Or they could be oblivious to what's really going on."

Tom made a note on his pad. "Fair point. We'll need to look closer at Stubbs' movements, see if his story holds up to scrutiny."

They lapsed into silence again as Harry turned onto the quiet, tree-lined street where David Walker lived. Her grip tightened on the steering wheel as the sleek modern lines of Walker's home came into view.

"What are your thoughts on Walker?" she asked. "Think there's any truth to his claims about Margaret's resentment towards Roger?"

Tom frowned. "Hard to say. Jealous, bitter ex-husbands aren't exactly the most reliable sources. For all we know, he could be trying to deflect suspicion onto her."

"By pointing out her potential motive?" Harry shook her head. "That's a risky gambit, even for someone as arrogant as Walker seems to be."

"You think he's telling the truth then? That there was real animosity between Margaret and her husband?"

Harry pulled the car to a stop, killing the engine. She turned to face Tom, her expression grim.

"I think at this point, we can't rule anything out. Jealousy, obsession, secrets and lies...this whole community is a powder keg of potential motives. We need to keep our eyes open to any possible angle, no matter how ugly it gets."

Tom nodded slowly, his jaw set in determination. "Then let's see what skeletons Mr. Walker has hiding in his closet. I've got a feeling this is only the beginning."

Chapter 16 The Hidden Shrine

The first light of dawn bathed Vivary Park in a gentle, golden glow. The once vibrant and bustling Flower Show had come to an end, leaving behind an atmosphere of quiet reflection and bittersweet memories. The vibrant colours of the floral displays were now muted, and the cheerful chatter of visitors had been replaced by the soft rustling of leaves in the early morning breeze.

Alice Turner, a local volunteer in her late 20s, moved briskly across the dew-kissed grass, her hands deftly folding up the canvas of a large marquee that had held the competition entries. Her cheerful demeanour, a constant source of positivity throughout the event, now carried a note of sombre reflection. The recent events had cast a shadow over the community, and even Alice's ever-present smile seemed tinged with sadness.

"Morning, Alice," greeted Ben Harris, the middle-aged groundskeeper with a gruff exterior but a kind heart. He had worked at Vivary Park for over a decade, and his deep connection to the place was evident in the careful, respectful way he handled the park's upkeep.

"Good morning, Ben," Alice replied, her voice brightening a little at the sight of her long-time friend and colleague. "Ready to tackle this marquee?"

Ben nodded, his weathered hands already busy untying the ropes securing the canvas. "Let's get to it. This place won't clean itself up," he said, his tone gruff but not unkind.

As they worked together to dismantle the structure, the silence was filled with the sounds of their labour—the creak of wooden poles, the clink of metal stakes, and the soft thud of folded canvas. Despite the physical effort, their movements were practiced and efficient, a testament to years of experience and countless events.

"How are you holding up?" Ben asked after a while, his voice softening with genuine concern. "It's been a rough few days."

Alice paused, her hands stilling for a moment on the canvas. "I'm okay," she said, her eyes reflecting a mix of emotions. "It's just hard to believe everything that's happened. The Flower Show is supposed to be a time of joy and celebration, but this year..."

Ben nodded, understanding without needing to ask for details. The recent murders had left a mark on everyone, turning a beloved tradition into a source of fear and uncertainty. "We'll get through it," he said firmly. "We always do."

They continued working in companionable silence, each lost in their own thoughts. Ben's mind wandered to the early years of his tenure at Vivary Park, remembering the countless hours spent nurturing the grounds and preparing for events like the Flower Show. His gruff exterior masked a deep love for the park and the community it served, and the recent tragedies had affected him more than he cared to admit.

Alice, on the other hand, thought about the friends she had lost and the ones who were still grappling with their grief. She had always been the one to lift others' spirits, to bring light into the darkest of times, but now she found herself needing that same support.

"Do you remember the first time we set up this marquee?" Alice asked suddenly, a small smile tugging at her lips.

Ben chuckled, the sound a rare but welcome break in his usual gruffness. "How could I forget? The wind nearly took it—and us—halfway across the park."

Alice laughed, the memory bringing a moment of levity. "We've come a long way since then."

"Indeed we have," Ben agreed. "We've weathered worse storms, and we'll weather this one too."

As they folded the last of the canvas and began stacking the chairs, the sun rose higher, casting a warm, golden light over the park. The once-vibrant flower beds, now a little less radiant, still held the promise of renewal and resilience. The cleanup was more than just a physical task; it was a symbolic act of moving forward, of reclaiming the park's beauty and purpose despite the darkness that had touched it.

Alice and Ben paused to take in the view, their hearts heavy but hopeful. The Flower Show would return next year, and with it, the promise of new beginnings. For now, they would do what they always did—take care of their beloved park and each other, one day at a time.

The early morning sun climbed steadily higher, casting a gentle warmth over Vivary Park. Birds chirped softly from the trees, their songs a stark contrast to the sombre mood that lingered. Alice Turner and Ben Harris continued their work, moving to another section of the park to pick up litter and dismantle smaller tents.

Alice pushed a wheelbarrow filled with discarded paper cups, napkins, and other remnants of the

Flower Show's bustling days. Ben followed with a large trash bag, his steady pace and careful movements reflecting his years of experience.

"Funny how quiet it is now," Alice remarked, her voice breaking the silence. "You'd never guess how lively it was just a couple of days ago."

Ben grunted in agreement, his eyes scanning the ground for any overlooked debris. "Yeah, it's always like this after an event. A bit eerie, but I suppose that's part of the charm."

They worked together seamlessly, their camaraderie evident in the ease with which they coordinated their efforts. The smaller tents were quickly taken down, folded neatly, and placed in the wheelbarrow. Despite the physical labour, Alice's cheerful demeanour never waned, and Ben's gruff exterior softened with each passing moment.

As they approached the children's play area, the mood shifted. The cheerful colours of the playground equipment—bright reds, blues, and yellows—seemed muted under the weight of recent events. The area where Dawn had been murdered held a haunting silence, a stark reminder of the darkness that had touched their community.

Alice paused, her hands trembling slightly as she picked up a piece of litter near the swings. "It's hard to believe she's gone," she said quietly, her voice tinged with sadness. "She was always so full of life."

Ben nodded, his face grim. "Yeah, Dawn was a good one. Always had a smile and a kind word for everyone. This whole thing... it's just not right."

They continued their work, the usual banter giving way to a shared moment of silent reflection. The swings swayed gently in the breeze, the metal creaking softly, as if mourning the loss of the vibrant woman who once graced the park with her presence.

"Do you remember the last time we saw her?" Alice asked, her voice barely above a whisper.

Ben sighed, his expression troubled. "She was here, helping set up the booths. Always the first to arrive and the last to leave. It's a damn shame what happened."

As they picked up the last bits of litter, a sense of unease settled over them. The playground, once a place of joy and laughter, now felt like a memorial to the lost. The juxtaposition of the colourful play structures and the dark memories created an unsettling atmosphere.

Alice looked around, her eyes lingering on the spot where Dawn's body had been found. "I hope they catch whoever did this," she said, determination edging into her voice. "She deserves justice."

"They will," Ben replied firmly. "Harry and Tom are good at what they do. They'll get to the bottom of it."

With the litter collected and the tents dismantled, Alice and Ben moved on, their steps heavy with the weight of their thoughts. The park's serene beauty was tinged with sorrow, a reminder of the fragility of life and the importance of community.

As they walked towards the park's storage shed to unload their collected items, a shadow flickered at the edge of the playground, unnoticed by either of them. The early morning light, once comforting, now cast long, eerie shadows that seemed to move with a life of their own.

Alice and Ben's conversation turned to lighter topics, attempting to lift the mood. They talked about upcoming community events, the weather, and plans for the next Flower Show. But the underlying tension remained, a silent acknowledgment of the recent horrors that had touched their lives.

"Thanks for helping out, Ben," Alice said, offering him a small smile. "It's good to have you here."

"Wouldn't be anywhere else," Ben replied, his voice gruff but sincere. "This park means a lot to me. So do the people in it."

As they neared the storage shed, the sun climbed higher, casting the park in a warm, golden light. The tranquillity of the morning offered a momentary respite, a brief pause in the midst of their sorrow and uncertainty. They knew the days ahead would be challenging, but for now, they found comfort in each other's presence and the simple act of tending to their beloved park.

Alice and Ben finished unloading the last of their collected items into the storage shed and decided to take a well-deserved break. They made their way to a wooden bench that offered a clear view of the now-empty park. The remnants of the Flower Show lay scattered around them—crumpled banners, empty tents, and trampled flowers—all signs of the vibrant event that had just ended.

Alice sank onto the bench with a sigh, stretching her legs out in front of her. "It feels good to sit down," she said, her voice carrying a mix of exhaustion and relief.

Ben grunted in agreement, lowering himself onto the bench beside her. "Aye, it does," he replied, his eyes scanning the park. "Feels different now, doesn't it? Quieter."

The park was indeed quieter. The usual hum of activity had been replaced by a stillness that felt almost eerie. The early morning light bathed the scene in a soft, golden hue, casting long shadows that stretched across the grass. A gentle breeze rustled the leaves, and the distant sound of birdsong provided a soothing backdrop.

Alice leaned back, her eyes closed as she enjoyed the moment of peace. "I always loved this park," she said softly. "It's like a little oasis in the middle of town. Even after everything that's happened, it still feels special."

Ben nodded, his gaze lingering on the play area where Dawn had been found. "It is special," he agreed. "Been here a long time, seen a lot of changes. But it's always been a place where people come together."

They sat in companionable silence for a few moments, each lost in their thoughts. The events of the past few days weighed heavily on their minds, but the familiar surroundings offered a measure of comfort.

"I remember my first Flower Show," Alice said suddenly, a smile tugging at her lips. "I was just a kid, running around, helping my mom with her booth. I thought it was the most magical thing in the world."

Ben chuckled, the sound low and warm. "I remember that too. You were always full of energy, darting here and there. Your mom was so proud of you."

Alice's smile widened, and she opened her eyes, turning to look at Ben. "She loved the Flower Show. Said it was the heart of the community. I think that's why I keep volunteering. It's my way of keeping her memory alive."

Ben's expression softened, and he placed a hand on Alice's shoulder. "You're doing a good job, Alice. Your mom would be proud."

They fell silent again, the weight of their shared memories settling between them. The park, with its empty flower beds and dismantled booths, seemed to hold its breath, waiting for the next chapter to unfold.

"Do you think we'll ever find out who did it?" Alice asked quietly, her voice tinged with uncertainty.

Ben's jaw tightened, and he glanced towards the playground, his eyes hardening. "I hope so," he said firmly. "Harry and Tom are good men. They'll find the truth. And when they do, this community will heal. It'll take time, but we'll get there."

Alice nodded, taking comfort in Ben's words. She knew he was right. The community was strong, and they had faced hardships before. They would find a way to move forward, to reclaim their park and their sense of safety.

As they sat there, the sun continued its ascent, casting the park in a brighter, more hopeful light. The breeze picked up, rustling the leaves and carrying the scent of freshly cut grass. It was a new day, a chance for renewal and reflection.

"We should probably get back to work," Alice said reluctantly, though she made no move to stand. "Still a lot to do."

"Yeah, we should," Ben agreed, but he too remained seated, savouring the moment of quiet. "But a few more minutes won't hurt."

They stayed on the bench a while longer, watching as a few early risers jogged through the park, their presence a reminder that life went on. The remnants of the Flower Show might have left a mark on Vivary Park, but it was still a place of beauty and community, a place where people came together to celebrate and to heal.

Eventually, Alice and Ben stood, stretching their tired muscles and preparing to face the day's tasks. They shared a look of mutual respect and understanding, knowing that together, they would help the park—and the community—find its way back to normalcy.

Alice and Ben eventually stood, stretching their tired muscles and preparing to resume their tasks. The heaviness of their earlier conversation lingered, but they both felt a renewed sense of purpose. The park, with its blend of beauty and sorrow, needed them.

"Right, let's get back to it," Ben said, picking up his trash bag with a determined nod.

"Lead the way," Alice replied, grabbing the handle of the wheelbarrow and following him.

As they walked towards the next section of the park, Alice glanced around at the familiar sights. The lush greenery of the trees, the neat flower beds, and the winding pathways all held a certain charm, even in the aftermath of the Flower Show.

"So, Ben," Alice began, trying to lighten the mood, "when are you finally going to enter the flower arranging competition? I've seen your garden, you know. It's spectacular."

Ben let out a hearty laugh, a sound that seemed to lift the weight of the morning. "Me? Compete? Nah, I just grow 'em for the fun of it. Leave the competing to the experts."

Alice smiled, pleased to see him in better spirits. "Come on, your roses could give Mrs. Jenkins a run for her money. And you know how seriously she takes her gardening."

Ben shook his head, his eyes crinkling at the corners with amusement. "Mrs. Jenkins would have my head if I tried to outdo her. Besides, gardening's my escape. No pressure, no competition. Just me and the plants."

As they reached the next cluster of smaller tents, Alice noticed a few children's toys scattered around—a forgotten ball, a small toy truck, a stuffed animal. The sight tugged at her heart, a reminder of the park's role as a haven for families and children.

"Remember when we used to have those big picnics here?" Alice asked, picking up the stuffed animal and dusting it off. "Families from all over town would come, spread out their blankets, and spend the whole day here."

Ben nodded, his expression fond. "I do. Those were the days. The smell of barbecues, kids running around, and everyone just enjoying themselves. We should bring those back."

"Definitely," Alice agreed, placing the stuffed animal on a nearby bench, hoping its owner would come back for it. "We need more of that. More reasons for people to come together and celebrate."

They worked side by side, dismantling the smaller tents and picking up litter. The physical activity, coupled with their light-hearted conversation, began to lift the oppressive mood that had settled over them earlier.

"Hey, did you hear about the new bakery opening on High Street?" Alice asked, her eyes sparkling with interest. "I heard they have the best pastries."

Ben chuckled, shaking his head. "You and your pastries, Alice. But no, I hadn't heard. Maybe we should check it out. A good pastry can make any day better."

"Oh, absolutely," Alice replied enthusiastically. "We should go together. I bet they have those croissants you love."

Their conversation flowed easily, filled with banter and shared memories. They talked about upcoming events, their favourite spots in the park, and plans for future projects. With each word, the heaviness of the morning seemed to lift, replaced by a sense of camaraderie and hope.

As they finished dismantling the last tent, Alice looked around the park, now much cleaner and tidier than it had been an hour ago. "We did good today, Ben. The park's looking better already."

Ben nodded, satisfaction evident in his expression. "We did. It's a start. And we'll keep at it. This place deserves the best."

Alice smiled, feeling a sense of accomplishment. "Yes, it does. And so do the people who come here."

They loaded the last of the equipment into the wheelbarrow and began making their way back to the storage shed. The sun was higher in the sky now, casting a warm, golden light over the park. The shadows that had seemed so menacing earlier were now just a part of the park's natural beauty.

As they walked, Alice turned to Ben. "Thanks for being here, Ben. I know it's been tough, but it's good to have you by my side."

Ben's expression softened, and he placed a reassuring hand on her shoulder. "Always, Alice. We're a team. And together, we'll get through this."

With renewed determination, they continued their tasks, their spirits lifted by the lighter conversation and the promise of better days ahead. Vivary Park, with its blend of beauty and sorrow, remained a symbol of their community's resilience and strength. And as long as they had each other, they knew they could face whatever challenges lay ahead.

Chapter 17 Notes from the Shadows

The first rays of dawn pierced through the curtains of Stephen Smith's modest home, casting a warm, golden glow on the room. The light played off the framed photographs and awards that adorned the walls, each telling a story of his passion for photography and his dedication to capturing the beauty of the world around him.

Stephen stirred in his bed, the familiar creak of the mattress a reminder of another day beginning. He sat up slowly, running a hand through his tousled hair, and glanced around his bedroom. The pictures on the walls showed smiling faces, vibrant landscapes, and moments of triumph—each a testament to his talent and hard work.

With a sigh, he swung his legs over the edge of the bed and stood up, stretching his muscles. The morning air was cool, and he shivered slightly as he made his way to the kitchen. The smell of freshly brewed coffee soon filled the small space, offering a comforting start to the day.

Stephen poured himself a cup and carried it to the dining table, where the daily newspaper awaited. He unfolded it carefully, his eyes skimming the headlines. The recent murders had been the talk of the town, casting a pall over the usually serene community. Even as he tried to focus on other news, his mind kept drifting back to the unsettling events.

He took a sip of coffee, savouring the warmth and bitterness, and forced himself to concentrate on the articles. The world outside his window seemed calm, but the underlying tension was palpable. It was as if the very air was charged with unspoken fears and uncertainties.

After finishing his coffee, Stephen moved to his small home office where his camera equipment was neatly arranged on a sturdy wooden desk. The cameras, lenses, and various accessories were meticulously maintained, each item placed just so. He checked each piece of equipment with practiced precision, ensuring everything was in perfect working order.

Photography had always been his escape, a way to capture the fleeting beauty of the world and hold it still for just a moment. But lately, even this refuge felt tainted by the shadows lurking in the community.

As he adjusted the settings on one of his cameras, Stephen couldn't shake the feeling of unease. The murders had touched everyone, and he was no exception. He had known some of the victims, had captured their smiles in candid moments at town events. The thought of their lives cut short sent a shiver down his spine.

He put down the camera and took a deep breath, trying to steady his nerves. "Keep it together, Stephen," he muttered to himself. "Focus on the present."

Determined to maintain a sense of normalcy, he glanced at his planner. There was a note about a photo shoot scheduled for later in the day—some portraits for a local family. It was a small job, but it would keep him busy and give him a reason to venture out.

Stephen finished his preparations and returned to the kitchen to clean up. The sun was now higher in the sky, casting brighter beams through the curtains. He opened the window, letting in the fresh morning air. Birds chirped cheerfully outside, their songs a stark contrast to the dark thoughts that had plagued him.

As he stood there, taking in the peaceful scene, Stephen made a silent promise to himself. He would do what he could to help the community heal, to bring back some semblance of normalcy through his work. Capturing moments of joy and beauty was more important now than ever.

With a renewed sense of purpose, he grabbed his camera bag and slung it over his shoulder. He took one last look at the photographs on the wall, drawing strength from the memories they held. Then, with a determined stride, he left his home, ready to face whatever the day might bring.

The morning light bathed the streets of Taunton in a warm glow as Stephen walked towards his car. The town, though scarred by recent events, still held a quiet resilience. And as long as there were moments worth capturing, Stephen knew he had a role to play in the community's recovery.

Stephen Smith parked his car in the car-park of the Castle Hotel, next to the Castle Museum, he planned to have lunch in the Brazz restaurant there later. The museum, with its old stone walls and historical charm, stood proudly in the morning light. He grabbed his camera bag from the back seat and walked towards the entrance, feeling a mix of anticipation and unease. The recent events in Taunton had cast a shadow over everything, but today he had a job to do.

The museum was bustling with visitors, a testament to the community's resilience. Families, tourists, and school groups wandered through the exhibits, their chatter blending into a lively hum. Stephen navigated through the crowd, his focus already shifting to the task at hand.

The Cheddar broach exhibit was a new addition, and it had quickly become one of the museum's highlights. The broach, a delicate piece of craftsmanship from the medieval period, was displayed under soft lighting that accentuated its intricate details. Stephen set up his tripod and began adjusting his camera settings, the familiar routine helping to calm his nerves.

He knelt down, angling his lens to capture the broach from various perspectives. The light played off the precious stones and fine metalwork, creating a mesmerising effect. Stephen became engrossed in his work, his world narrowing down to the delicate artifact in front of him.

As he moved to get a different angle, a shadowy figure appeared in the background. The figure stood still, watching Stephen intently. Oblivious to the silent observer, Stephen continued to snap photos, adjusting his focus and exposure to capture the broach in all its glory.

The museum's curator, a middle-aged woman named Jane, approached him with a warm smile. "Stephen, it's good to see you," she greeted, her voice filled with genuine pleasure. "How's it going?"

Stephen glanced up, returning her smile. "Hi, Jane. It's going well. This broach is incredible. The detail is just stunning."

Jane nodded, her eyes sparkling with pride. "It really is. We're so lucky to have it on loan. The community has been really excited about it."

They chatted for a few moments about the exhibit and the museum's upcoming events. Stephen mentioned his admiration for the meticulous work that had gone into preserving the broach, and Jane shared anecdotes about the process of acquiring and preparing the exhibit.

Despite the light-hearted nature of their conversation, an underlying tension was palpable. The recent murders had left everyone on edge, and the museum staff were no exception. The usual buzz of excitement was tinged with a sense of unease.

"Have you been getting many visitors?" Stephen asked, curious about how the recent events had affected attendance.

Jane sighed, glancing around the room. "It's been a mixed bag. Some days are busier than others. People are trying to go about their lives, but there's definitely a sense of caution in the air."

Stephen nodded, understanding all too well. "It's hard to find a balance between being cautious and trying to live normally. But it's good to see people here, appreciating the history and beauty we have."

Jane smiled, though it didn't quite reach her eyes. "Yes, it is. We need these moments of normalcy, now more than ever."

As they spoke, the shadowy figure lingered at the edge of the exhibit, blending into the background. Stephen remained unaware, his attention fully on Jane and the task at hand.

"Well, I should let you get back to it," Jane said, patting Stephen on the shoulder. "Thanks for doing this. Your photos always bring our exhibits to life."

"Happy to help," Stephen replied, giving her a reassuring smile. "I'll send you the best shots by the end of the day."

Jane nodded and walked away, leaving Stephen to his work. He adjusted his camera once more, trying to capture the broach from a few final angles. The morning light filtering through the museum windows added a soft, ethereal quality to the scene, making the broach sparkle even more.

As he reviewed his photos, Stephen felt a sense of satisfaction. The images were beautiful, a testament to the broach's artistry and his own skill. He packed up his equipment, ready to move on to his next assignment.

The shadowy figure, still watching from a distance, slipped away unnoticed as Stephen turned to leave. The museum's vibrant atmosphere seemed to dim slightly, the sense of foreboding lingering in the air.

Stephen walked out of the museum, his mind already on his next task. The recent events in Taunton weighed heavily on him, but moments like these, capturing the beauty of history, gave him a sense of purpose and hope. He knew the community needed more of these moments to heal and move forward.

After finishing his photo shoot at the Castle Museum, Stephen decided to treat himself to lunch at Brazz, a charming part of the Castle Hotel known for its lively atmosphere and delicious food. As he walked through the hotel's elegant entrance, he felt a sense of comfort in the familiar surroundings. The hotel's grandeur, with its historic architecture and inviting decor, provided a temporary respite from the tensions of recent days.

The restaurant was buzzing with activity. The sound of clinking glasses, the murmur of conversations, and the occasional burst of laughter created a warm, welcoming ambiance. Stephen was greeted by the hostess and led to a cozy table by the window, offering a perfect view of the bustling scene inside.

As he settled into his seat, Stephen took a deep breath, allowing the lively energy of the place to wash over him. He ordered his favourite dish—a hearty steak and ale pie with a side of seasoned vegetables—and a glass of red wine. The familiar ritual of dining at Brazz brought a sense of normalcy to his day.

While waiting for his meal, Stephen let his gaze wander around the restaurant. Couples chatted animatedly, friends shared stories, and families enjoyed their time together. The staff moved efficiently between tables, their friendly smiles and attentive service adding to the restaurant's charm.

Despite the lively atmosphere, a nagging sense of unease lingered at the back of Stephen's mind. He dismissed it as paranoia, a byproduct of the recent events that had shaken the community. He tried to focus on the here and now, appreciating the simple pleasure of a good meal in a familiar place.

As he sipped his wine, Stephen noticed a shadowy figure seated at a corner table, partially obscured by a large potted plant. The figure seemed to be watching him, but Stephen brushed off the thought, convincing himself it was just a coincidence. He had been feeling jumpy ever since the murders, and it was affecting his judgment.

His meal arrived, and the enticing aroma of the steak and ale pie helped to distract him from his worries. He cut into the flaky crust, savouring the rich, savoury filling. For a while, he allowed himself to get lost in the simple pleasure of good food.

Unbeknownst to Stephen, the shadowy figure was indeed watching him closely. The figure's eyes tracked his every movement, their intent hidden behind the casual facade of a diner enjoying lunch. As Stephen ate, the figure remained still, blending into the background noise and activity of the restaurant.

After a few bites, Stephen glanced around the restaurant again, his photographer's eye naturally drawn to the details. The soft lighting, the tasteful decor, the diverse group of patrons—it was a scene worth capturing, if only in his memory.

His attention was drawn to a table nearby, where an elderly couple was celebrating their anniversary. Their hands were clasped together, their faces illuminated with joy as they exchanged loving glances. The sight brought a smile to Stephen's face, reminding him of the enduring beauty of simple, heartfelt moments.

He finished his meal and leaned back in his chair, feeling more relaxed than he had in days. The sense of unease had diminished, replaced by a feeling of contentment. He signalled for the bill, deciding to take a leisurely stroll through the park afterward to enjoy the afternoon sun.

As he left Brazz, he remained blissfully unaware of the shadowy figure who slipped out shortly after him, maintaining a discreet distance. The bustling activity of the restaurant gave way to the quieter, more contemplative atmosphere of the hotel's lobby.

Stephen stepped outside, the warm sunlight greeting him as he walked home through Vivary Park. The events of the day had been a welcome distraction, but the underlying tension of recent weeks still loomed large in his mind. He resolved to stay vigilant, even as he tried to maintain a semblance of normalcy.

The shadowy figure followed at a safe distance, their intentions unclear but their presence a silent reminder that the darkness in Taunton had not yet lifted. As Stephen strolled through the park, the world around him seemed both familiar and subtly altered, the line between safety and danger blurred by unseen eyes.

The park, usually a place of solace, now felt fraught with hidden threats. Stephen's senses were heightened, every rustle of leaves and distant footstep causing his heart to race. He reminded himself to stay calm, to focus on the beauty of the park and the work he loved.

The shadowy figure continued to follow, blending into the background, ever watchful and waiting. As Stephen walked deeper into Vivary Park, he couldn't shake the feeling that he was not alone. But for now, he was determined to enjoy the day, to capture the fleeting moments of peace and beauty that still existed amidst the turmoil.

Stephen returned home, the comforting familiarity of his modest abode greeting him as he stepped through the door. The warmth of the morning light had shifted to the softer hues of the late afternoon, casting long shadows across the room. He placed his camera bag on the kitchen table and went to make himself a cup of tea, needing something to help him unwind after the day's events.

As he walked towards the living room, something caught his eye—a letter, stark white against the worn wood of the floor, had been posted through the letterbox. Stephen felt a strange sense of foreboding as he picked it up. There was no return address, just his name written in a hurried scrawl on the front.

He tore open the envelope, his heart pounding. Inside was a single sheet of paper with a brief, urgent message:

Stephen,

I need to talk to you. Meet me at the lake in Vivary Park at 10 PM tonight. It's important.

David Walker

Stephen stared at the note, a cold chill running down his spine. David Walker was one of the suspects in the recent murders, a fact that made this sudden communication all the more unsettling. He tried to recall the last time he had spoken to David. They had always had a cordial, if distant, relationship, bonded by mutual acquaintances and the occasional town event.

The request to meet at such a late hour, and in such an isolated spot, set off alarm bells in Stephen's mind. He pulled out his phone and dialled David's number, his fingers trembling slightly. The phone rang and rang, but there was no answer. He left a brief, cautious message, hoping for some clarification or reassurance.

"David, it's Stephen. I got your letter. Please call me back when you get this. I need to know what's going on."

He hung up, feeling the weight of uncertainty settling in his chest. Every instinct told him to be wary, but his curiosity and the urgency in David's note compelled him to find out more. The thought of the recent murders made him shudder, but he resolved to proceed cautiously.

Stephen spent the afternoon in his darkroom, a sanctuary of dim light and quiet amidst the chaos of recent events. The small room was filled with the pungent aroma of developing chemicals, a scent that had become oddly comforting to him over the years. Red safety lights cast a warm, eerie glow over the rows of hanging negatives, their ghostly images waiting to be brought to life.

He carefully removed the film from his camera and began the meticulous process of developing the photographs of the Cheddar broach. Each step required precision and patience: mixing the chemicals, soaking the film, and watching as the images slowly emerged. The routine was a welcome distraction, offering a temporary escape from the grim reality outside.

As he worked, his mind wandered back to his recent interactions with Dawn Menzies and Larry Stubbs.

Dawn, with her bright smile and infectious enthusiasm, had been a fixture in the community. Her untimely death had sent shockwaves through the town, leaving a void that was painfully felt by everyone who knew her.

He remembered the last time he saw her at a community event, her laughter ringing out as she organised volunteers. The memory was bittersweet, a reminder of the joy she brought to others and the senseless tragedy of her murder.

Then there was Larry Stubbs, the quiet but friendly groundskeeper who had worked alongside Dawn. Larry's reserved demeanour hid a deep well of knowledge about the town and its people. Stephen had always admired Larry's dedication and attention to detail, qualities that made the recent suspicion surrounding him all the more unsettling.

The darkroom's quiet provided a stark contrast to the turmoil in Stephen's mind. He tried to focus on the task at hand, carefully adjusting the exposure and contrast of each photograph. The intricate details of the broach slowly came into sharp relief, its ancient beauty preserved through his lens. He found solace in the delicate patterns, each curve and line a testament to the craftsmanship of a bygone era.

But the gnawing unease remained, a constant undercurrent to his thoughts. The murders had cast a long shadow over Taunton, and the sense of safety that once defined the town had been irrevocably shattered. Every interaction, every familiar face, now carried a hint of suspicion and fear.

Stephen's reflection in the darkroom's dim light seemed to blur with the images he was developing. The faces of Dawn and Larry, the enigmatic beauty of the broach, all melded together in his mind. He wondered if there was a connection, some thread that linked the seemingly disparate events.

As the final photograph emerged, Stephen hung it up to dry and stepped back to admire his work. The broach glistened under the red light, a symbol of history and mystery. He hoped that capturing its essence would bring some clarity, some sense of accomplishment amidst the chaos.

He leaned against the counter, closing his eyes and taking a deep breath. The familiar routine of the darkroom had done little to ease his mind, but it had given him a sense of purpose. He knew he couldn't ignore the feeling of dread that lingered, but for now, he had to focus on the present.

Stephen decided to take a break and stepped out of the darkroom into the brighter, more inviting light of his home. The contrast was jarring, but it reminded him of the world outside, the world he needed to navigate with caution.

He glanced at the clock. It was still a few hours until his meeting with David Walker at the lake. The thought filled him with a renewed sense of apprehension, but also determination. He had to see this through, to find out what David knew and how it connected to the unfolding events.

As the evening shadows lengthened and the sky deepened to twilight, Stephen felt a growing sense of dread. The letter from David Walker weighed heavily on his mind. He tried to call David again, hoping for some clarification or reassurance, but once more, there was no answer. The silence on the other end of the line only amplified his unease.

Stephen paced his living room, his thoughts racing. The recent murders had cast a dark pall over Taunton, and this mysterious meeting with David seemed fraught with potential danger. Yet, he felt compelled to go, driven by the need to uncover the truth and perhaps find some connection that could explain the recent events.

He moved to his study and meticulously checked his camera equipment, ensuring everything was in working order. The familiar ritual helped to calm his nerves somewhat. He packed his camera bag with care, adding a small flashlight to the mix. He paused for a moment, taking a deep breath, and steeling himself for whatever lay ahead.

The air was cool and crisp as Stephen stepped out of his house, the chill a sharp contrast to the warm safety he was leaving behind. He glanced around his quiet street, the familiar houses now shrouded in darkness. The night seemed to amplify every sound—the rustling of leaves, the distant hum of traffic, the occasional bark of a dog. Each noise heightened his sense of alertness.

Stephen locked his door and began his walk towards Vivary Park. The path was familiar, yet tonight it felt different, cloaked in an eerie stillness. As he walked, the events of the past few weeks played over in his mind. Dawn Menzies' vibrant presence, now extinguished; Larry Stubbs' quiet reliability, now clouded by suspicion. The community had been rocked to its core, and Stephen felt the weight of it pressing down on him.

The streets were largely deserted, the townsfolk preferring the safety of their homes. Stephen's footsteps echoed in the stillness, a lonely sound that seemed to underscore his isolation. He clutched his camera bag a little tighter, feeling the reassuring weight of his equipment against his side.

Entering Vivary Park, the darkness seemed to close in around him. The familiar pathways were cloaked in shadow, the trees looming like silent sentinels. He switched on his flashlight, the beam cutting through the blackness and casting long, flickering shadows. The lake lay ahead, its surface a mirror reflecting the sliver of moonlight that pierced the cloud cover.

Stephen's heart pounded as he approached the meeting spot, the letter's words echoing in his mind. He checked his watch—9:50 PM. He was early, but he preferred it that way. It gave him a chance to survey the area, to ensure there were no surprises.

He found a bench near the water's edge and sat down, the cool metal seeping through his clothing. The park was eerily silent, the usual sounds of the night seeming to hold their breath. He scanned the surroundings, the beam of his flashlight sweeping over the landscape, revealing nothing out of the ordinary.

As the minutes ticked by, Stephen's unease grew. He tried to focus on the task at hand, to steel himself for whatever David had to reveal. The night air was crisp, carrying with it the faint scent of the lake and the earthy aroma of the surrounding vegetation.

At exactly 10 PM, he heard a rustling in the bushes nearby. Stephen's grip tightened on the flashlight, his heart racing. The beam of light revealed David

Walker emerging from the shadows, his face drawn and anxious.

"Stephen," David called out softly, his eyes darting around nervously. "Thank you for coming."

Stephen rose from the bench, keeping a safe distance. "David, what's going on? Why did you want to meet here, and at this time?"

David glanced over his shoulder, his expression filled with fear. "I can't explain everything now, but I know something about the murders. Something important. It's not safe to talk here."

Stephen's mind raced. "Then why here, David? Why not somewhere safer, or during the day?"

David's eyes were wide with urgency. "Because they're watching. They're always watching. I had to make sure we weren't followed."

Stephen felt a chill run down his spine. "Who, David? Who's watching you?"

Before David could respond, a sudden noise from the darkness made both men jump. Stephen swung the flashlight around, its beam revealing only shadows and trees. The sense of being watched, of an unseen presence lurking just out of sight, was almost unbearable.

"Let's move," David whispered urgently. "We can't stay here."

Stephen nodded, his instincts screaming at him to flee, yet he felt compelled to find out more. They moved quickly, sticking to the shadows, both acutely aware of the unseen eyes that seemed to follow their every move.

As they walked deeper into the park, the world around them seemed both familiar and subtly altered, the line between safety and danger blurred by unseen threats. Stephen knew that the path ahead was fraught with uncertainty, but he was determined to uncover the truth, no matter where it led.

Chapter 18 The Last Meeting

David and Stephen stood by the lake in Vivary Park, the moon casting a silvery glow over the water. David's eyes darted around nervously, and he leaned closer to Stephen. "We can't talk here," he whispered. "I feel like we're always being watched." Without waiting for a response, David led Stephen down a narrow woodland path that snaked through the trees at the back of the lake. The canopy above them thickened, shrouding the path in darkness, and the sounds of the park faded into an eerie silence, broken only by the distant hoot of an owl and the occasional quack of a duck.

The night sky over Vivary Park was an expanse of inky blackness, dotted with glistening stars. The full moon cast a silvery glow over the serene landscape, making the lake shimmer with an ethereal beauty. The air was cool and crisp, filled with the distant hoot of an owl and the occasional quack of a duck.

David stood by the water's edge, his silhouette barely discernible against the dark backdrop of trees. He peered into the shadows, alert for any sign of movement. His heart raced with a mix of anxiety and determination. He knew that tonight was crucial. Stephen had to understand—he had to believe him.

The soft crunch of footsteps on the gravel path signalled Stephen's arrival. David turned to see his friend approaching, a sceptical expression etched on his face.

"David," Stephen greeted, his tone cautious. "What's so urgent that it couldn't wait until morning?"

David took a deep breath, steadying himself. "Thanks for coming, Stephen. I know it sounds crazy, but I had to tell you in person. We're being watched."

Stephen raised an eyebrow, folding his arms across his chest. "Watched? By whom?"

David glanced around nervously before lowering his voice. "By members of the Flower Show committee. I think some of them are involved in the murders."

Stephen let out a disbelieving laugh. "David, you've been under a lot of stress. Are you sure you're not just imagining things?"

"No, Stephen, listen to me," David insisted, his voice urgent. "I've been watching them. They're too involved in everything that's been happening. The accidents, the deaths—none of it is coincidental."

Stephen sighed, shaking his head. "You've always had a vivid imagination, but this is too much. The Flower Show committee? They're just a bunch of enthusiasts. What motive could they possibly have?"

David stepped closer, his eyes intense. "Power and control. They have a vested interest in the Flower Show, and they're willing to do anything to protect their secrets. Think about it—Roger Morgan's death, the sabotage of Stephen's entries, the whispers about bribery and corruption. It all points back to them."

Stephen's scepticism deepened. "Even if that's true, why would they target us? We're just photographers."

"Because we're getting too close to the truth," David replied, his voice barely above a whisper. "We've seen things we shouldn't have. They know we're a threat."

Stephen shook his head again, a mixture of frustration and pity in his eyes. "David, this is madness. You're letting your paranoia get the best of you. I don't believe a word of it."

David's face fell, the weight of Stephen's disbelief crushing his spirit. "Please, Stephen. I need you to trust me. Just this once."

Stephen turned away, his resolve firm. "I can't, David. I'm sorry. I need to get home."

David watched as Stephen walked away, his figure disappearing into the darkness. The sound of his footsteps faded, leaving David alone by the lake, a profound sense of isolation settling over him.

As Stephen's figure disappeared into the darkness, David stood alone by the lake, frustration and despair weighing heavily on him. He muttered to himself, "Nobody understands. Nobody believes me. They all think I'm crazy, but I know I'm right."

As the night grew colder, David's mind raced with thoughts of what might come next. He knew he couldn't give up. Somehow, he had to find a way to prove his theory and uncover the truth behind the murders. But for now, all he could do was wait and hope that his friend would come around before it was too late.

Lost in his thoughts, David didn't notice the subtle movement in the bushes behind him. A lone figure, cloaked in shadows, silently stepped forward, eyes fixed on David. The night seemed to hold its breath, the usual nocturnal sounds hushed as if sensing the impending violence.

Before David could react, the figure raised a heavy object and brought it down hard on the back of his head. There was a sickening thud, and David crumpled to the ground, his last thought a fleeting mix of surprise and betrayal.

The figure moved quickly, dragging David's limp body across the damp grass towards the weir at the edge of the lake. The moonlight glinted off the water, providing a ghostly illumination as the killer struggled to push David's body into the stream.

With a final, determined shove, the figure kicked David's body into the water. The current caught him, pulling him slowly but inexorably towards the weir. David's body drifted over the edge, disappearing into the dark, churning waters below.

The night sky, indifferent and silent, offered no answers, only the persistent call of an owl in the distance. The ripples on the lake's surface gradually smoothed out, erasing any trace of the violent act that had just occurred.

Vivary Park returned to its tranquil state, the serene beauty of the night masking the dark deed done in its depths.

Chapter 19 Murder by the Weir

The first rays of dawn barely kissed the horizon as Henry "Hank" Thompson grumbled his way through the back fields of Vivary Park. A craggy old man with hands as rough as the land he cherished, Hank was known throughout the town as a fixture of stubborn resolve and unwavering dedication. His weathered face bore the marks of countless seasons spent battling the elements, each wrinkle a testament to his no-nonsense attitude and deep love for his land.

It was a rare soul who saw Hank without his battered brown hat, its wide brim casting a perpetual shadow over his piercing eyes. This morning was no different. He had risen before the birds, compelled by a gnawing irritation. The fence at the edge of his property, running alongside the Sherford River, had once again been vandalised. Hank had no doubt it was the doing of local youths, their idle hands and reckless disregard for others' property making them the prime suspects in his book.

With a heavy sigh, Hank dropped his toolbox to the ground. The dull thud echoed in the quiet morning, a signal of his readiness to set things right. The familiar sounds of hammering and the creak of old wood under strain soon filled the air, mingling with his muttered curses about "kids these days." He worked with a practiced efficiency, each swing of his hammer fuelled by a mix of frustration and an ingrained sense of duty.

Hank straightened up, wiping his brow with a calloused hand and letting out a sigh that seemed to carry the weight of his many years. He leaned against the freshly mended fence, taking a rare moment to appreciate the tranquillity of the early morning. It was then that his gaze drifted to the Sherford River, its waters glinting softly in the rising sun. A frown creased his brow as he noticed the river looked more swollen than usual, the current faster and more forceful than he'd seen in days.

"Must be somethin' cloggin' it up," he muttered, puzzled by the unexpected surge. There hadn't been a drop of rain in the past week, and the usual causes of such a swell seemed unlikely. Hank's curiosity, mixed with a hint of concern, urged him to investigate. He grabbed his walking stick, a sturdy branch worn smooth by years of use, and made his way down to the riverbank.

As he approached, the sound of rushing water grew louder, a persistent gurgle that seemed almost urgent. Hank's keen eyes scanned the surface, searching for the source of the disturbance. It didn't take long for him to spot it—a bulky, brown shape caught in the current, just upstream from where he stood. From a distance, it looked like a large log, lodged against a cluster of rocks.

"Blasted thing's prob'ly been floatin' downstream for days," he grumbled, pushing through the tall grass that fringed the river. But as he drew closer, the details of the object began to emerge, and Hank's frown deepened. The shape wasn't quite right for a log—too round in some places, too angular in others. The colour, a muddy brown, seemed unnatural, almost like fabric.

"What's this now?" he muttered under his breath, his pace quickening despite himself. The object was caught in the rocks, bobbing slightly as the water rushed past. Hank's heart skipped a beat as he realized what he was seeing. It wasn't a log at all.

His boots slipped on the slick riverbank as he knelt down for a closer look. The bulky shape resolved into something all too familiar: a human form, facedown in the water, the brown fabric of a jacket blending eerily with the muddy hues of the river. Hank's stomach churned as the reality of his discovery hit him. The water swirled around the body, creating a macabre dance that held him transfixed for a moment.

The jacket, soaked through and clinging to the figure, looked well-worn, its seams strained and its colour dulled by the elements. Hank's eyes moved from the jacket to the pallid, lifeless hand that protruded from a sleeve, the fingers curled slightly as if in a final, desperate grasp.

"Bugger me!" Hank whispered, his voice barely audible over the rush of the river. He stood up slowly, his mind racing. This was no ordinary day, and the swollen river had brought more than just water to his doorstep. The urgency of the situation pushed him into action, his earlier grumbles forgotten as he turned and hurried back towards his farmhouse, the image of the body burned into his mind.

The discovery was a stark reminder of the unpredictable nature of life, and as Hank made his way to call the authorities, he couldn't help but feel a chill that had nothing to do with the morning air. The peaceful rhythm of his morning had been shattered, replaced by a grim mystery that demanded answers.

Hank's boots pounded against the dirt path as he hurried back to his farmhouse, the image of the lifeless body haunting his every step. His heart raced, but his mind remained focused. He had to call the authorities—there was no time to waste.

Bursting through the farmhouse door, Hank grabbed the old rotary phone from its cradle and dialled the emergency number with a steady hand. The line clicked, and a calm, professional voice answered.

"Emergency services, what's your emergency?"

Hank took a deep breath, keeping his voice steady. "This is Hank Thompson. I found a body in the Sherford River, near my property in Vivary Park. It's a man, facedown in the water. Looks like he's been there a while."

The operator's tone remained composed. "Can you confirm the location, sir?"

"Yeah, it's by the riverbank, just upstream from my farmhouse. The current's strong, and the body's caught in some rocks."

"Understood, Mr. Thompson. Are you in a safe location?"

"I'm at my farmhouse now. Just get someone here quick."

"Help is on the way, sir. Please stay on the line until the officers arrive."

Hank grunted in acknowledgment, his eyes fixed on the distant river. The minutes felt like hours, but soon the wail of sirens pierced the air, growing louder as the police approached.

Flashing lights illuminated the early morning gloom as a police cruiser pulled up to Hank's farmhouse. Two officers stepped out, their faces set with professional determination. A constable, young and eager, approached Hank with a notepad in hand.

"Mr. Thompson? I'm Constable Davies. Can you show us where you found the body?"

Hank nodded curtly, leading the officers down the path to the riverbank. The constable's questions came rapid-fire, and Hank answered with gruff efficiency.

"How did you come across the body, sir?"

"I was fixin' my fence when I noticed the river was swollen. Went to check it out and saw the body caught in the rocks."

"Did you touch or move the body at all?"

"No. Just got close enough to see it was a man. Didn't want to disturb anything."

"Do you recognise the deceased?"

Hank shook his head. "No. Never seen him before."

The constable scribbled notes, his brow furrowed in concentration. "Thank you, Mr. Thompson. We'll take it from here. Please stay nearby in case we have more questions."

Hank nodded again, stepping back as the officers moved to secure the scene. The flashing lights cast eerie shadows on the water, and Hank's mind churned with unanswered questions. But for now, his part was done. He had called for help, and the authorities were on the case.

The morning birdsong was shattered by the shrill wail of sirens piercing the air, shattering the idyllic calm that had blanketed Vivary Park. Within minutes, a sleek police cruiser screeched to a halt near the fountain, and two figures emerged, their contrasting demeanours reflecting the yin and yang of the investigative process.

Harry was the first to stride purposefully towards the crime scene, her sharp eyes already scanning the surroundings for clues. Close on her heels was Tom, his methodical gaze sweeping over the scene with meticulous precision.

As they approached the riverbank, the sight of the victim's body sent a ripple of unease through even their experienced ranks. Harry's brow furrowed, her mind already whirring with possibilities, while Tom's eyes narrowed, his focus zeroing in on the smallest details that could unravel the mystery.

A constable, young and eager, approached them with a notepad in hand. "Detectives, the body was found by Mr. Hank Thompson. He's over there by the farmhouse," he said, pointing to a gruff-looking man standing a few yards away.

Harry nodded, her gaze shifting to the constable. "What can you tell us about the scene?"

The constable cleared his throat, his voice steady despite the macabre sight before them. "The victim is a male, facedown in the water. No immediate signs of struggle, but the body is caught in some rocks. We haven't moved him yet, waiting for your instructions."

Tom crouched beside the body, his brow furrowed as he studied the positioning of the limbs. "There are no obvious signs of defensive wounds," he murmured, his voice tinged with grim professionalism. "The attack was likely swift and unexpected."

Harry's gaze was drawn to the victim's body, partially submerged in the shallow waters of the river. The man's face was frozen in a ghastly expression, his eyes wide with terror, and his mouth agape as if he had tried to cry out in his final moments.

"Let's get the body out of the water and have forensics take a closer look," Harry instructed, her voice steady despite the grim scene. "We need to know who this man is and why he ended up here."

As the constables moved to follow her orders, Harry and Tom exchanged a grave look. The weight of the case was already bearing down on them, but they knew they had to move quickly to identify the killer before more innocent lives were claimed.

With the body now being carefully extracted from the river, Harry and Tom made their way over to Hank Thompson, who stood by the farmhouse, his face set in a grim expression.

"Hank Thompson?" Harry asked, her voice gentle but firm.

Hank nodded, his eyes flicking between the detectives. "That's right. I found the body this morning."

"Can you walk us through what happened?" Tom asked, his tone professional.

Hank took a deep breath, his voice steady. "I was fixin' my fence when I noticed the river was swollen. Went to check it out and saw the body caught in the rocks. Didn't touch it, just called the police right away."

"Did you see anyone else around? Anyone suspicious?" Harry pressed.

Hank shook his head. "No. Just me and the river. Didn't see or hear anything unusual."

"Thank you, Mr. Thompson," Tom said, his voice sincere. "We'll need you to stay nearby in case we have more questions."

Hank nodded, his eyes lingering on the river. "I'll be here."

As they approached the riverbank, the sight of the body sent a chill down their spines.

Harry and Tom exchanged a glance, the weight of the revelation settling heavily upon them. David Walker, the man they had been investigating, now lay dead before them.

He had a reputation for being fiercely competitive, often clashing with his peers, particularly Roger Morgan. His aggressive nature and history of instability had made him a prime suspect in Roger's murder, but now, he was the latest victim in this twisted game.

The medical examiner, Dr. Eliza Hawthorne, had arrived on the scene while Harry and Tom had been talking to Hank, crouched beside the body. Her latex gloves were stained with the grim remnants of her examination. She looked up as Harry and Tom approached, her expression grave.

"Detectives," she greeted them with a curt nod. "I've just started the preliminary examination, but I can tell you this much: the cause of death appears to be a single, forceful blow to the back of the head. The body was then placed in the river, likely to obscure the time of death."

Harry knelt beside the body, her eyes scanning the scene for any clues. "Any signs of a struggle?"

Eliza shook her head. "None that I can see. It looks like he was taken by surprise."

Tom furrowed his brow, his mind racing with possibilities. "Could it be the same killer? The method seems different from the other murders."

Eliza nodded thoughtfully. "It's possible. The killer might be adapting their methods to throw us off. But the precision of the blow suggests someone with strength and knowledge of anatomy."

Harry's gaze drifted to the river, the water flowing gently past the rocks where David's body had been found. "We need to find out who had the opportunity and motive to kill David. His connection to Roger can't be a coincidence."

Tom made a note in his pad. "We'll need to re-interview everyone connected to both victims. There has to be a link we're missing."

Harry turned back to Eliza. "Anything else you can tell us about the body?"

Eliza hesitated for a moment before speaking. "There are some unusual marks on his wrists, like he was bound at some point. And there's a faint smell of chemicals on his clothes, something I can't quite place yet. I'll need to run some tests back at the lab."

Harry nodded, her mind already racing with the implications. "Thanks, Eliza. Keep us updated."

As they stood up, Tom glanced around the scene, his eyes narrowing. "We need to find out where he was before he ended up here. Someone must have seen or heard something."

Harry agreed, her resolve hardening. "Let's get to work. The killer's left us another puzzle, and we need to solve it before they strike again."

As they walked back to their car, Harry's mind was already racing with questions. Who had the strength and knowledge to deliver such a precise blow? What was the significance of the chemicals on

David's clothes? And most importantly, how did this murder connect to the death of Roger Morgan?

As Hank trudged back to his farmhouse, the image of the lifeless body in the river lingered in his mind, casting a shadow over his thoughts. The discovery had shaken him to his core, stirring up a maelstrom of emotions he hadn't felt in years. Life and death, two sides of the same coin, had collided in a way that left him grappling for understanding.

"Life's a fragile thing," he mused, his steps heavy with the weight of his thoughts. "One moment you're fixin' a fence, the next you're starin' at a body in the river. Makes you wonder what it's all about, really. All the years I've spent workin' this land, fightin' the elements, and for what? To end up like that poor soul, forgotten and washed away?"

The river, usually a source of tranquillity and life, now seemed a harbinger of death, its waters carrying away the remnants of a life once lived. Hank's mind wandered to the inevitability of his own mortality, the thought both sobering and humbling.

As he neared his farmhouse, Hank's thoughts turned to David Walker. He had known David in passing, their interactions limited to the occasional nod or brief conversation at town events. David was a talented photographer, but his reputation was marred by a fierce competitiveness and a tendency to rub people the wrong way.

"David Walker," Hank muttered, shaking his head. "Always thought he was a bit of a hothead, but never figured he'd end up like this. Remember that time at the Flower Show, he got into it with Roger Morgan over some photograph? Thought they were gonna come to blows right there in front of everyone. Guess that fire in him burned too bright, and now it's snuffed out."

Hank recalled the last time he had seen David, fussing over his photographs at the town exhibition. There had been a tension in the air, a sense of unresolved conflict that now seemed eerily prophetic. David's arrogance and disdain had masked a deeper turmoil, one that had ultimately led to his untimely demise.

Back at the farmhouse, Hank picked up his toolbox and returned to the fence, his earlier irritation now replaced by a sombre resolve. The rhythmic sound of hammering filled the air once more, but this time, it was accompanied by a quiet reflection.

"Life goes on," he thought, driving a nail into the wood with a steady hand. "Can't let this shake me too much. Got work to do, and this land ain't gonna tend to itself. But I'll be damned if I don't take a moment to appreciate what I've got. Every sunrise, every breath, it's all a gift. Can't take it for granted."

As he worked, Hank's gaze occasionally drifted to the river, its waters now a reminder of the fragility of life. The fence, once a symbol of his battle against the encroaching wild, now seemed a testament to his resilience in the face of life's uncertainties.

With each swing of the hammer, Hank's resolve hardened. He would continue to care for his land, to fight the good fight, but with a newfound appreciation for the fleeting nature of existence. The discovery of David Walker's body had cast a pall over his morning, but it had also ignited a deeper understanding of the preciousness of life.

"Rest in peace, David," he murmured, his voice barely audible over the sound of his work. "Hope you find the peace you couldn't find in life."

And with that, Hank Thompson, the craggy old man with hands as rough as the land he cherished, returned to his work, his heart a little heavier but his spirit unbroken.

Chapter 20 The Murder Board

Harry and Tom stepped into the CID room, the atmosphere heavy with the weight of David Walker's recent murder. The dim overhead lights cast a sombre glow, barely illuminating the space and deepening the shadows in the corners. The air felt dense, thick with the urgency and tension of the investigation that seemed to permeate every inch of the room.

In the centre of the room stood the "murder board," a chaotic yet meticulously detailed tapestry of the case. It dominated the space, an imposing reminder of the complexities they were untangling. Photographs of the victims, including a freshly pinned one of David Walker, formed a grim gallery of faces, each looking out with haunting stillness. Notes were scattered across the board, some neatly typed, others hastily scribbled in a rush of revelation. Red and blue lines crisscrossed the board, connecting suspects, locations, and pieces of evidence, creating a web of intrigue and suspicion.

The clutter on the board mirrored the cluttered thoughts in Harry and Tom's minds. There were maps with highlighted routes, timelines detailing each victim's last known movements, and sketches of potential crime scenes. Newspaper clippings added another layer, their sensational headlines screaming out in bold type about the string of murders that had rocked Taunton.

The room itself seemed to echo the urgency. The desks were strewn with open case files, their contents spilling out in a disarray that bespoke the frantic search for answers. A faint hum from the ancient air conditioning unit did little to dispel the stifling heat, adding a sense of claustrophobia to the already oppressive atmosphere.

Harry walked over to the murder board, her eyes scanning the myriad of details, looking for a thread they might have missed. Tom followed, his footsteps muffled on the worn carpet, the sound barely audible above the hum of the air conditioner.

As they stood before the board, the enormity of their task weighed heavily on them. The room seemed to close in, the dim light focusing their attention solely on the grim mosaic of evidence before them. This was the heart of their investigation, a nerve centre where every clue, every piece of information, converged into a single, daunting puzzle.

Here, in this dimly lit room, surrounded by the faces of the victims and the maze of evidence, Harry and Tom prepared to dive once more into the depths of the case, driven by the silent urgency that filled the air.

Harry, her brow furrowed, carefully pinned a new set of crime scene photos to the board. The images of David Walker's lifeless body were stark and unsettling, capturing the violent final moments of his life. Each photograph was methodically placed, forming a chronological narrative of the crime scene. Tom, standing beside him, held a stack of witness statements, his eyes scanning the pages for any shred of useful information.

"Let's start with the crime scene," Harry murmured, more to herself than to Tom. She adjusted the position of a photograph showing David Walker had floating in the river.

Tom placed a statement from a nearby resident who had heard a commotion. "This witness heard noises around midnight," he said, pinning the statement next to the photo. "It matches the estimated time of death."

They moved with practiced efficiency, their movements a dance of investigation. Red lines of string connected the new photos and statements to those already on the board, weaving a complex web of connections and clues. Harry picked up a marker and began drawing lines between Walker and the other victims, tracing possible links.

"Look at this," Harry said, highlighting a connection between Walker and one of the earlier victims. "They both worked for the same company five years ago. Could be significant."

Tom leaned in, scrutinising the connection. "And there's this," he added, tapping a photo of another victim. "She lived just two streets away from Walker. Maybe they crossed paths more often than we thought."

The room seemed to hum with the energy of their investigation. The board, once a chaotic collage, began to take on a more structured appearance as they meticulously reviewed and connected each piece of evidence. The smell of stale coffee hung in the air, a testament to the long hours they had spent poring over the details.

As they worked, the murder board became a living document, evolving with each new piece of information. The connections between the murders grew clearer, revealing a pattern that had previously eluded them. Harry stepped back, squinting at the board, her mind racing with possibilities.

"We're missing something," she said finally, his voice tinged with frustration. "There's a link here that we're not seeing."

Tom nodded, his eyes never leaving the board. "We need to think like the killer. What's the motive? What's the common thread?"

The room, heavy with the weight of unsolved mysteries, seemed to close in around them. They knew that every second counted, that the murderer could strike again if they didn't find the answers soon. The board, with its labyrinth of clues, held the key to unravelling the truth—they just had to see the pattern.

With renewed determination, Harry and Tom continued their meticulous work, knowing that somewhere within the tangle of photos, statements, and lines, lay the solution to David Walker's murder and the dark secret connecting all the victims.

Harry stood back from the murder board, her arms crossed, eyes narrowing as she scrutinized the intricate web of connections. The dim lighting cast long shadows, giving the room an almost oppressive atmosphere. The air was thick with the scent of stale coffee and the faint tang of anxiety.

"I'm telling you, Tom," Harry said, her voice low but intense, "there's a personal angle to all of this. Look at the victims – they weren't random targets. There's a direct link between them. Someone close to them is orchestrating this."

Tom, leaning against a cluttered desk, shook his head slowly. "I'm not so sure, Harry. Jealousy, revenge, sure. But what if it's a cover-up?

Something deeper? Maybe one of these victims knew something they weren't supposed to."

Harry paced in front of the board, her movements quick and precise, like a tigress in a cage. "David Walker and the others, they all had connections to that old company. But it's not just professional. There are personal ties, too. Friends, family... someone with access to their lives."

Tom stepped closer to the board, pointing at a photograph of an earlier victim. "Okay, but look at this. She had no known enemies, no debts, nothing. Her murder was the cleanest. If it's personal, why her? Why not leave her out?"

Harry's eyes flashed with frustration. "It's because of what she represented, Tom. Maybe she was a threat in a different way. Maybe she saw something, knew something."

The tension in the room was palpable. The steady hum of the air conditioning did little to cool the rising heat of their argument. Tom's calm demeanour contrasted sharply with Harry's fiery intensity, creating a charged atmosphere that crackled with every exchange.

"Harry, we need concrete evidence," Tom urged, his voice steady but firm. "We can't just jump to conclusions. We need to build a case, not a theory."

Harry turned to face him fully, her eyes blazing. "And how do you suggest we do that if we don't follow the leads we have? Every second we waste, the killer gets further away. We have to trust our instincts."

Tom ran a hand through his hair, exhaling sharply. "I get that. I do. But we have to be methodical. We have to be sure. We can't afford to be wrong on this."

For a moment, the room fell silent, the only sound the distant murmur of office noise beyond their door. Harry's gaze softened slightly, and she took a deep breath, trying to rein in her frustration.

"Alright," she said, her voice quieter but still resolute. "We'll be methodical. But we can't ignore the personal connections. There's something there, Tom. I can feel it."

Tom nodded, a hint of a smile tugging at the corner of his mouth. "Fair enough. We'll dig deeper into those personal ties. But we'll do it by the book. Agreed?"

Harry nodded, a reluctant smile breaking through her intensity. "Agreed. Let's find this bastard."

With a renewed sense of purpose, they turned back to the murder board, ready to tackle the mystery from every angle, determined to uncover the truth, no matter where it led them. The conflict had only strengthened their resolve, forging a stronger partnership in the crucible of their heated debate.

Harry and Tom stood before the murder board, the debate still lingering in the charged air between them. They exchanged a glance, a silent agreement passing between them to pursue their next lead. Harry's eyes hardened with determination.

"We need to get Eliza's preliminary report on David Walker's autopsy," she said, breaking the silence.

Tom nodded. "Agreed. Let's head over to the Medical Examiner's office."

The two detectives gathered their notes and made their way out of the dimly lit CID room. The fluorescent lights of the hallway seemed overly bright in contrast, flickering slightly as they walked. Their footsteps echoed off the linoleum floors, a rhythmic reminder of the urgency propelling them forward.

As they stepped outside, the afternoon sun had dipped low, casting long shadows across the parking lot. The sky was a gradient of orange and purple, hinting at the approaching evening. Harry and Tom moved quickly to their unmarked car, the tension of their earlier argument still palpable but now channelled into a focused drive.

The ride to the Medical Examiner's office was quiet, each lost in their thoughts. The city seemed almost serene, a deceptive calm that contrasted sharply with the turmoil of their investigation. Harry's mind raced with theories and connections, while Tom reviewed their notes, looking for anything they might have missed.

They arrived at the Medical Examiner's office, a stark, utilitarian building that housed the city's morgue. The air was cooler here, with a slight antiseptic scent that hinted at the clinical procedures performed within. Harry and Tom entered the building, their badges flashing to the security guard who nodded them through with a sombre understanding.

The hallway leading to Eliza's office was lined with doors, each marked with sterile, professional plaques. They reached the door marked "Dr. Eliza Hawthorne, Medical Examiner" and paused for a moment. Tom knocked lightly, and they heard Eliza's voice call them in.

The office was spacious but cluttered, a testament to Eliza's meticulous yet frenzied work pace. The walls were lined with shelves of medical textbooks and files, and the desk was strewn with papers and reports. In the centre of it all stood Eliza, a figure of composed efficiency in a white lab coat, her eyes sharp and focused.

"Harry, Tom," she greeted them, a slight smile softening her otherwise serious demeanour. "I've been expecting you. I've got the preliminary results on David Walker."

Harry and Tom took seats opposite Eliza, the atmosphere in the room shifting to one of intense concentration. Eliza's desk lamp cast a pool of light on the autopsy report she had prepared, the rest of the room fading into shadows.

"Tell us what you've got, Eliza," Harry said, leaning forward, her earlier intensity now channelled into a laser focus on the information Eliza was about to reveal.

Eliza opened the file, her eyes scanning the details before she began. "Walker's cause of death was blunt force trauma to the head, consistent with the murder weapon we discussed.

Eliza continued, "There's also a substance under his fingernails. I've sent it for further analysis, but preliminary results suggest it's some kind of soil or dirt. Could be a clue to where he was before he was brought to the scene."

The room fell silent as Harry and Tom absorbed the information. Each detail added another layer to the puzzle, deepening the mystery but also bringing them closer to the truth.

"And then there's this," Eliza added, pulling out a small evidence bag. Inside was a silver locket, tarnished and old. "We found this in his pocket."

Harry took the bag, examining the locket closely. "This could be a significant clue. It might belong to the killer or someone connected to them."

"Thanks, Eliza," Harry said finally, her voice steady. "This is exactly what we needed. We'll follow up on these leads."

"We need to figure out our next steps. We have a lot of pieces, but we need to see how they fit together" she continued.

Eliza nodded, her eyes scanning the autopsy report spread out before her. "The soil under Walker's fingernails is key. If we can pinpoint where it came from, we might find the place he was held before he was killed."

Tom leaned forward, tapping a photograph of the soil sample. "We need to get this analysed as quickly as possible. I'll call the lab and push for a rush on the results."

Harry nodded, her mind racing. "And the locket. We need to find out who it belongs to. It could be a significant lead. Maybe it was left behind by mistake, or maybe it was placed there deliberately."

Eliza picked up the locket, examining it closely. "It's old and worn, which suggests it's been kept for a long time. There might be something inside—an inscription, a photo—that could give us more information."

Tom added, "We should also re-interview Walker's family and friends. Someone might recognise the locket or remember something about his recent activities that didn't seem important before."

The room fell silent as they each considered the potential suspects and their next moves. Harry's eyes were intense as she spoke. "We need to focus on people who had personal connections with Walker. Someone close to him had the motive and opportunity."

Tom nodded, his voice thoughtful. "Let's review the list of suspects again. We need to tighten the noose around the killer. We can't afford to miss anything."

They moved to a whiteboard on one side of the room, where they began to list potential suspects and their alibis. The tension in the room was palpable, driven by the urgency to solve the case before the killer struck again.

Harry, with her usual intensity, said, "Let's start with Walker's colleagues at the company. We know there were some connections to the other victims. We need to dig deeper into those relationships."

Tom added, "And what about his personal life? Any recent changes, any new relationships or breakups? We need to explore every angle."

Eliza, ever the meticulous professional, chimed in. "We also need to consider the physical evidence. The soil, the locket—they tell a story. We need to make sure we're reading it correctly."

Their differences in approach became apparent as they brainstormed. Harry, driven by intuition and a keen sense of human nature, pushed for a focus on personal connections and emotional motives. Tom, ever the methodical detective, emphasized the need for concrete evidence and logical analysis. Eliza, with her clinical perspective, bridged the gap, providing crucial insights from the physical evidence.

Despite the underlying tension, their teamwork was evident. They challenged each other's assumptions, tested each other's theories, and combined their strengths to form a comprehensive strategy. The clock was ticking, but they were united in their determination to catch the killer.

Harry concluded, her voice resolute, "We split up. Tom, you handle the soil analysis and the lab. I'll visit Walker's family and friends. Eliza, keep digging into the physical evidence. Let's reconvene tonight and compare notes."

They all nodded in agreement, a shared sense of purpose driving them forward. As they left Eliza's office, the cool evening air greeted them once again, invigorating them for the tasks ahead. They had a plan, and they were ready to tighten the noose around the murderer, knowing that every second counted.

Chapter 21 The Soil and the Locket

Tom stepped out of his car, the late afternoon sun casting long shadows across the parking lot of the forensics lab. The modern building stood stark against the backdrop of Taunton's more historic structures, its sleek lines and glass facade reflecting the seriousness of the work conducted within. The lab exuded a sense of sterility and precision, a world apart from the chaotic scenes of crime that Tom was accustomed to.

As he approached the entrance, the automatic doors slid open with a soft whoosh, releasing a gust of cool, sterile air that carried the faint scent of chemicals. The lobby was a pristine expanse of white and chrome, with polished floors that gleamed under the bright fluorescent lights. The sound of his footsteps echoed slightly, a stark reminder of the clinical environment he was entering.

Tom's heart pounded in his chest, each beat a reminder of the importance of this visit. He wiped his slightly sweaty palms on his trousers, trying to quell the nervous energy bubbling within him. The findings from the lab could be the key to cracking the case wide open.

"Detective Reed, right?" A voice called out, pulling him from his thoughts.

Tom looked up to see a young woman in a lab coat approaching him. She had a warm smile, her eyes bright with professionalism and curiosity.

"Yes, that's me," Tom replied, extending his hand. "And you must be Sarah?"

Sarah nodded, shaking his hand firmly. "Welcome. Dr. Miller is expecting you. Follow me, please."

Tom followed Sarah down a corridor lined with glass-walled rooms where technicians in lab coats worked diligently over microscopes and test tubes. The soft hum of machinery filled the air, underscoring the high-tech environment. As they walked, Sarah gave him a brief overview of the lab's capabilities, but Tom's mind was already racing ahead, eager to hear what Dr. Miller had discovered.

They reached a door at the end of the corridor. Sarah knocked lightly before opening it and gesturing for Tom to enter. Inside, Dr. Miller stood up from behind a large desk cluttered with charts and soil samples.

Tom stepped into Dr. Miller's office, immediately struck by the meticulous order of the space. The walls were adorned with geological charts and maps, each meticulously labelled and detailed. Shelves lined one side of the room, filled with jars of soil samples, their contents ranging in colour and texture, reflecting the diversity of the earth's composition. A large desk occupied the centre of the room, cluttered with equipment, microscopes, and a computer displaying magnified images of soil particles.

Dr. Miller, a man in his late forties with silver streaks in his hair and an air of precision, gestured for Tom to take a seat. The forensic expert adjusted his glasses, his keen eyes twinkling with the excitement of sharing his findings.

"Detective Tom, thank you for coming. I believe we have some significant findings regarding the soil sample you provided," Dr. Miller began, his voice steady and authoritative.

"Thank you, Dr. Miller. I'm eager to hear what you've discovered," Tom replied, leaning forward in his chair.

Dr. Miller, adjusted his glasses again, the lenses catching the light as he leaned over to point at an enlarged image of Roger Morgan's body displayed on a large monitor. His expression was one of focused determination, the kind that comes from years of unravelling the secrets hidden within forensic evidence.

"Here," Dr. Miller said, tapping the screen to highlight the area where the photograph had been pinned to Roger's forehead. The image was gruesome, yet clinically analysed, with every detail scrutinized. "We found traces of a unique adhesive on the photograph. It's not something you'd find at a regular store. This adhesive is a speciality product, typically used in professional-grade mounting for photography exhibits."

Tom furrowed his brow, his mind racing to connect this new piece of the puzzle with what they already knew. "So, we're looking for someone who has access to professional photography supplies. That narrows it down to a specific group of people, likely within the photography community."

Dr. Miller nodded, his face reflecting the gravity of the situation. "This type of adhesive is known for its durability and precision. It's designed to keep photographs mounted securely, often used by professionals who need their work displayed perfectly."

The monitor switched to another image, this one a close-up of the adhesive residue, magnified to show its unique chemical composition. Harry could see the intricate details, the complex structure that differentiated it from common adhesives. Dr. Miller continued, "This adhesive isn't available at general craft stores. It's distributed through speciality suppliers who cater to high-end photographers and art galleries."

Tom, was deep in thought, his arms crossed as he processed the new information. The lab was filled with the soft clinks and rustles of other technicians working on various pieces of evidence, but their corner of the room seemed to hold a weightier silence, the importance of this discovery pressing down on them.

"We need to cross-reference this with our list of suspects," Tom said, his voice firm. "Who in the community has access to these materials and also had a motive to harm Roger?"

"And we should also check with local photography supply stores. If someone bought this adhesive recently, there might be a record of the purchase."

Dr. Miller handed them an evidence bag containing a sample of the adhesive, his fingers precise and careful. "Here are the samples for your investigation. I've also included a list of distributors for the adhesive. It might help you trace where it was purchased."

"We found some interesting fibres on Roger Morgan's clothing," Dr. Miller continued, his voice carrying the weight of a significant discovery. "These fibres match those of a particular type of fabric used in high-end photography bags."

Tom leaned in closer, their interest piqued. Dr. Miller gestured to a large monitor displaying a magnified image of the fibres. The intricate weave and unique texture of the fabric were clearly visible, setting it apart from more common materials.

"This fabric is not something you'd find in everyday items," Dr. Miller explained. "It's specifically designed to protect delicate photography equipment. The weave is tight and durable, meant to withstand heavy use while safeguarding the contents of the bag."

Tom's mind raced, connecting this new information with what they already knew about the case. "So, we're looking at someone who not only had access to high-end photography supplies but also owned or used one of these specialized bags. That suggests a professional or a very serious enthusiast."

Tom's gaze fixed on the monitor. "It narrows down our suspect pool. We need to find out who in Roger's circle owned one of these bags. If we can link these fibres to a specific person, it could be a significant break in the case."

Dr. Miller continued, "I've cross-referenced the fibres with several manufacturers. There are only a few companies that produce this type of fabric, and even fewer that supply these high-end bags. I've compiled a list of potential brands and suppliers."

He handed Tom a neatly organised report, the pages filled with detailed information about the fabric and its uses. Tom skimmed through it, his mind already formulating a plan. "This is exactly what we needed. We'll start by identifying who among Roger's acquaintances might have had access to these bags."

Dr. Miller picked up a clear jar containing a sample of dark, loamy soil. "Soil analysis is a fascinating process. We start by examining the physical characteristics—texture, colour, and composition. This sample, for instance, is quite rich in organic matter, giving it a darker colour and a finer texture."

He placed the jar down and turned to a chart on the wall. "We then move on to chemical analysis, where we test the pH levels and the presence of minerals. This is done using techniques like spectroscopy, which allows us to detect specific elements within the soil."

Tom nodded, trying to absorb the information. "And how does that help in identifying where the soil came from?"

Dr. Miller smiled, appreciating Tom's interest. "Each geographic location has a unique soil signature, much like a fingerprint. This is determined by the local vegetation, the underlying bedrock, and human activity in the area. For instance, soil near a lake will have different characteristics compared to soil from a forest or an urban area."

He pointed to another chart displaying various soil compositions. "The sample you provided had a specific blend of clay minerals, micro-fossils, and a slightly acidic pH level. We compared this to our database of local soil samples and found a match with the soil from the area around Vivary Park's lake."

Dr. Miller turned to his computer, pulling up a detailed report. "Here, you can see the breakdown. The presence of kaolinite and illite, which are types of clay minerals, along with diatomaceous earth, suggests a freshwater environment. The slightly acidic pH is typical of soil influenced by the surrounding vegetation and water runoff from the lake."

Tom examined the screen, the technical terms making more sense with Dr. Miller's explanations. "So, this definitely confirms that the soil on the victim's shoes came from Vivary Park's lake area?"

"Absolutely," Dr. Miller affirmed. "The combination of these factors creates a unique profile that is highly specific to that location. It's as close to a definitive match as we can get."

Tom felt a surge of determination. "This is exactly the breakthrough we needed. Thank you, Dr. Miller."

Dr. Miller nodded. "I'm glad we could help. If you need any further analysis or additional samples tested, don't hesitate to reach out."

As Tom stood to leave, he felt a renewed sense of purpose. The sterile, analytical environment of Dr. Miller's office had provided clarity and direction. With the soil analysis as a solid piece of evidence, he was one step closer to unravelling the mystery that had gripped Taunton.

As Tom walked out of Dr. Miller's office, his mind buzzed with the weight of the new information. The sterile scent of the lab lingered in his nostrils, a reminder of the precision and clarity that now seemed within reach. He could almost feel the pieces of the puzzle shifting into place, each one aligning with the newfound certainty of the soil analysis.

Tom turned back to Dr. Miller, who was still reviewing the data on his computer.

"Dr. Miller," Tom said, his voice steady with newfound purpose, "this information is invaluable. It aligns perfectly with other clues we've gathered. The soil composition, the specific location—it all points to the lake at Vivary Park as a crucial site in our investigation."

Dr. Miller looked up, meeting Tom's gaze. "I'm glad we could provide clarity, Detective. Soil can often tell a story that witnesses cannot."

Tom nodded. "You've helped us piece together a significant part of this puzzle. With this evidence, we can narrow down our suspect list and focus on the areas that matter most."

Dr. Miller smiled slightly. "If you need any further analysis or have additional samples, don't hesitate to bring them in. We're here to assist in any way we can."

"Thank you, Dr. Miller," Tom said, extending his hand once more. "We'll definitely be in touch. This has been a turning point in the investigation."

Tom's mind was already racing with the next steps. He needed to revisit Vivary Park, reexamine the evidence with this new perspective, and talk to witnesses with renewed urgency. The path was clearer now, the destination within sight. The soil analysis had not just provided answers; it had reignited his determination to solve the case and bring justice to the victim.

Tom pushed open the heavy glass door of the forensics lab, stepping into the cool evening air. The sun was setting, casting a warm, golden glow across the parking lot. Long shadows stretched out, mingling with the fading light, creating a stark contrast that mirrored the clarity and complexity of the case he was unravelling.

The soil analysis is a major breakthrough, Tom thought, his mind racing. *But there are still so many pieces to fit together. Stephen Smith, David Walker, Larry Stubbs, Margaret Morgan... each of them had a motive, but which one had the opportunity?*

He walked towards his car, the crunch of gravel under his shoes a steady rhythm that accompanied his thoughts. The evidence was pointing more clearly towards the area around Vivary Park's lake, but the suspects' actions and alibis were still a tangled web.

Stephen Smith's resentment over the disqualification, David Walker's bitterness about Roger's success, and Margaret's anger over the affair... each had their reasons. But who had the means and the cold-blooded intent to follow through?

The weight of the case pressed heavily on his shoulders. Tom felt the responsibility keenly—the need to bring justice to Roger Morgan and to prevent further tragedy. The town of Taunton was looking to him for answers, and he couldn't afford any missteps.

As Tom reached his car, he paused, leaning against the door for a moment. The horizon was a blaze of oranges and purples, the sun dipping below the skyline, leaving a trail of fading light. The tranquillity of the scene stood in stark contrast to the turmoil within him.

He took a deep breath, the cool air filling his lungs and momentarily clearing his mind. The lab results had given him a solid lead, a direction to pursue with renewed vigour. The connection to Vivary Park's lake was a critical piece of the puzzle, and it brought a new sense of purpose.

I can't let the pressure get to me, he reminded himself. *I have to stay focused, follow the evidence, and keep pushing forward.*

He straightened up, feeling a renewed sense of determination. The shadows were growing longer, the night approaching, but instead of feeling overwhelmed, Tom felt his resolve solidify. The path ahead was fraught with challenges, but he was ready to face them head-on.

This is what it means to be a detective, he thought, gripping the car door handle. *To carry the weight of the case, to feel the pressure, but to keep moving forward regardless.*

As he got into the car and started the engine, the hum of the motor blended with his thoughts. He had a clear plan now: revisit Vivary Park, re-interview key witnesses, and dig deeper into the suspects' backgrounds. The answers were there, hidden beneath the surface, and he was determined to uncover them.

Chapter 22 Cover-Ups and Confessions

Harry pulled up to the Walker family home, a modest brick house nestled in a quiet neighbourhood on the outskirts of Taunton. The afternoon sun cast long shadows across the street, but even in the soft light, the signs of recent stress were evident. The once neat and tidy garden, which likely had been a source of pride, now showed signs of neglect. Overgrown weeds choked the flowerbeds, and the grass was a patchwork of brown and green, hinting at missed mowing sessions.

The driveway, which Harry suspected had once been meticulously swept, was now littered with leaves and debris. A child's bicycle lay on its side near the front porch, its bright colours a stark contrast to the subdued, almost sombre, atmosphere of the house. The front door, a faded red with chipped paint, stood slightly ajar as if waiting for someone to finally come and close it properly.

As Harry approached, she noticed the curtains drawn tightly across the front windows, blocking out the sunlight and giving the home an air of seclusion. The windows themselves were smudged with grime, a subtle indication that the usual routine of cleaning and upkeep had been interrupted by recent events.

The porch steps creaked under her weight as she climbed them, and she paused at the door, taking a deep breath. She could hear the muffled sounds of a television inside, a low murmur that barely broke the heavy silence surrounding the house. The air was thick with the scent of blooming roses, their untended branches sprawling wildly, adding a bittersweet note to the scene.

Harry knocked gently, the sound echoing in the stillness. She waited, glancing around at the signs of life that persisted despite the overshadowing grief. A wind chime, hanging from the eaves, tinkled softly in the breeze, a delicate melody that contrasted with the heavy mood.

The front door of the Walker residence creaked open slowly, revealing a petite woman with dishevelled hair and red-rimmed eyes. She looked at Harry with a mix of curiosity and apprehension.

"Hello," the woman greeted softly, her voice carrying the weight of recent grief. "Can I help you?"

"Good afternoon, Mrs. Walker. I'm Detective Inspector Harriet Lambert," Harry said, offering a gentle smile. She held up her badge for the woman to see. "I'm very sorry for your loss. May I come in and speak with you about David?"

Mrs. Walker's eyes widened slightly as she took in the information, and then she stepped back, opening the door wider. "Of course, Detective. Please, come in."

Harry stepped into the hallway, immediately feeling the heavy atmosphere of the house. She could sense the grief that clung to the walls, the air thick with the sorrow of a family in mourning.

"I'm sorry to intrude at such a difficult time," Harry began, following Mrs. Walker into the living room. "But it's important that we understand more about David's life and his relationships. It will help us find who did this."

Mrs. Walker managed a weak smile and led Harry into the living room. The room was cluttered with family photos, their smiling faces a stark contrast to the present sorrow. The air was heavy with the scent of stale coffee and a faint hint of lavender from an air freshener struggling to mask the underlying grief.

Harry took a seat on the worn-out sofa, noting the stack of newspapers and unopened mail on the coffee table. "I know this is an incredibly difficult time," she began gently, "but I appreciate you speaking with me. I'm here to understand more about David's life and his relationships. Anything you can share will be very helpful."

Mrs. Walker nodded, her hands nervously wringing a handkerchief. "David was such a good boy," she began, her voice trembling. "He was always so kind and hardworking. He loved his photography, you know? It was his passion."

Harry listened intently, her eyes never leaving Mrs. Walker's face. "He sounds like a wonderful person. Were there any recent changes or stresses in his life that you noticed?"

"Well," Mrs. Walker hesitated, "he had been under a lot of pressure lately. The Flower Show meant everything to him, and he worked so hard to make his mark. But there were... tensions. Rivalries with other photographers."

At that moment, Mr. Walker entered the room, his face a mask of stoic endurance. He looked at Harry, then at his wife, and finally took a seat in the armchair by the window. "You're here about David," he said, more as a statement than a question.

"Yes, Mr. Walker," Harry confirmed. "I'm Detective Inspector Harriet Lambert. I want to express my deepest condolences for your loss. I'm here to gather any information that might help us understand what happened to David."

Mr. Walker nodded solemnly, and Mrs. Walker took a deep breath before beginning to share her memories. "David was such a good boy. Always kind, always hardworking. He loved his photography more than anything else."

Harry listened intently, her focus unwavering. "You were saying that David was under a lot of pressure recently, especially with the Flower Show. Can you tell me more about that?"

Mrs. Walker hesitated, glancing at her husband for support. "Yes, he was. The competition meant a lot to him. He worked so hard, but there were... tensions with other photographers. Rivalries."

"Stephen Smith and Roger Morgan, for example," Mr. Walker added, his voice low but firm. "David mentioned them a few times. There were disagreements."

Harry leaned forward slightly. "Can you tell me about any specific disagreements he had and with who?"

Mr. Walker sighed deeply. "Roger Morgan was one of the main ones. David always felt that Roger used his influence to overshadow him. There were several incidents where David believed Roger had sabotaged his chances of winning."

Mrs. Walker added, "Roger had a lot of pull in the community. He'd been a judge at the Flower Show for years, and David thought he wasn't always fair. There was one year when David was sure he had the winning shot, but Roger found a technicality to disqualify him."

"That must have been incredibly frustrating for David," Harry said, jotting down notes. "Were there any other photographers he had issues with?"

Mr. Walker nodded. "Yes, Stephen Smith. They had a pretty intense rivalry. Stephen accused David of stealing his ideas and techniques. They had a few public arguments about it. Stephen felt that David was copying his style and getting credit for it."

"Did David ever talk about feeling threatened by either Roger or Stephen?" Harry asked, watching their reactions closely.

Mrs. Walker hesitated before answering. "David didn't like to talk about it much. He didn't want to worry us. But I could see it was getting to him. He was more stressed and anxious than ever before."

Mr. Walker added, "David was a good man, but he was under a lot of pressure. The Flower Show meant everything to him, and the thought of someone trying to undermine his hard work really ate at him."

Harry made a few more notes. "Do you think these rivalries could have escalated to the point where someone might want to harm David?"

Mr. Walker's face hardened. "I never wanted to believe it, but after what's happened, I can't rule it out. Those competitions can bring out the worst in people. When pride and reputation are on the line, some people might go too far."

Mrs. Walker's eyes filled with tears. "David just wanted to be recognised for his talent. He didn't deserve any of this."

Harry leaned forward slightly, her notebook open on her lap. "Mrs. Walker, Mr. Walker, I appreciate your cooperation. I need to ask a few more questions about David. Can you tell me about his recent activities? Was there anything unusual or different about his routine?"

Mrs. Walker sighed, looking down at her hands. "David was always busy with his photography. He loved it so much. But recently, he seemed more stressed than usual. The Flower Show was coming up, and he was determined to make a mark this year. He spent a lot of time at Vivary Park, taking photos and preparing his entries."

"Vivary Park?" Harry asked, making a note. "Was there a specific reason he chose that location?"

Mrs. Walker nodded. "It's a beautiful place, and David always found inspiration there. But he also mentioned meeting someone there regularly, a man named Stephen Smith. He never said why, and I didn't press him. I thought it was something to do with his work."

Harry looked at Mr. Walker. "Did David ever talk about any disputes or enemies? Anyone he had conflicts with?"

Mr. Walker's jaw tightened, and he looked out the window for a moment before responding. "David was a good man, but he had his share of disagreements. He mentioned having issues with a few people, particularly in the photography community. Roger Morgan and Stephen Smith were the names that came up the most. There was a lot of rivalry and tension, especially with the Flower Show coming up."

"Can you tell me more about these rivalries?" Harry pressed gently. "Did David feel threatened or particularly stressed by anyone in particular?"

Mr. Walker took a deep breath. "Roger Morgan had been a thorn in David's side for years. They were always competing, and it seemed like Roger had it out for him. David felt that Roger used his influence to undermine him whenever he could. As for Stephen Smith, they had some pretty heated arguments. Stephen accused David of stealing his ideas and techniques."

Mrs. Walker added, "David never wanted to talk too much about it at home. He didn't want to worry us, but I could see the toll it was taking on him. He was exhausted, constantly on edge. The pressure to succeed, to prove himself... it was a lot for him to handle."

Harry nodded, absorbing the information. "And what about David's involvement in the Flower Show? Was he a regular participant?"

"Yes," Mr. Walker replied. "David loved the Flower Show. It was his chance to showcase his work and gain recognition. He won a few awards over the years, but it also brought a lot of competition and jealousy. This year, he was more determined than ever to win."

As the conversation in the Walker's living room continued, the atmosphere grew increasingly sombre. Harry sensed there was something more the family might know, something they were hesitant to share. She leaned forward, her voice gentle yet probing.

"Mrs. Walker, Mr. Walker, is there anything else you can tell me about David's routine or any unusual activities in the weeks before his death?" Harry asked, her eyes scanning their faces for any hint of withheld information.

Mrs. Walker glanced at her husband before looking down at her hands, which were twisting the handkerchief even more tightly. "There is something," she said hesitantly. "David mentioned meeting someone regularly at Vivary Park. A man named Stephen Smith."

Harry's interest piqued. "Stephen Smith? Do you know why they were meeting?"

Mrs. Walker shook her head. "He never told us. He was always so private about his work. I thought it had something to do with the Flower Show, but I can't be sure."

Mr. Walker frowned, his brows knitting together. "David said it was important, but he never went into details. It seemed like a regular thing, almost like a routine. He would go to the park, sometimes for hours, and come back looking... I don't know, troubled."

As Harry gathered her notes, she noticed a young man, lingering near the doorway. His expression was a mix of frustration and concern, clearly wanting to contribute but hesitant to interrupt. Harry beckoned him over with a gentle nod.

"Hello there young man, do you have a moment?" Harry asked, her tone inviting.

"That's Simon, David's younger brother" said Mrs Walker.

Simon stepped forward, nodding. "Yeah, I do. I think there's something you should know about David."

Harry motioned for him to sit down. "Please, go ahead."

Simon took a deep breath, his eyes flicking to his parents before settling back on Harry. "David had been spending a lot of time at Vivary Park. He mentioned meeting someone there, often late at night."

Harry's interest piqued. "Late at night? Did he ever tell you who he was meeting?"

Simon shook his head. "No, he was pretty secretive about it. But I had a feeling it wasn't just a casual acquaintance. He seemed... anxious, like there was more to it."

"Anxious how?" Harry pressed gently. "Did he seem afraid, or more like he was hiding something?"

"More like he was hiding something," Simon clarified. "He'd get this nervous energy before leaving, and when he'd come back, he was always lost in thought, like he was trying to figure something out."

Harry made a note of this. "Did you ever see this person he was meeting, or hear anything about what they talked about?"

Simon shook his head again. "No, he was always careful to keep it private. But I know it was happening regularly. He'd make up excuses to leave the house, and when I'd ask him about it, he'd brush me off."

"Do you think these meetings could be connected to his work or the Flower Show?" Harry asked.

Simon hesitated, then nodded slowly. "It's possible. David was under a lot of pressure with the Flower Show coming up. He was determined to make a name for himself, and he might have been looking for an edge. But it also felt like there was something more personal involved."

"Personal?" Harry echoed, leaning forward. "Do you mean like a relationship or a personal matter he was dealing with?"

"Maybe," Simon said, frowning. "I don't know for sure. But I got the sense that whoever he was meeting was important to him in some way. It wasn't just business."

Harry nodded thoughtfully. "This is very helpful, Simon. If you think of anything else, no matter how small, please let me know."

Simon nodded, his expression earnest. "I will. I just want to help find out who did this to David. He didn't deserve it."

"We're going to find out," Harry assured him. "Thank you for sharing this with me."

Harry's mind raced as she processed this new information. The regular, mysterious meetings with Stephen Smith at the park were a significant lead. If Stephen Smith was involved, or at least knew something crucial, he could be the key to unravelling the mystery behind David's murder.

"Thank you for telling me this," Harry said, her tone thoughtful. "These meetings could be very important. I'll need to speak with Stephen Smith and find out more about their nature and purpose."

Mrs. Walker looked up, her eyes filled with worry. "Do you think Stephen had something to do with David's death?"

"I can't say for certain at this point," Harry replied carefully. "But I promise you, we'll investigate every lead. If Stephen Smith knows anything, we'll find out."

Mr. Walker's expression hardened. "Good. We need to know why our son was taken from us."

As Harry prepared to leave, the weight of the conversation hung heavily in the air. Mrs. Walker, still clutching her handkerchief, looked at Harry with eyes full of unspoken questions. The silence in the room was thick with grief and confusion.

"Detective," Mrs. Walker began, her voice trembling. "Why would anyone want to hurt David? He was such a good person. He didn't deserve this."

Harry took a deep breath, choosing her words carefully. "I understand how difficult this is for you. David's death is a tragedy, and I promise you, we are doing everything in our power to find out who did this and why."

Mr. Walker, who had remained stoic throughout most of the conversation, finally let his emotions show. His eyes glistened with tears he had been holding back. "We just want to understand. We want to know what happened to our son."

"I know," Harry said gently. "And I promise you, we will uncover the truth. Your information has been invaluable, and it will help us piece together what happened."

Simon stepped forward, his expression a mix of anger and sorrow. "Detective, please don't let this case go cold. We need justice for David. We need to know that whoever did this is brought to account."

Harry met his gaze with a determined look. "I promise you, we won't stop until we find the person responsible. David's case is a priority for us. I will personally make sure you are kept informed about our progress."

Mrs. Walker nodded, tears streaming down her cheeks. "Thank you, Detective. It means a lot to know that you're taking this seriously. David was our world, and we just can't fathom why anyone would do this to him."

Harry reached out and gently squeezed Mrs. Walker's hand. "I understand. Your family's strength and love for David are evident, and it will help us in our investigation. We'll find the answers you deserve."

Mr. Walker cleared his throat, his voice thick with emotion. "Please, keep us updated. We need to know every step of the way. It's the only way we can cope with this."

"I will," Harry assured them. "You have my word."

As Harry left the Walker home, she felt the gravity of the promise she had made. The Walkers' grief and their need for closure weighed heavily on her mind. She knew that the path ahead would be challenging, but she was determined to see it through.

The mysterious meetings with Stephen Smith, the rivalries within the photography community, and the pressures David faced all needed to be examined closely. Harry walked to her car with a renewed sense of purpose, ready to follow every lead and uncover the truth behind David Walker's tragic death. The Walkers deserved answers, and Harry was committed to providing them, no matter how long it took.

Chapter 23 Silent Testimonies

The sky above Taunton was a canvas of soft blues and greys, promising a fair afternoon with just a hint of drizzle later. East Street bustled with its usual weekday energy; a symphony of hurried footsteps, snippets of conversation, and the occasional honk of a car horn. Shops flaunted their eclectic wares, and the smell of freshly fried food wafted from various fast-food eateries, creating an irresistible blend of aromas.

Amidst this lively atmosphere, the East Street McDonald's stood as a beacon of familiarity. Its bright signage, a stark contrast to the quaint charm of the surrounding architecture, invited a steady stream of customers. Inside, families juggled trays laden with Happy Meals, students hunched over textbooks with coffees at their side, and local workers grabbed a quick bite before hurrying back to their routines.

Helen Carter, chairwoman of the Flower Show Committee, approached the entrance with her usual purposeful stride. Her mind raced with thoughts about the recent show, analysing every detail to ensure its flawless execution. Despite the recent success, the shadow of the recent murders still lingered, casting a pall over the event's memory. As she reached for the door, a familiar voice called out to her.

"Helen! Fancy seeing you here."

She turned to see Bill Thompson, the committee's treasurer, smiling warmly. Practical and straightforward, Bill had always been more focused on the financial aspects of their events, but his dedication was undeniable.

"Bill! What a pleasant surprise," Helen replied, her face lighting up. "How have you been?"

"Busy as ever," Bill said with a chuckle. "I'm still wrapping up some of the financial reports from the show. Care to join me for a coffee?"

Helen nodded, and they entered the bustling restaurant together. As they approached the counter, a tall, cheerful girl greeted them warmly. Her name tag read 'Louise.'

"Hi there! What can I get for you today?" Louise asked, her smile infectious.

"Two black coffees, please," Bill said, returning her smile.

As Louise prepared their order, she made small talk. "You folks look familiar. Were you involved in the

Flower Show? I was there on Saturday and really enjoyed the birds of prey demonstration."

"Yes, we're both on the committee," Helen said. "It was a lot of work, but it turned out well, despite everything."

Louise nodded, her expression turning serious for a moment. "I also heard about those terrible murders in town. Everyone's pretty shaken up. It's hard to believe something like that could happen here."

Helen and Bill exchanged a look of visible concern. "Yes, it's been quite distressing," Helen admitted. "We managed to pull off the show, but the aftermath is still weighing heavily on all of us."

Bill added, "The safety of our attendees was a top priority, and we worked closely with the authorities to ensure everything was under control. But it's going to take time for the community to heal."

Louise handed them their coffees, her smile returning but with a hint of sympathy. "I hope everything works out. The Flower Show is such a lovely event for the community."

"Thank you, Louise," Helen said, taking her coffee. "We appreciate the support."

After receiving their coffees, Helen and Bill found a quiet corner to sit in the bustling McDonald's. The rhythmic hum of conversations around them created a comfortable background noise as they settled into their seats.

"I'm glad we bumped into each other," Helen began, stirring her coffee absently. "We need to debrief about the show and start planning for next year, but I can't shake the feeling that we need to address the impact of those recent events more directly."

Bill's expression grew serious. "I agree. The community is still on edge, and we need to find a way to reassure them. Maybe a memorial or a community gathering to honour the victims and show solidarity."

Helen sighed, her meticulous nature fighting to maintain control. "That's a good idea. We need to remind everyone that the Flower Show is still a symbol of our community's spirit and resilience."

Helen took a sip of her coffee, the warm liquid providing a brief moment of solace. "It's hard to believe it's over," she said, her voice tinged with exhaustion. "The Flower Show went off without a hitch, but the shadow of those murders still lingers."

Bill nodded, his expression serious. "Roger's death was a shock to everyone. He was such a beloved figure in the community. His photographs captured the very essence of Taunton."

"Yes," Helen agreed. "I keep replaying the events in my mind, trying to make sense of it. Who would want to kill Roger Morgan? He had his rivals, sure, but murder?"

Bill leaned forward, lowering his voice. "I've been thinking the same. Stephen Smith and David Walker come to mind immediately. Both had clear motives."

Helen's brow furrowed. "Stephen was disqualified from the show a few years back because of Roger's insistence on following the rules. He never forgave Roger for that."

"Exactly," Bill said. "And then there's David. Remember how angry he was when Roger won last year's competition with that stunning photo of the Castle Hotel? David claimed Roger had stolen his shot."

"David's anger was palpable," Helen recalled. "But could it really have driven him to murder? It seems so extreme."

Bill sighed, taking a sip of his coffee. "In the world of art, emotions run high. Jealousy, envy, and resentment can fester. Still, murder is a different level. We need to consider if there might be more to it. Perhaps someone we haven't thought of yet."

Helen nodded thoughtfully. "True. We need to look at all possibilities. But David's behaviour during the show was off. Did you notice how agitated he was, especially when he saw Roger's entries displayed?"

"I did," Bill said, his eyes narrowing. "He was pacing, muttering to himself. It was as if he was on the verge of losing control."

Helen shivered slightly. "And then there's the matter of the photograph stapled to Roger's forehead. 'The first of many,' it said. It's a chilling message, and it suggests a deeper, more calculated plan."

Bill frowned. "It could mean the killer has a list of targets. If that's the case, we need to warn the others."

"Yes," Helen agreed. "We can't let anyone else fall victim. But who else could be on that list? Who else had such a significant rivalry or grudge with Roger?"

Bill rubbed his chin, deep in thought. "There were always rumours about Roger's personal life. His marriage to Margaret wasn't exactly harmonious. And then there were whispers about his relationships with his models."

Helen's eyes widened. "The model, Dawn Menzies. She was his latest muse, wasn't she? Could she be involved somehow?"

"It's possible," Bill said. "Dawn was certainly close to Roger, and if Margaret found out about an affair, her reaction could be severe. But we can't jump to conclusions."

Helen took another sip of her coffee, then leaned forward. "We need to think about how to reassure everyone, Bill. The community is still reeling from the murders, and our sponsors are getting jittery."

Bill nodded, his brow furrowed in thought. "Increased security is a must. We need to show everyone that their safety is our top priority. Maybe we can hire extra security personnel for all future events and make sure their presence is visible."

"That's a good start," Helen agreed. "But we also need to address the public directly. A statement from the committee could go a long way in calming fears."

Bill tapped his fingers on the table thoughtfully. "Yes, a public statement would help. We need to be transparent about the steps we're taking to ensure safety. Maybe a press conference or a detailed letter to the local newspapers."

Helen's eyes brightened with an idea. "What if we organise a memorial segment during the next Flower Show? We could honour the victims, turning this tragedy into a moment of community solidarity. It would show that we stand together in the face of adversity."

Bill looked at her, considering the suggestion. "That could work, Helen. But we need to be cautious about how we present it. We don't want to come off as insensitive or like we're using the tragedy for publicity."

"Absolutely," Helen agreed. "It has to be genuine. We should involve the families of the victims, get their input and blessing. Maybe even invite them to speak if they're comfortable with it."

Bill nodded. "And we should ensure that any proceeds from the event go towards something meaningful, like a scholarship fund in the victims' names or donations to a local charity."

Helen smiled. "Exactly. It has to be about healing and coming together as a community. If we do this right, it could turn a terrible situation into something positive."

Bill sighed, the weight of the situation evident on his face. "It's a fine line to walk, but I think it's the right thing to do. Let's start by drafting a proposal for the committee and reaching out to the families."

Helen reached across the table, giving Bill's hand a reassuring squeeze. "We'll get through this, Bill. The Flower Show is more than just an event—it's a symbol of our community's spirit. We'll make sure it continues to shine, even in these dark times."

As they finished their coffees, Helen and Bill resolved to meet with the rest of the committee to discuss their plans. They stood up, gathering their things and preparing to face the challenges ahead.

"Let's arrange a meeting for tomorrow," Helen suggested. "We need to get everyone on the same page as soon as possible."

"Agreed," Bill said, nodding. "I'll send out an email to the committee members tonight. We'll meet at the community centre first thing in the morning."

As they stepped out into the busy street, Helen and Bill parted ways, each carrying the heavy burden of ensuring the Flower Show's success and the community's healing. The streets of East Street bustled around them, but their minds were focused on the tasks ahead.

Inside McDonald's, Louise was wiping down the counter, her cheerful demeanour masking a sense of curiosity about the conversations she'd overheard from Helen and Bill. Just as she was finishing up, she couldn't help but notice a group of teenagers gathered around a table near the back, their voices hushed but animated.

"Did you hear what Emily said about the murders?" one of the teenagers, a girl with bright red hair, whispered excitedly.

"Yeah," another replied, leaning in closer. "She said her brother saw someone sneaking around Roger Morgan's place the night he was killed."

Louise's ears perked up, her cleaning motions slowing as she tried to catch more of the conversation.

"Who was it?" a third teenager asked, his eyes wide with curiosity.

"Emily didn't say, but her brother thinks it was someone from the Flower Show committee," the red-haired girl continued, her voice barely above a whisper. "He said they looked really suspicious, like they were trying to hide something."

Louise's heart skipped a beat. She glanced around to make sure no one was paying attention to her before moving a bit closer to the teenagers' table, her curiosity getting the better of her.

"Do you think it could be true?" one of the boys asked, his tone both sceptical and intrigued.

"Who knows," the red-haired girl shrugged. "But if it is, that means the killer could be someone we all know."

The group fell silent, the weight of their speculation hanging in the air. Louise, feeling a mix of dread and excitement, quickly finished her cleaning and headed to the back room. She needed to tell someone about what she had overheard, but she wasn't sure who to trust.

As the teenagers continued their discussion, oblivious to the world around them, the sense of impending discovery and danger grew. Louise knew that the small town of Taunton was on the brink of uncovering secrets that could shake the community to its core. She just hoped that the truth would come to light before anyone else got hurt.

Outside, Helen and Bill walked away from McDonald's, unaware of the new piece of gossip that was now circulating. As Helen walked away, she felt a renewed sense of purpose. The Flower Show had always been a beacon of beauty and community spirit, and she was determined to ensure it remained so, even in the face of tragedy. Bill, watching her go, felt the same resolve harden within him. They would not let the darkness overshadow the light of their beloved event.

Chapter 24 Eliza's Examination

The sun had just dipped below the horizon, casting long shadows across the quiet streets of Taunton. The air was heavy with the lingering warmth of the day, now cooling into a comfortable evening chill. Streetlights flickered to life, their soft glow illuminating the path to the medical examiner's office, a solitary building standing sombrely against the deepening twilight.

Harry arrived first, her footsteps echoing against the pavement as she approached the entrance. The office was housed in a brick building that seemed to absorb the weight of the cases it handled. Its windows were dark, reflecting the orange and pink hues of the setting sun. She paused at the door, glancing over her shoulder as if expecting the shadows to yield some hidden observer, then entered, the door creaking slightly in the stillness.

Inside, the atmosphere was markedly different. Fluorescent lights buzzed softly, casting a stark, clinical brightness over the room. The scent of antiseptic hung in the air, a sharp contrast to the earthy smells outside. The reception area was empty, save for a few chairs lined up against the wall and a counter cluttered with forms and files.

Tom arrived shortly after, his arrival heralded by the soft murmur of voices as he exchanged a few words with the receptionist. His expression was set, eyes focused, carrying the weight of the day's investigation like a mantle. He spotted Harry and gave a brief nod, a silent acknowledgment of the gravity of their meeting. Together, they waited, the silence between them heavy with unspoken thoughts and shared purpose.

The sound of hurried footsteps announced Eliza's arrival. She entered briskly, her white lab coat flaring slightly with her movements. Her usually composed demeanour was tinged with a hint of urgency, her eyes betraying the pressure of the mounting case. She greeted them with a tight smile, the lines of fatigue etched subtly around her eyes.

"Let's head to the back," Eliza said, her voice steady but underscored with a sense of urgency. She led them through a set of double doors into a dimly lit hallway. The walls were lined with cabinets and bulletin boards plastered with charts and notes, the detritus of countless cases past and present.

They walked in silence, the only sound the soft scuffing of their shoes against the linoleum floor. The hallway seemed to stretch interminably, each step echoing the weight of their collective burden. Finally, they reached the door to the examination room, a sturdy barrier between them and the sterile, clinical world where Eliza conducted her work.

Eliza pushed open the door, revealing a room bathed in stark white light. The stainless steel of the examination tables gleamed coldly, and the air was cooler here, the hum of the ventilation system a constant, soothing background noise. Instruments were meticulously arranged on trays, ready for use, and the walls were lined with shelves holding jars and containers, each meticulously labelled.

The three of them gathered around a central table, the epicentre of their grim work. Eliza's notes were spread out, an array of photographs, diagrams, and reports that painted a chilling picture of the investigation. They stood there for a moment, the gravity of their mission settling heavily upon them.

The tension in the room was palpable as Harry, Tom, and Eliza took their seats around the central table. The stark white light of the examination room cast sharp shadows, accentuating the lines of worry etched on their faces. A digital clock on the wall ticked relentlessly, a constant reminder of the time slipping away.

Harry broke the silence first. She leaned forward, placing a small stack of notes and photographs on the table. Her eyes were sharp, focused, as she began to speak.

"I spent the day talking to David's family," she said, her voice steady but with an edge of urgency. "His mother mentioned something interesting. David had been acting strangely in the weeks leading up to his death. He was more secretive than usual, and she overheard a few heated phone calls. She couldn't make out much, but one name came up repeatedly: Stephen Smith."

Tom leaned back in his chair, his fingers steepled thoughtfully. "Stephen Smith again. He seems to be at the centre of all this."

Harry nodded. "David's brother also mentioned that he had been spending a lot of time at Vivary Park, meeting someone late at night. He didn't know who, but he had a feeling it wasn't just a casual acquaintance."

Tom scribbled a few notes before speaking. "I received the lab reports from the evidence we collected at the crime scene and Roger's house. For starters, we found traces of a unique adhesive on the photograph pinned to Roger's forehead. It's a specialty product, not something you can buy at a regular store. We're tracking down suppliers in the area."

He paused, flipping through his notes. "Additionally, the fibres found on Roger's clothing match those of a particular type of fabric used in high-end photography bags. We're cross-referencing purchase records to see if we can link it to any of our suspects."

Eliza, who had been listening intently, cleared her throat and leaned forward. "The autopsy and forensic analysis have provided some crucial insights, and not just about Roger. Let's start with him. The wound on Roger's chest was indeed inflicted by the monopod found at the scene, but the angle and depth of the wound suggest it was delivered with significant force, likely from someone who was standing very close to him, possibly someone he trusted."

She glanced at her notes before continuing. "We also found traces of a particular type of pollen on Roger's clothes, which is unique to Vivary Park. This corroborates the theory that the park is a significant location in this case. Additionally, there were microscopic traces of photographic chemicals on his hands, consistent with those used by professionals."

Harry frowned, absorbing the information. "So, we're looking at someone within the photography community, someone who had access to these chemicals and the type of adhesive used on the photograph. The connection to Vivary Park is becoming more apparent, too."

Eliza nodded and continued. "Now, onto David. The autopsy revealed bruises on his arms, consistent with being grabbed or restrained. He also had defensive wounds on his hands, indicating a struggle. There were similar traces of pollen and photographic chemicals on his clothing, linking him to both Roger and Vivary Park."

Tom leaned forward, interested. "And what about Dawn?"

Eliza took a deep breath. "Dawn's body showed no signs of defensive wounds, which suggests she might have been taken by surprise. However, there were similar traces of the same adhesive found on her clothing. Additionally, a distinct perfume, not commonly available, was detected on her clothes, and it matches the scent found on both Roger and David."

Harry's eyes widened slightly. "So, the same person was likely close enough to all three victims to leave these traces."

Eliza nodded. "There's more. I found a partial DNA match under Roger's fingernails. It's not conclusive enough for an arrest, but it's a partial match to Stephen Smith. This, combined with the other evidence, strongly suggests his involvement."

Harry frowned, absorbing the information. "So, we're looking at someone within the photography community, someone who had access to these chemicals and the type of adhesive used on the photograph. The connection to Vivary Park is becoming more apparent, too."

Tom nodded. "It also means the killer is likely someone who knew Roger personally and had the means and opportunity to meet him in a place where they wouldn't be immediately noticed."

Eliza added, " I also found some residual DNA under Roger's fingernails. It's a partial match to Stephen Smith, but not conclusive enough for an arrest. We need more to solidify our case."

The evening deepened outside, casting the room in a sombre twilight as the team reconvened after their initial discussion. Eliza stood by the examination table, a small reel of photo film in her hand. Her expression was grave, and the tension in the room heightened as Harry and Tom joined her.

Eliza cleared her throat, breaking the silence. "During the autopsy, I found something in David's pocket that I believe may be crucial to our investigation."

She held up the reel of film, its presence almost ominous in the sterile light of the room. "It's a reel of photo film. I had it developed earlier today, and the images... well, they reveal quite a bit."

Harry and Tom leaned in, their curiosity piqued and a sense of foreboding settling over them. Eliza carefully laid out a series of photographs on the table, each one more revealing than the last.

Harry picked up the first photograph, her eyes narrowing as she studied it. "These are of David and Stephen Smith... meeting at Vivary Park."

Tom's brow furrowed as he looked over Harry's shoulder. "Why were they meeting in secret? What's the connection?"

Eliza's voice was steady but tinged with the weight of the revelation. "It gets more complicated. Look at the next few photos."

Harry's hands trembled slightly as she flipped through the images. The sequence showed David and Stephen in increasingly intimate poses, culminating in a photograph of the two men kissing.

A heavy silence fell over the room as the implications of the photographs sank in. The images not only revealed a hidden relationship but also suggested a motive that was far more personal and tangled than they had previously considered.

Tom exhaled slowly, his mind racing. "This changes everything. We need to reconsider the dynamics between our suspects."

Harry nodded, her eyes still fixed on the photographs. "Stephen's involvement just became a lot more significant. We need to question him again, and this time, we don't hold back."

Eliza gathered the photographs, her expression serious. "I agree. These images not only reveal a secret relationship but also suggest a potential motive rooted in personal and emotional turmoil."

As the team absorbed the gravity of this new evidence, the sense of urgency deepened. The path ahead was fraught with complexity, and the lines between professional rivalry and personal vendetta had blurred beyond recognition.

The atmosphere in the room was charged with tension as Harry, Tom, and Eliza sat around the table, the photographs spread out before them like pieces of a jigsaw puzzle. The overhead light cast a harsh glare on the images, highlighting the stark reality of the revelations they contained.

Harry's gaze was fixed on the photograph of David and Stephen kissing. "This isn't just about professional jealousy anymore. There's a deep, personal connection here that we need to understand."

Tom nodded, his mind working through the possibilities. "If their relationship was secret, it could explain a lot. But why would Stephen kill David and Roger? And what about Dawn?"

Eliza interjected, her voice measured. "We need to consider the possibility that someone else found out about their relationship. Someone who felt betrayed or threatened by it."

Harry's eyes flashed with determination. "Or maybe Stephen himself felt threatened. If their relationship was on the verge of being exposed, it could have pushed him to take drastic measures."

Tom shook his head. "But to kill all three of them? That seems extreme, even for a jealous lover."

Eliza leaned forward, her gaze intense. "We need to explore every angle. These photographs are a window into a hidden world, and we need to understand what was happening behind the scenes."

Harry picked up another photograph, studying it closely. "We need to talk to Stephen again. And we need to dig deeper into David's life. Who else knew about this relationship? And what did it mean for the dynamics within the photography community?"

Tom's expression was resolute. "We'll start with Stephen. Confront him with the photographs and see how he reacts. But we also need to be prepared for the possibility that there's another player in this game. Someone we haven't identified yet."

The team sat in silence for a moment, the weight of their task settling heavily on their shoulders. The photographs had added a new layer of complexity to an already intricate case, and the path to the truth was fraught with uncertainty and danger.

Tom broke the silence, his voice laced with curiosity and frustration. "Whoever took these photos must have been close enough to know about the meetings. They had to be aware of the secret relationship."

Harry nodded, her brow furrowed in thought. "It's someone who had access to Vivary Park, who knew their schedule and had the skill to take these pictures without being noticed. This wasn't a random person."

Eliza leaned forward, her eyes scanning the photographs once more. "The quality of these images suggests a professional hand. The framing, the clarity... this isn't the work of an amateur."

Tom's eyes narrowed as he considered Eliza's point. "Which means it could be someone within the photography community. Someone with a motive to keep an eye on David and Stephen."

Harry's gaze was distant, her mind racing through the possibilities. "What if the photographer was trying to gather evidence? Maybe they wanted to expose the relationship for personal gain or to manipulate one of them."

Eliza tapped her finger thoughtfully on the table. "But how did the film end up in David's pocket? If he was the target, why would he be carrying the evidence against himself?"

Tom pondered this for a moment. "It's possible that David discovered the photographer's identity and took the film from them, intending to confront them or use it as leverage. But before he could do anything with it, he was killed."

Harry's eyes widened slightly as a new thought struck her. "What if David didn't know the film was in his pocket? What if someone planted it there to frame him or to mislead us?"

Eliza's expression grew serious. "That would imply a level of premeditation and cunning. The killer wanted us to find this film, to draw us into this web of secrets and deceit."

Tom exhaled sharply, the weight of the situation pressing down on him. "We need to identify everyone who had close contact with David and Stephen. Anyone who might have had a reason to spy on them and the skill to take these photographs."

Harry nodded, her resolve hardening. "And we need to consider the possibility that there's another player involved, someone pulling the strings from the shadows."

The room fell silent as they absorbed the implications of their conversation. The photographs had not only revealed a hidden relationship but also suggested a deeper, more complex plot at play. The team was now faced with the daunting task of unravelling this intricate web, knowing that the answers they sought were likely to bring them face-to-face with a cunning and dangerous adversary.

Chapter 25 Confrontation in the Café

Harry and Tom walked down the cobbled street of Taunton, the sun casting a warm glow on the historic buildings that lined the road. They approached a charming brick building with a modest sign above the door that read "Stephen Smith Photography." The large windows of the studio revealed a glimpse of the artistry within, each pane framing an exquisite photograph that hinted at the talent of the photographer.

The exterior of the studio was well-maintained, with climbing ivy adding a touch of nature to the sophisticated facade. As they drew closer, the subtle scent of lavender from a nearby flower box mixed with the faint aroma of freshly brewed coffee from a nearby café, creating an inviting atmosphere.

Harry knocked on the door, and they waited for a moment. The door opened to reveal Stephen Smith, a man in his late thirties with an air of meticulous professionalism. He had dark hair neatly styled and wore a crisp, tailored shirt that suggested both style and precision. His eyes, though welcoming, held a hint of wariness as he took in the sight of the two detectives.

"Detectives Lambert and Reed, I have been expecting you" Stephen said, his voice calm but with an edge of apprehension. He offered a polite, if not slightly tense, smile.

"Hello Mr. Smith," Harry replied, her tone respectful yet authoritative. "We'd like to ask you a few questions regarding the recent events. May we come in?"

Stephen stepped aside, allowing them to enter the studio. As they crossed the threshold, Harry and Tom were immediately struck by the ambiance of the space. The studio was a blend of quaint charm and modern sophistication. Polished wooden floors reflected the soft, natural light that streamed in through the large windows. The walls were adorned with Stephen's work—each photograph a testament to his skill, capturing moments of breathtaking beauty and raw emotion.

A series of black-and-white portraits drew the eye, their subjects' expressions hauntingly real. Landscapes in vibrant colours showcased the serene beauty of the Somerset countryside, while candid street scenes brought the hustle and bustle of daily life into sharp focus. The room was arranged with a meticulous eye for detail, from the placement of the photographs to the tasteful selection of vintage furniture that added a touch of elegance.

"Please, have a seat," Stephen said, gesturing to a pair of leather chairs by a small coffee table adorned with photography books and a vase of fresh lilies. He took a seat opposite them, his demeanour composed but guarded.

"Thank you," Tom said as they settled in. "We appreciate your cooperation."

Stephen nodded, his smile remaining but his eyes betraying a flicker of concern. "Of course, detectives. Anything I can do to help."

The stage was set, the tranquil beauty of the studio contrasting sharply with the tension of the investigation that had brought them there. The initial pleasantries exchanged, they were ready to delve into the questions that could unravel the mystery hanging over Taunton.

The quiet hum of a ceiling fan filled the space as Harry and Tom settled into the leather chairs, the smell of fresh lilies mingling with the subtle scent of polished wood. Stephen's studio, though serene and filled with artistic beauty, was now charged with an undercurrent of tension.

Harry leaned forward slightly, her gaze steady on Stephen. "Stephen, we would like you to come with us to the police station for an interview," she began, her voice firm but gentle. "It's about the recent murders."

Stephen's face paled slightly, but he maintained his composure. He nodded, understanding the gravity of the situation. "Of course, I understand," he replied, his voice steady. "Let me grab my coat."

Stephen stood up from his seat, his movements deliberate and controlled, as though each step was measured to maintain his calm demeanour. He walked over to a coat rack near the door, where a dark, tailored coat hung neatly. As he reached for it, his fingers trembled ever so slightly, betraying the anxiety he tried to mask.

The detectives exchanged a brief glance, their silent communication acknowledging the stress Stephen must be feeling. The soft click of the coat rack echoed in the quiet studio as Stephen slipped the coat over his shoulders, straightening it with a practiced hand. He turned back to face Harry and Tom, his expression now resolute.

"Shall we?" he asked, gesturing towards the door.

Harry and Tom rose from their seats, the leather chairs creaking softly in the stillness. "Thank you for your cooperation, Stephen," Tom said, his tone professional but with a hint of empathy.

As they moved towards the door, the ambient sounds of the studio—the ticking of a clock, the distant hum of traffic outside, the faint rustling of leaves against the window—seemed to fade into the background. The trio stepped out into the bright daylight, the sudden contrast to the dimly lit studio making them blink momentarily.

Outside, the world carried on as usual, with passersby unaware of the tension that accompanied their steps. The detectives led Stephen to their car, parked a short distance away. The journey to the police station was silent, the weight of the unspoken questions and looming interrogation hanging heavily in the air.

As they arrived at the station, the building's stark, functional design stood in sharp contrast to the artistic elegance of Stephen's studio. The detectives guided him through the entrance, the cool, clinical atmosphere of the police station replacing the warmth of the sunlit street outside.

The police station's interrogation room was a stark contrast to Stephen's elegant studio. The room was small and utilitarian, with bare walls painted a dull, institutional grey. A single fluorescent light hummed overhead, casting a harsh, unforgiving glow on the plain metal table and the uncomfortable plastic chairs arranged around it. The air was cool, almost sterile, devoid of any comforting scents or sounds.

Harry and Tom sat across from Stephen, their expressions serious and focused. The room's starkness seemed to amplify the tension, every rustle of clothing or creak of the chairs magnified in the oppressive silence. Harry opened a folder, glancing at its contents before meeting Stephen's gaze.

"Can you tell us where you were on the nights Roger, Dawn, and David were killed?" Harry asked, her voice calm but probing.

Stephen took a deep breath, steadying himself before responding. "I was at my studio on the night Roger was killed," he began, his tone measured and precise. "You can check with my assistant; she was there with me until late."

Tom nodded, making a note in his pad. "And on the night of Dawn's murder?" he prompted.

"I was at a friend's house," Stephen replied, his eyes flicking between the two detectives. "We were having dinner. You can contact them to verify that."

"And the night David was killed?" Harry asked, leaning slightly forward, her gaze unwavering.

Stephen's expression softened slightly, a flicker of sadness passing over his features. "I was at an exhibition opening," he said quietly. "David was supposed to be there too, but he never showed up. The event organizers and several attendees can confirm my presence."

Harry and Tom exchanged a glance, their silent communication acknowledging the thoroughness of Stephen's responses. Harry turned her attention back to Stephen, her voice gentle but firm. "We'll need the contact information for your assistant, your friends, and the event organisers."

Stephen nodded, reaching into his coat pocket for a small notebook. He carefully wrote down the details, his handwriting neat and precise, a reflection of his meticulous nature. He handed the paper to Harry, who took it with a nod of thanks.

The room seemed to grow quieter, the weight of the conversation settling heavily over them. Stephen's alibis, while seemingly solid, would need to be verified. The detectives knew that the truth often lay hidden beneath layers of seemingly straightforward facts.

The fluorescent lights of the police station's interrogation room cast a stark, cold glow on the bare walls, amplifying the tension in the small space. The air was thick with unspoken questions as

Harry and Tom settled back into their seats across from Stephen. The hum of distant conversations and the occasional ringing phone were muted, creating a bubble of uneasy quiet around them.

Stephen sat rigidly in his chair, his hands clasped tightly in front of him on the metal table. His usually composed demeanour showed cracks under the pressure of the situation, his eyes flicking between the two detectives as they prepared to delve deeper into his personal life.

Tom leaned forward slightly, breaking the silence with a measured tone. "What was your relationship with David?"

Stephen's breath hitched almost imperceptibly, and he took a moment before responding. "David and I have been lovers for years," he said, his voice steady but tinged with a quiet sadness. "He pretended to fancy Dawn to keep our relationship a secret."

The admission hung in the air, altering the dynamic in the room. The stark, sterile environment seemed to close in around them, the walls bearing silent witness to the unveiling of hidden truths. The emotional weight of Stephen's revelation contrasted sharply with the clinical surroundings, adding a layer of poignancy to the moment.

Harry studied Stephen's face, noting the mix of sorrow and relief that flickered across his features. "Why did you feel the need to keep it a secret?" she asked gently, her voice softening in empathy.

Stephen sighed, his gaze dropping to the table. "David was afraid of the backlash. He thought that if people knew about us, it would ruin his career, his reputation. Taunton can be...unforgiving." He paused, gathering his thoughts. "So, we kept it hidden. Dawn was a friend, and she agreed to play along."

The detectives absorbed this new information, the pieces of the puzzle shifting slightly but not yet falling into place. The personal complexities of Stephen's relationship with David added depth to the investigation, revealing potential motives and connections that had previously been obscured.

Tom made a note in his pad, his pen scratching softly against the paper. "Did anyone else know about your relationship?" he asked, his tone neutral but probing.

Stephen shook his head. "No, we were very careful. Only Dawn knew, and she was supportive."

The room fell silent again, the hum of the fluorescent light the only sound. Harry and Tom exchanged a glance, their minds working through

the implications of Stephen's revelation. The stark
setting of the interrogation room seemed to
underscore the gravity of the secrets being
uncovered, each revelation adding another layer to
the intricate web of relationships and motives.

Harry leaned forward, her expression earnest.
"Thank you for your honesty, Stephen. We know
this isn't easy."

Stephen nodded, a flicker of gratitude in his eyes. "I
just want to help find out who did this. David didn't
deserve to die like that."

The revelations about his relationship with David
had left an emotional residue in the air, but there
were still more layers to peel back, more truths to
uncover.

Harry leaned forward, her voice steady and probing.
"Do you know anyone who would want to kill
David?"

Stephen's brow furrowed in genuine confusion, his
eyes searching Harry's for answers he didn't have.
"No," he said slowly, shaking his head. "I can't
think of anyone. David was well-liked, as far as I
knew."

The room fell silent again, the weight of Stephen's
words settling over them like a heavy blanket. The

detectives studied him closely, looking for any sign of deceit or hidden knowledge, but all they saw was a man deeply shaken by the loss of his lover and the bewildering situation he found himself in.

Tom scribbled a note in his pad, the scratch of his pen a small, steady sound in the otherwise silent room. "Think carefully, Stephen," he urged. "Anyone who might have had a grudge against him, any disagreements or conflicts he had recently?"

Stephen's gaze dropped to his hands, clasped tightly together on the table. He seemed to be searching his memory, sifting through interactions and events for any clue that might help. "I really don't know," he finally said, his voice heavy with frustration and sorrow. "David was a kind person. He avoided conflict whenever he could. He was dedicated to his work, and people respected him for that."

Harry and Tom exchanged a glance, their expressions reflecting the complexity of the case. The starkness of the interrogation room seemed to emphasize the dead ends they kept encountering, each unanswered question another shadow in the already dimly lit mystery.

"Is there anyone who might have been jealous of David's success?" Harry pressed gently. "Anyone who might have felt overshadowed by him?"

Stephen sighed deeply, running a hand through his hair. "In our field, there's always competition, but nothing that I ever thought was serious. Jealousy, maybe, but murder? It just doesn't make sense."

The detectives leaned back in their chairs, the gravity of the situation hanging heavily in the air. Stephen's genuine bewilderment and lack of knowledge about any potential threats only added layers of complexity to the mystery they were trying to unravel. The sterile environment of the interrogation room served as a stark backdrop to the emotional turmoil and confusion playing out before them.

As the session drew to a close, the atmosphere remained thick with unspoken questions and unresolved tensions. The cold, clinical environment seemed to emphasise the gravity of the situation, every sound magnified in the otherwise silent room.

Tom closed his notebook and looked across the table at Stephen, who sat with his hands still clasped tightly in front of him. "Thank you for your cooperation, Stephen," Tom said, his voice professional but carrying an undercurrent of empathy. "You can go now, but please stay available in case we need to ask more questions."

Stephen nodded, a mixture of relief and lingering anxiety visible in his eyes. "Of course, detectives.

I'll be at my studio," he replied, his voice steady but subdued.

Harry stood up first, the legs of her chair scraping softly against the tiled floor. She gathered her papers, her movements precise and deliberate, reflecting the seriousness of the investigation. Tom followed suit, and together they walked Stephen to the door of the interrogation room.

The corridor outside was a hive of activity, with officers moving briskly and the low hum of conversations creating a backdrop of controlled chaos. The stark fluorescent lighting continued here, casting sharp shadows and highlighting the polished surfaces of the desks and walls. The contrast between the bustling hallway and the isolated interrogation room was striking, underscoring the shift from intense scrutiny to the routine operations of the police station.

As they walked, the sounds of the police station grew louder—the ringing of phones, the clicking of keyboards, and the occasional burst of laughter or raised voice. It was a reminder of the world outside the closed room, a world that continued to move forward despite the dark undercurrents running beneath the surface.

At the entrance to the station, Harry paused and turned to Stephen. "Remember, if you think of anything else, don't hesitate to contact us," she said, her tone both firm and encouraging.

Stephen nodded, his expression earnest. "I will. Thank you, detectives."

Tom opened the door, and the three of them stepped out into the bright daylight. The sudden change from the artificial lighting inside to the natural light outside was almost blinding, and Stephen blinked a few times as his eyes adjusted. The fresh air was a welcome relief from the sterile environment of the police station, carrying with it the familiar scents of the town—freshly cut grass, distant traffic, and the faint aroma of coffee from a nearby café.

"Take care, Stephen," Tom said, giving him a nod.

Stephen managed a small smile. "You too, detectives."

With that, he turned and walked away, his figure gradually blending into the flow of people and cars on the busy street. Harry and Tom watched him go, their minds already shifting back to the myriad details of the case that still demanded their attention.

Harry and Tom re-entered the police station, the door closing behind them with a soft thud, the sense of urgency returned. The investigation was far from over, and each piece of information, each interaction, brought them one step closer to uncovering the truth. The next part of the story awaited, with new leads to follow and more questions to answer.

As Stephen walked back towards his photo studio, the familiar streets of Taunton seemed different, cloaked in an unsettling tension that mirrored his own anxiety. The sun had begun its slow descent, casting long shadows that stretched across the cobbled paths. The hustle and bustle of the town seemed muted, as if the very air was holding its breath.

He approached his studio, the charming brick building now appearing almost foreboding in the waning light. The ivy that climbed its facade rustled softly in the evening breeze, but the usual sense of calm and creativity that the place inspired was conspicuously absent. Instead, a sense of unease settled over Stephen like a shroud.

The large windows, which once framed his art with pride, now reflected a man burdened by suspicion and fear. He reached for the door, the familiar feel of the handle offering little comfort. As he turned the key and pushed the door open, something caught his eye—a piece of paper taped to the door at eye level.

Stephen's heart skipped a beat. He pulled the note from the door, his hands trembling slightly as he unfolded it. The words, scrawled in thick, black ink, seemed to leap off the page:

"I know what you did - you are an abomination that needs cleansing!"

The air around him seemed to grow colder, the chilling message sending a shiver down his spine. He looked around, but the street was empty, the silence only broken by the distant hum of traffic. The usually inviting entrance to his sanctuary now felt like the threshold of a nightmare.

Inside the studio, the atmosphere was markedly different from the serene, sophisticated space it had been just hours earlier. The photographs on the walls, once sources of pride and beauty, seemed to cast accusatory glances. The soft light filtering through the windows did little to dispel the darkness that had settled within Stephen's heart.

He closed the door behind him, the click of the lock sounding unnaturally loud in the oppressive silence. Stephen's mind raced, the implications of the note swirling chaotically. Who could have left it? How did they know? And, most importantly, what did they want?

Stephen moved through his studio, the familiar surroundings now tinged with an eerie sense of foreboding. His gaze fell on his work, the images that had once brought him joy and recognition now seeming to mock him with their tranquil beauty.

He sank into a chair, the note still clutched in his hand. The weight of the words bore down on him, each one a sharp blade cutting into his peace of mind. The studio, filled with the quiet hum of distant traffic and the soft creaks of the old building, felt like a cage closing in on him.

The last rays of sunlight faded, leaving the studio bathed in the soft, artificial glow of his lamps. Stephen knew he had to stay calm, to think clearly. The note was a threat, but it was also a clue. Someone knew more than they should, and that someone was watching him.

Chapter 26 Behind Locked Doors

When Stephen first read the note, he felt an overwhelming sense of shock. The words were harsh and unexpected, jolting him from his usual sense of safety and routine.

"What is this? Who would write something like this?" he thought, his mind struggling to process the implications. The accusation was not just personal; it was deeply hostile and filled with an almost archaic sense of condemnation.

Stephen's immediate reaction was to deny the note's validity. *"This must be some kind of mistake. Maybe it's meant for someone else. Surely, no one could seriously believe this about me."*

He tried to rationalize the situation. *"Someone's playing a sick joke. Or maybe it's a misunderstanding. There's no way this is real."* But even as he thought these things, the certainty behind the words on the note gnawed at him.

As the initial shock wore off, a deep-seated fear began to take hold. The note's message suggested someone knew something about him—something he thought was hidden or forgotten. The phrase "I know what you did" echoed ominously in his mind.

"Who knows? What do they think they know? What could they be referring to?" Each question only heightened his paranoia. He began to feel watched, as if the walls of his apartment were closing in on him.

Stephen took a deep breath, wiping his chemical-smeared hands on a rag as he surveyed his work. It had been a productive day, but now it was time to head home. He glanced at the clock on the wall, noting the time. "I need to wrap this up," he murmured to himself, though the thought of leaving his sanctuary always filled him with a bit of reluctance.

He gathered his things, carefully placing cameras and lights back in their designated spots. After ensuring that everything was in order, he flipped off the lights, plunging the studio into shadows, save for the shafts of light filtering through the high windows. The echo of his footsteps accompanied him as he walked across the hardwood floor to the door.

Locking the door behind him, Stephen stepped out into the bustling city street. The contrast between the quiet, creative cocoon of his studio and the noisy, vibrant life of the city was always jarring. He blended into the crowd, his mind still lingering on his art even as his body moved through the throng of people. The cacophony of car horns, distant conversations, and the hum of city life filled his ears as he made his way home.

Stephen's home was a courtyard townhouse, a white-bricked structure that exuded charm and understated elegance. The front of the house faced a narrow cobblestone street, while the back opened up to a secluded courtyard enclosed by a red-bricked garden wall topped with intricate iron railings. The garden within was meticulously maintained, with neatly trimmed hedges, blooming flowers, and a small fountain that gurgled softly, providing a soothing background melody.

The townhouse itself was a perfect blend of old-world charm and modern comfort. The white brick façade stood out against the surrounding buildings, its large windows framed with dark green shutters. Ivy climbed up one side of the house, adding to the picturesque quality of the setting. The iron gate leading to the courtyard was ornate, with swirling patterns that spoke of craftsmanship from a bygone era.

Stephen unlocked the gate and stepped into the courtyard, feeling an immediate sense of calm wash over him. The stresses of the day seemed to melt away as he walked up the stone path to the back door. The garden was his oasis, a place where he could disconnect from the outside world and find peace.

As he entered the house, the cool air greeted him, a stark contrast to the warmth outside. The interior of the townhouse was just as inviting as its exterior. The walls were painted in soft, neutral tones, creating a soothing backdrop for the eclectic mix of furniture and décor. The living room featured a comfortable, overstuffed sofa and mismatched armchairs, inviting relaxation. Shelves lined with books, knick-knacks, and potted plants added a personal touch, reflecting Stephen's tastes and interests.

However, as Stephen moved through the space, he began to notice subtle changes that gave him pause. The photo frame on the mantel, usually cantered and showcasing a picture of his family, was now tilted to the side. A book that he distinctly remembered placing on the bookshelf was now lying open on the coffee table, its pages fluttering slightly from the draft. His favourite coffee mug, which he always kept by the sink, was now on the kitchen counter, filled with cold coffee.

He dismissed these changes initially, attributing them to his own forgetfulness. He had been preoccupied with work and the recent discovery of a cryptic note on his studio door. The note, written in an unfamiliar hand, simply read: "I know what you did - you are an abomination that needs cleansing!" Stephen had shrugged it off as a prank, but the sense of unease lingered.

Stephen tried to shake off the unsettling feeling creeping over him. "It's nothing," he muttered to himself, trying to sound convincing. "I've just been distracted lately, that's all."

But as he wandered through the townhouse, his mind kept returning to the note. What did it mean? He had no enemies, no one who would play such a prank. He tried to rationalise the situation. "Maybe it's just someone trying to scare me. Some bored teenager or an annoyed neighbour."

Yet the changes in his home were undeniable. Each small, seemingly insignificant shift in his surroundings felt like a jigsaw piece falling into place, forming a picture he didn't want to see. The eerie silence of the house, usually a comfort, now felt oppressive. He could hear every creak of the floorboards, every whisper of the wind against the windows.

Stephen's thoughts raced. "Am I losing it? Did I move these things and just forget?" He shook his head, trying to clear the fog of doubt. But deep down, a knot of fear was tightening in his chest. The note's message echoed in his mind, a sinister whisper that refused to be silenced.

Stephen walked over to the mantel and straightened the photo frame, his fingers trembling slightly. "I must have knocked it over," he murmured, though he couldn't recall doing so. He picked up the book from the coffee table, "The Collected Works of Edgar Allan Poe," and placed it back on the shelf. "I probably left it out when I was looking for something to read."

In the kitchen, he dumped the cold coffee from the mug and washed it, placing it back by the sink where it belonged. "Maybe I was half-asleep this morning," he reasoned, though his routine was usually meticulous.

The townhouse's usual comforting quiet now felt ominous, every sound magnified in the stillness. The creak of the floorboards under his feet, the hum of the refrigerator, even the distant murmur of the city outside seemed to conspire against his peace of mind. Stephen rubbed his temples, trying to dispel the headache forming from his mounting anxiety.

The kitchen was dimly lit, the soft glow from the under-cabinet lights casting long shadows across the countertops. Outside, the night had fallen, blanketing the courtyard townhouse in darkness. The only sound was the faint humming of the refrigerator and the occasional creak of the old building settling.

Stephen had just finished washing the last of the dishes from his solitary dinner. He wiped his hands on a dish towel, feeling the quiet of the evening settle around him like a heavy blanket. The comfort of his home seemed distant tonight, replaced by an inexplicable unease.

As he turned to place the towel on the counter, his eyes caught something unusual on the kitchen table. A single piece of paper lay in the centre, stark and out of place. Stephen frowned, his steps hesitant as he approached it. The note was simple, written in crude, block letters:

"I'm watching you."

For a moment, Stephen stood frozen, his mind struggling to process the message. His heart began to pound in his chest, each beat reverberating in his ears. He picked up the note with trembling hands, the paper rustling slightly as he held it.

"This can't be real," he thought, a cold sweat breaking out on his forehead. *"Who could have left this? How did they get in?"* The questions raced through his mind, each one more alarming than the last.

"I'm watching you." The words seemed to pulse on the paper, a sinister promise that sent chills down his spine. Was someone really watching him? Had they been inside his home? The thought was almost too terrifying to contemplate.

Panic setting in, Stephen began to search the apartment frantically. He moved through the rooms with increasing desperation, his movements erratic. He checked the locks on the doors and windows, each one secure and showing no signs of forced entry.

His hands shook as he pulled back curtains, opened closets, and checked under furniture. Each empty space only heightened his paranoia. *"Where could they be hiding?"* he wondered, his breath coming in short, rapid gasps.

The silence of the apartment was oppressive, the creak of the floorboards under his feet magnified in the stillness. He felt eyes on him, imagined shadows moving just out of sight. His head whipped around at every imagined sound, his mind playing tricks on him in the dim light.

"Should I call the police?" he thought, pausing in the middle of the living room. *"What would I tell them? That I found a note? They won't believe me without proof. They'll think I'm paranoid or imagining things."*

He clenched his fists, frustration and fear mingling in his chest. *"But what if someone is watching me? What if they come back?"* The thought of spending the night alone, knowing that someone might be out there, was almost unbearable.

Stephen's rational mind battled with his growing paranoia. *"I can't let this person scare me into a panic. I need to stay calm and think clearly."* But even as he tried to reassure himself, his eyes kept darting to the shadows, his ears straining for any hint of an intruder.

Stephen returned to the kitchen, the note still clutched in his hand. He placed it back on the table, staring at it as if it might reveal some hidden clue. His hands were shaking uncontrollably now, his breath coming in shallow, rapid bursts.

He sat down heavily in a chair, running his hands through his hair. *"What am I going to do? I can't live like this, constantly looking over my shoulder."* The thought of being watched, of not knowing who was behind it or why, gnawed at his sanity.

His eyes flicked to the windows, the dark panes reflecting the faint light from the kitchen. He imagined eyes staring back at him, unseen but ever-present. The note was a physical manifestation of his worst fears, a tangible proof that his sanctuary had been violated.

Stephen's thoughts spiralled into darker and darker territory, the fear feeding on itself. *"I need to find out who did this. I need to make sure it doesn't happen again."* The determination was there, but it was shaky, undermined by the deep-seated terror that had taken root in his mind.

He glanced at the clock on the wall, noting the late hour. *"I need to get some sleep, clear my head. Maybe in the morning, things will seem clearer."* But even as he thought it, he knew sleep would not come easily. The note had shattered his sense of security, leaving him vulnerable and afraid in his own home.

Stephen forced himself to stand, his legs feeling weak and unsteady. He double-checked the locks once more, then made his way to the bedroom, every creak of the floorboards sounding like a whisper of doom. The note's message echoed in his mind, a constant reminder of the unseen threat lurking in the darkness.

As he lay down, his eyes wide open and staring at the ceiling, Stephen knew that tonight, peace and rest were beyond his reach. The fear had taken hold, and it would not let go.

Chapter 27 A Note in the Kitchen

Stephen sat on the edge of his bed, the note he had found in his kitchen still fresh in his mind. The sense of unease that had settled over him since discovering the message made the walls of his apartment feel like they were closing in. He needed to get out, to be around people, to convince himself that the world was still normal and that he wasn't being watched.

He decided to go to his favourite cafe in Taunton. It was a place where he often found solace, surrounded by the comforting hum of life going on around him. He hoped the familiar environment and the presence of other people would help dispel the creeping paranoia that had taken root in his mind.

Stephen grabbed his coat and keys, casting one last wary glance around his apartment. The shadows seemed to shift and loom, making his heart race. *"I just need a change of scenery,"* he thought, trying to calm his nerves. He locked the door behind him, the click of the deadbolt sounding louder than usual in the silence of the hallway.

The walk to the cafe was brisk, the cool evening air a welcome relief from the stifling atmosphere of his apartment. He kept his hands in his pockets, his fingers absently tracing the outline of his phone.

The streets of Taunton were alive with activity, people going about their evening routines, oblivious to the turmoil churning inside him.

Stephen tried to blend into the crowd, focusing on the rhythm of his footsteps and the familiar sights of the town. He passed shop windows glowing with warm light, their displays filled with seasonal decorations. The normalcy of it all was both reassuring and surreal, given the fear that gnawed at his thoughts.

The cafe was a lively oasis in the heart of Taunton, a place where the hum of conversation blended with the clinking of cups and the hiss of the espresso machine. The decor was a charming mix of rustic and modern, with exposed brick walls adorned with local artwork and shelves lined with jars of coffee beans and colourful mugs. Wooden tables and chairs were scattered throughout the space, each occupied by patrons enjoying their morning rituals.

The aroma of freshly brewed coffee mingled with the sweet scent of pastries, creating an inviting atmosphere that drew people in from the bustling street outside. Baristas moved behind the counter with practiced efficiency, their movements a blur as they prepared lattes, cappuccinos, and espressos. The sound of milk frothing and orders being called out added to the vibrant symphony of the cafe.

Stephen sat at a small table near the window, nursing a cup of black coffee. The warmth of the mug was comforting in his hands, but his mind was far from the cozy ambiance of the cafe. He tried to lose himself in a book, but the words blurred on the page as his thoughts drifted back to the note he had found in his apartment. The unease that had taken root in his mind refused to let go.

As he absentmindedly stirred his coffee, Stephen glanced out the window. The street outside was busy with pedestrians going about their day, cars passing by, and the occasional cyclist weaving through traffic. Amid the bustle, a figure standing across the street caught his eye.

The person was partially obscured by a lamppost, their features hidden under the brim of a hat and a long coat. Even from this distance, Stephen felt a prickle of recognition and unease. The figure seemed to be staring directly at him, an unwavering gaze that sent a shiver down his spine.

He blinked, his heart pounding in his chest. *"Am I imagining this?"* he wondered, glancing back down at his book. But curiosity and fear compelled him to look again. When he did, the figure was gone, vanished into the crowd as if they had never been there.

"Did I really see someone? Or is my mind playing tricks on me?" Stephen's paranoia spiked, the sense of being watched now an oppressive weight on his shoulders. He tried to focus on his book, but the words swam before his eyes, refusing to make sense. His hands, still wrapped around the coffee cup, began to tremble.

"I need to act normal," he told himself, but the effort was monumental. Every time the door to the cafe opened, he tensed, expecting the mysterious figure to walk in. He scanned the faces of the other patrons, searching for any sign that someone might be watching him.

The cafe's atmosphere, normally a balm for the soul, now felt suffocating. The cheerful chatter of friends catching up, the laughter of children, and the soothing background music were all stark contrasts to Stephen's internal turmoil. The world around him continued to move in a rhythm of normalcy, while his own world was fracturing under the weight of fear.

A couple at a nearby table leaned in close, sharing a private joke. Their smiles and easy laughter felt like a mockery of Stephen's anxiety. A student hunched over a laptop, typing furiously, oblivious to the outside world. A businessman scrolled through his phone, his expression one of calm concentration.

To Stephen, these scenes of everyday life felt surreal. *"How can everyone be so at ease when I'm falling apart?"* The question echoed in his mind, amplifying his sense of isolation. He took a sip of his coffee, the bitter liquid doing little to steady his nerves.

He forced himself to take deep breaths, trying to regain some semblance of composure. *"It's just your imagination,"* he repeated silently, a mantra against the rising tide of panic. *"No one is watching you. You're safe here."* But the memory of the figure across the street lingered, a shadow on the edge of his consciousness.

Stephen's eyes darted to the window again, scanning the street for any sign of the mysterious watcher. He saw only the normal hustle and bustle of Taunton, but the sense of unease remained, a constant undercurrent to his thoughts.

He checked his phone, hoping for a distraction, but found no new messages or notifications. The familiar routine of scrolling through social media offered no comfort. Instead, it only heightened his awareness of his own solitude.

As the minutes ticked by, Stephen's attempts to act normal became increasingly strained. He decided to finish his coffee and leave the cafe, seeking the safety of his apartment despite the lingering fear it now held. He gathered his things, trying to move casually, but his hands were still shaking.

He cast one last glance out the window before stepping into the street, half expecting to see the figure again. But the sidewalk was empty, save for the usual passersby. He pulled his coat tighter around him and began to walk, the feeling of being watched following him like a shadow.

Stephen's mind raced with possibilities and questions, each one more troubling than the last. The bustling cafe had done little to ease his paranoia, and as he made his way home, the fear gnawed at him, a relentless reminder that his sense of security had been irrevocably shattered.

The morning sun was rising, casting a soft golden light over Vivary Park. The air was crisp and fresh, filled with the scent of blooming flowers and damp earth. Dew clung to the grass, sparkling like tiny diamonds in the gentle sunlight. Birds chirped merrily from the treetops, and the park seemed to be waking up with a serene and peaceful energy.

Vivary Park was a sprawling expanse of green in the heart of Taunton, featuring winding paths, lush gardens, and tranquil ponds. Tall trees bordered the walkways, their leaves rustling softly in the morning breeze. The park was a favourite spot for early morning joggers and walkers, but at this hour, it was still relatively quiet.

After leaving the cafe, Stephen had felt restless. The note, the mysterious figure, and his heightened sense of paranoia had left him unable to relax. He decided that a walk through Vivary Park might help clear his mind. His daily walks had always been a source of comfort, a time when he could collect his thoughts and find some peace amidst the beauty of nature.

As Stephen walked through the park, he tried to focus on the calming surroundings. The gentle sway of the branches, the soft chirping of birds, and the rhythmic crunch of gravel underfoot were all familiar and soothing. However, a nagging sense of unease lingered, a remnant of the fear that had plagued him since finding the note.

As he rounded a bend in the path, Stephen suddenly felt a prickling sensation at the back of his neck, as if he were being watched. He slowed his pace, glancing over his shoulder. At first, he saw nothing unusual—just the empty path behind him and the trees swaying gently in the breeze.

But then, out of the corner of his eye, he caught a fleeting glimpse of movement—a shadow darting behind a tree. His heart rate quickened. *"Is someone following me?"* he wondered, trying to keep his breathing steady. He turned fully to look, but saw only the peaceful, empty park.

Determined not to let his paranoia get the better of him, Stephen decided to confront whoever might be lurking in the shadows. He left the path, walking briskly toward the spot where he had seen the movement. As he approached the tree, he called out, "Is someone there?"

There was no response. He rounded the tree, but found nothing—just an empty space where the morning light filtered through the branches. His eyes scanned the area, searching for any sign of another person, but the park seemed deserted.

Stephen's unease grew as he continued his walk. Every so often, he would catch another glimpse of movement—behind a bush, near a bench, or among the flowerbeds. Each time he tried to confront the person, he found nothing but empty spaces, as if the park itself were playing tricks on him.

The juxtaposition of the park's serene beauty with Stephen's growing fear created a surreal atmosphere. The early morning light cast long shadows that seemed to move and shift, creating an eerie play of light and darkness. The vibrant colours of the flowers, the rich green of the grass, and the sparkling dew all seemed muted by the tension that gripped him.

The park's usual tranquillity felt oppressive. The rustling leaves sounded like whispers, and the chirping birds seemed to be mocking him with their carefree tunes. The pond, usually a place of reflection and calm, now looked like a dark, ominous pool.

As Stephen walked deeper into the park, the feeling of being watched intensified. He began to walk faster, his breaths coming in short, sharp bursts. The path ahead seemed to stretch endlessly, and the trees on either side loomed larger and more menacing.

Finally, unable to shake the feeling that someone was following him, Stephen stopped and turned around one last time. He called out again, louder this time, "Whoever you are, show yourself!"

The park remained silent, save for the gentle rustling of leaves and the distant chirping of birds. Stephen felt a wave of frustration and fear wash over him. *"Am I imagining all this?"* he wondered, his mind racing.

Stephen walked briskly through Vivary Park, the early morning light casting a soft, golden glow on the dew-covered grass. The park, usually a place of solace, felt different today. His mind was preoccupied with the unsettling events of the past few days—the cryptic note he had found on his studio door and his kitchen table and the growing sense of unease that someone was watching him. The tranquil beauty of the park did little to soothe his frayed nerves.

He tried to focus on the familiar sights and sounds around him: the cheerful chirping of birds, the rustling of leaves in the gentle breeze, the occasional jogger or dog walker passing by with a nod or a wave. But his thoughts kept returning to the mysterious note and the questions it raised. Who could have left it? What did they want? And why him?

As he completed his usual circuit and headed back towards his home, Stephen made a decision. He needed to visit his photographic studio. Maybe the familiar routine of work would help clear his mind and provide some much-needed distraction.

Leaving the park, Stephen made his way through the quiet streets of Taunton, the town slowly coming to life as people began their day. The walk to his studio was short, but with each step, his anxiety grew. He couldn't shake the feeling that something was terribly wrong, that his life was being watched and manipulated by unseen forces.

He arrived at the studio, a small but well-equipped space that had been his creative sanctuary for years. The walls were lined with his photographs, each one a testament to his passion and skill. The sight of his work, usually a source of pride and comfort, did little to calm his nerves today.

Stephen unlocked the door and stepped inside, the familiar scent of developer fluid and paper greeting him. He flicked on the lights, illuminating the space filled with cameras, tripods, and editing equipment. The studio, normally a haven of creativity, felt oppressive today, the walls closing in around him.

On his desk, amidst the organized chaos of lenses and memory cards, lay an envelope. It was plain, unmarked, and ominously out of place. His heart began to pound as he approached it, a sense of dread settling over him like a heavy cloak.

With trembling hands, Stephen picked up the envelope and tore it open. Inside, he found several notes and photographs. The first note read, "You can't hide from the truth." His breath caught in his throat as he pulled out the photographs. They were of him and David, taken without their knowledge, in various intimate moments. One photo showed them in a tender embrace, their faces close, eyes locked in a shared gaze of affection and trust.

The invasion of privacy was palpable, each photograph a violation, a snapshot of a private moment turned into a weapon. Stephen's hands shook as he examined each photo, the sense of exposure and vulnerability overwhelming him. The notes that accompanied the photos were filled with threats and accusations, each one more menacing than the last.

"We know what you did." "There's no escaping the past." "You will pay for your sins."

"How did they get these photos?" Stephen's mind raced, trying to piece together the who and the why. *"Who would do this to me? To us?"* The realization that someone had been watching him, had invaded his most private moments, sent a chill down his spine.

"I can't deal with this alone," he thought, the weight of the situation pressing down on him. *"This isn't just a prank or a simple threat. This is serious. This is dangerous."* His fear turned to desperation as he realized the full extent of the threat.

He looked closely at each photograph, searching for clues. The clarity of the images indicated they had been taken with a high-quality camera, possibly from a distance with a telephoto lens. The angles suggested the photographer had been hiding, watching, waiting for the right moments to capture.

Stephen felt a wave of nausea. The thought that someone had been so close, had watched him so intimately, was almost too much to bear. His studio, his home, his entire life felt tainted, corrupted by the unknown stalker.

He knew he couldn't handle this alone. The fear, the paranoia, the sheer invasion of his privacy was more than he could manage. He needed help. He needed someone who could get to the bottom of this, someone who could protect him and David.

Taking a deep breath, Stephen grabbed his coat and headed off to the police station to see Detective Inspector Lambert.

The Taunton Police Station was a bustling hive of activity. Officers moved briskly through the corridors, the hum of phones ringing and the clatter of keyboards creating a steady backdrop of sound. The fluorescent lights cast a stark glow over the room, illuminating the controlled chaos of law enforcement at work. The air was filled with the scent of coffee and the faint odour of cleaning supplies, mingling with the tension and urgency that permeated the station.

Stephen entered the station, feeling out of place amidst the order and discipline of the police environment. His hands were clammy, and his heart pounded in his chest. He approached the front desk, where a stern-faced officer glanced up from her paperwork.

"I'm here to see Detective Inspector Harry Lambert and Detective Sergeant Tom Reed," Stephen said, his voice tinged with desperation.

The officer nodded and made a quick call, then directed Stephen to a waiting area. He sat down, his mind racing with thoughts of the threatening notes and the invasive photographs. He clutched the envelope tightly, as if it were a lifeline.

A few minutes later, the door to the waiting area opened, and Harry Lambert and Tom Reed stepped in. Harry, with her sharp eyes and composed demeanour, immediately put Stephen at ease. Tom, with his methodical presence, provided a sense of stability. They both approached Stephen with an air of professionalism and genuine concern.

"Stephen," Harry said, extending a hand. "We understand you have something important to discuss."

Stephen shook Harry's hand, then Tom's, and gestured to the envelope. "Yes, I... I've been receiving these." His voice wavered as he handed over the envelope.

Harry took the envelope and led Stephen to a small, private interview room. The room was stark, with a simple table and chairs, a notepad, and a recording device. The walls were bare, save for a clock ticking steadily, marking the passing time. Tom closed the door behind them, ensuring they wouldn't be disturbed.

"Please, sit down," Harry said gently, as she and Tom took seats opposite Stephen.

Stephen sat, his hands still trembling slightly. "I don't know who's doing this or why, but I'm scared. These photos… they're of me and David. Someone has been watching us, taking pictures without our knowledge."

Harry opened the envelope and began to examine the contents. The photographs showed intimate moments between Stephen and David, each one more invasive than the last. The notes were filled with threats and accusations, each one more chilling than the previous.

"I found the first note on my studio door, the second in my kitchen," Stephen continued, his voice cracking. "And then these arrived at my studio. I don't feel safe. I don't know who's behind this or what they want."

Tom took detailed notes, his brow furrowed in concentration. "Stephen, we're going to take this very seriously. These threats are not something we can ignore."

Harry nodded, her expression serious. "We understand your fear and frustration. This is a clear case of stalking and harassment. We'll start by examining the photos and the notes for any clues. Have you noticed anyone unusual around your home or studio? Any strange behaviour from people you know?"

Stephen shook his head. "No, I've been wracking my brain, but I can't think of anyone who would do this. I just want it to stop."

Tom leaned forward, his voice steady. "We'll look into your recent interactions, your professional and personal circles. Sometimes these things can come from places we least expect. But rest assured, we'll find out who's behind this."

Stephen's eyes were filled with a mix of relief and residual anxiety. "Thank you. I didn't know where else to turn. I've been feeling so paranoid, like I'm constantly being watched."

Harry reached across the table, placing a reassuring hand on Stephen's arm. "You did the right thing by coming to us. We're going to handle this. In the meantime, we'll arrange for some additional security measures around your home and studio to ensure your safety."

The interview room, though simple and functional, felt like a sanctuary to Stephen. The professional demeanour of Harry and Tom, combined with their genuine concern, helped to ease his anxiety. Harry's eyes were sharp, missing nothing, while Tom's methodical approach instilled a sense of order and control.

Outside the room, the sounds of the station continued, but inside, there was a focused calm. The detectives' presence provided Stephen with a semblance of security amidst the chaos that had become his life.

As they concluded the meeting, Harry stood and extended her hand again. "We'll keep you updated on our progress, Stephen. Remember, you're not alone in this. We're here to help."

Stephen shook her hand, his grip firmer now. "Thank you, Detective. I really appreciate it."

Tom nodded, offering a reassuring smile. "Take care, Stephen. We'll get to the bottom of this."

As Stephen left the station, he felt a weight lift from his shoulders. The fear and uncertainty were still there, but now they were tempered by the knowledge that he had allies in Harry and Tom. The detectives' professionalism and concern had given him hope, and for the first time in days, he felt a glimmer of relief.

Outside, the morning sun shone brightly, casting long shadows on the pavement. Stephen took a deep breath, ready to face whatever came next, knowing he was no longer alone in his fight against the unknown threat that loomed over him.

Chapter 28 Pieces of Roger

The Taunton Police Station buzzed with the usual mid-morning activity, phones ringing and the low hum of conversations creating a backdrop of white noise. In the shared office of Harry and Tom, the atmosphere was tense and focused. The desks were a stark contrast to each other; Tom's was immaculately organized with neatly stacked files and a precise array of pens, while Harry's was a controlled chaos of notes, files, and photographs pinned up in a haphazard manner.

Harry Lambert, her brow furrowed in concentration, sifted through a box of Roger Morgan's personal effects. Tom Reed, meticulously taking notes on a yellow legal pad, glanced up occasionally, his eyes narrowing as he processed each new piece of information.

"Why are we going through all this again?" Tom asked, not looking up from his notes.

Harry paused, holding up a small, leather-bound journal. "Because, Tom, if there's anything we've learned from past cases, it's that the devil is in the details. We need to understand Roger's life—every aspect of it. His relationships, his secrets, his routines. Everything."

Tom nodded, conceding the point. "Right. We need to see if there's something we missed. Something that could give us a lead."

Harry continued, her voice thoughtful. "Exactly. Roger was a man with a public persona and a private life. The inconsistencies between those two could be where the truth lies. Affairs, hidden resentments, professional rivalries—these are the things that can lead to murder."

Tom's eyes met Harry's, a silent agreement passing between them. They had been partners long enough to know that sometimes the smallest piece of evidence could break a case wide open. Harry flipped open the journal and began to read aloud, hoping that Roger's own words might offer the insight they desperately needed.

"Look at this, Tom," Harry said, her eyes scanning the neatly written entries. "Roger's diary. This might give us some insight."

Tom leaned closer, his interest piqued. "Good find. Start from the beginning, let's see if there's anything that stands out."

Harry flipped to the first entry, her voice steady as she read, "April 3rd, 'Met with Dawn today. Her beauty is only matched by her grace in front of the camera. Our sessions are becoming the highlight of my week.'"

Tom tapped his pen on the desk, "Dawn Menzies. We need to look deeper into their relationship. An affair is a strong motive."

Harry nodded, flipping through more pages, each entry painting a clearer picture of Roger's secret life. "April 15th, 'Margaret confronted me about the long hours. She suspects but doesn't know. The guilt is weighing on me, but I can't stop seeing Dawn. She makes me feel alive in a way I haven't felt in years.'"

Tom scribbled notes furiously, "Margaret knew something was off. She might not have had concrete proof, but suspicion can be a powerful thing."

Harry continued to read, her voice tinged with curiosity, "May 2nd, 'Another beautiful session with Dawn. She's becoming more than just a model to me. I need to end things with Margaret, but it's so complicated.'"

Tom's eyes narrowed, "Roger was planning to leave Margaret. If she found out, it could have pushed her over the edge. What else do we have in his belongings?"

Harry moved to another item, a stack of letters bound with a red ribbon. She untied it and scanned the contents, her eyes widening as she read. "Letters from Dawn. Some are quite intimate. She was clearly invested in this relationship too. Here's one dated a week before his death. 'Roger, I can't continue like this. We need to make a decision. It's either me or Margaret. I love you, but I won't be the other woman forever.'"

Tom leaned back in his chair, processing the new information. "That's a strong ultimatum. If Roger was dragging his feet, it could have caused tension."

Harry agreed, "Let's not forget Margaret's resentment. She felt betrayed and humiliated. We need to speak with her again, dig deeper into her feelings and whereabouts the night of the murder."

Tom stood, grabbing the diary and the letters. "Agreed. It's a shame we cannot talk to Dawn again. She might have known more about Roger's plans and any threats he might have received."

As they were about to leave, Harry's phone buzzed. She glanced at the screen and her eyes widened. "Tom, it's the lab. They've found something on the monopod used in the murder."

Tom raised an eyebrow, "What is it?"

Harry answered, "Traces of female DNA. It's not a conclusive match yet, but it's a lead. Let's get down to the lab and see what they've got."

The Taunton Police Station's evidence room was a cavernous, dimly lit space. Rows upon rows of metal shelves, lined with case files and evidence boxes, stretched into the distance. The air was thick with the musty smell of old paper and dust, giving the room a sombre, almost oppressive atmosphere. Fluorescent lights flickered intermittently, casting eerie shadows on the concrete floor.

Harry and Tom sat at a cluttered table in the centre of the room, the surface barely visible under the spread of documents, photographs, and forensic reports related to Dawn Menzies' case. The table was their battlefield, each piece of evidence a weapon in their quest for justice.

Harry, her brow furrowed in concentration, rifled through a stack of photographs. Tom, ever the meticulous investigator, was cross-referencing notes and reports, his pen tapping rhythmically against his notebook.

"Let's go through Dawn's case files again. We might have missed something," Harry said, her voice steady but tinged with urgency.

Tom nodded, "Agreed. Her connection to Roger is too significant to ignore."

Harry picked up a photograph and held it up to the light. It was a candid shot of Dawn and Roger, their heads close together, smiling. The intimacy captured in the image was undeniable.

"Look at this, Tom. This wasn't just a professional relationship," Harry remarked, passing the photo to him.

Tom examined the photograph, his eyes narrowing. "Roger and Dawn were clearly more than just colleagues. This could have been the trigger for Margaret's rage."

Harry set the photograph aside and opened Dawn's diary, a small leather-bound book with pages filled with neat, flowing script. She began reading aloud, "September 10th, 'I'm scared. He says it's all under control, but I can't shake the feeling that something bad is going to happen. M's jealousy is getting worse. She's watching us.'"

Tom leaned in, his interest piqued. "She mentions 'M' several times. Margaret, no doubt. This diary entry confirms that Dawn was terrified of her."

Harry flipped through more pages, her eyes scanning for any additional clues. "October 1st,

'Roger wants to go public with our relationship, but I'm not sure. M's threats are becoming more intense. I found a note on my car windshield today. It said, 'Stay away from him, or else.' I'm living in fear.'"

Tom's face hardened. "Margaret had the motive and the opportunity. We just need to tie her to the actual murders."

The two detectives continued to sift through the evidence, their focus unwavering. They found more photographs, some showing Dawn and Roger in intimate settings, others capturing them at public events, always looking over their shoulders as if expecting someone to be watching.

Among Dawn's personal effects, they discovered crumpled notes and letters, some from Roger, expressing his love and commitment to her, others anonymous and threatening. Each note painted a picture of a woman caught in a web of fear and obsession.

Harry pulled out a forensic report and laid it on the table. "Look at this. The brutality of Dawn's death is chillingly different but still significant. Roger was killed with a monopod through the chest, while Dawn and David were hit from behind and then mutilated. Despite the different methods, the precision and personal nature of both attacks suggest the same killer. The level of violence and the intimate, targeted approach in both cases indicate someone who had a deep, personal connection to both victims."

Tom nodded, "The killer's method might vary, but the underlying rage and intent are consistent. They wanted to make sure their actions sent a clear message, leaving no doubt about their personal vendetta."

Harry's eyes lit up with a sudden realisation. "Margaret's jealousy and rage make perfect sense now. She found out about the affair, and her world fell apart. But to go from jealousy to murder... we need concrete evidence."

Tom leaned back, his mind racing. "We need to place her at the scenes. Witnesses, security footage, anything that can physically tie her to the murders."

Harry nodded, determination etched on her face. "We're getting closer, Tom. We just need to find that one piece of evidence that will tie it all together."

As they delved deeper into the case files, a palpable sense of urgency filled the room. They knew they were on the verge of a breakthrough, but time was not on their side. The killer was still out there, and the clock was ticking.

Harry's inner monologue echoed in her mind, "We're so close. Margaret's jealousy and rage make sense now. We just need concrete evidence to tie her to both murders. For David, for Dawn, for Roger, for justice."

The evidence room, with its dim lighting and dusty shelves, seemed to close in around them as they worked tirelessly, the weight of the case pressing down on their shoulders. Every photograph, every note, every report brought them one step closer to the truth. But until they had irrefutable evidence, the case remained a haunting puzzle, its pieces scattered in the shadows.

Hours passed as they meticulously combed through the evidence, their minds sharp despite the fatigue that gnawed at them. Harry's eyes fell on a small, inconspicuous box tucked away on a lower shelf. She pulled it out and opened it, revealing a collection of personal items that had belonged to Dawn.

Among the items was a small, silver locket. Harry opened it carefully, revealing two photographs inside—one of Roger, the other of Dawn. The significance of the locket was clear; it was a token of their secret love.

Tom looked over her shoulder, his expression thoughtful. "Sentimental value. It's the little things that matter. If we can find something like this at Margaret's house…"

Harry nodded, closing the locket and setting it aside. "We need to search Margaret's house again. Thoroughly. There might be something there that we missed the first time."

As they continued their review, they stumbled upon another crucial piece of evidence—an email exchange between Roger and Dawn. The emails were filled with plans for their future together, discussing the possibility of Roger leaving Margaret and starting a new life with Dawn.

"This is it, Tom," Harry said, her voice filled with conviction. "This email exchange shows that they were serious about their relationship. Margaret finding out about this would have driven her over the edge."

Tom agreed, his eyes scanning the printed emails. "We need to find out if Margaret saw these. If she did, it's another nail in the coffin."

Their determination grew with each piece of evidence they uncovered. The puzzle was slowly coming together, and the picture it formed was one of betrayal, jealousy, and cold-blooded murder.

Harry and Tom knew they had to move quickly. The pieces were falling into place, but they needed to act before the trail went cold. They packed up the evidence, their minds already racing ahead to their next steps.

As they left the dim confines of the evidence room, the weight of the case still pressed heavily upon them. But they were more determined than ever to see justice served. The connections between David, Dawn, Roger, and Margaret were becoming clearer, and they were closing in on the truth.

The corridors of the police station seemed brighter as they walked with purpose, their steps echoing with resolve. They had a plan, and they would not rest until the killer was brought to justice.

In Harry's mind, the pieces of the puzzle continued to shift and align. "We're getting closer," she thought. "Margaret's jealousy and rage make sense now. We just need concrete evidence to tie her to all three murders. And we will find it."

As they exited the police station, the cool evening air was a stark contrast to the stuffy evidence room. The stars began to twinkle in the twilight sky, a silent witness to the unfolding drama. Harry and Tom knew that the road ahead would be challenging, but they were ready to face whatever came their way.

The case was far from over, but they were closer than ever to uncovering the truth. With renewed determination, they set off into the night, ready to follow the trail of evidence wherever it might lead.

The evidence room had given up its secrets, but it was the detectives' relentless pursuit of justice that would ultimately bring the case to a close. And as they continued their investigation, they knew that the answers they sought were within their grasp. All they needed was that final piece of the puzzle to bring the killer to justice and bring peace to the memories of Dawn, David and Roger.

Chapter 29 The Tension Unravels

The morning sun hung low in the sky, casting a golden hue over the quaint streets of Taunton. Harry and Tom walked briskly through the bustling town, their eyes scanning for familiar faces among the crowds gathered for the Flower Show. The air was filled with the scent of blooming flowers and the hum of excited chatter.

Their first stop was the local tea-room, a popular spot where members of the Flower Show committee often took breaks. As they entered, the familiar smell of fries and burgers greeted them. They spotted Clara Bennett, the rising star in macro flower photography, seated in a corner booth, her camera bag slung over her shoulder.

Harry and Tom approached her, and Clara looked up, her eyes widening slightly at the sight of the detectives. "Detectives, what brings you here?"

"We're looking into Roger Morgan's, Dawn Menzies and David Walker's murders" Harry began, sliding into the seat across from her. "We need to ask you a few questions."

Clara nodded, her expression serious. "Of course, anything I can do to help."

Tom sat next to Harry, pulling out his notepad. "We're particularly interested in Margaret Morgan and her interactions with others. Did you ever notice anything unusual about her behaviour?"

Clara hesitated for a moment, then spoke quietly, "Margaret has always been... complicated. She had a sharp tongue and wasn't afraid to voice her opinions, especially when it came to topics she didn't agree with."

"Such as?" Harry prompted.

"Margaret was quite vocal about her disapproval of certain lifestyles," Clara said, choosing her words carefully. "She was particularly homophobic. There was an incident last year when she found out that one of the flower show participants, Warren Smith, was gay. She made some rather unpleasant comments."

Tom's eyes narrowed. "Do you think her homophobia could have played a role in her actions?"

Clara shrugged. "It's hard to say, but it definitely fuelled a lot of her anger. She was very traditional, and anything that deviated from her view of 'normal' seemed to set her off."

Harry exchanged a glance with Tom, then turned back to Clara. "Do you know anyone else who might have had issues with Margaret? Anyone who might have seen or heard something that could help us?"

Clara thought for a moment. "You should talk to Peter and Sarah, the couple who run the local nursery. They've had their fair share of run-ins with Margaret over the years."

Harry and Tom thanked Clara and left the team room, heading towards the nursery. The sun was beginning to set, casting long shadows across the town. As they approached the nursery, they spotted Peter and Sarah, busy organising plants for the next day's sales.

"Peter, Sarah, do you have a moment?" Harry called out as they approached.

Peter, a tall man with a kind face, looked up and smiled. "Of course, detectives. What can we do for you?"

"We're looking into the murders of Roger Morgan, Dawn Menzies and David Walker," Tom explained. "We've heard that you might have some insights into Margaret Morgan's behaviour."

Sarah, a petite woman with a warm demeanour, nodded. "Margaret was a difficult woman. She often clashed with people, especially those who didn't fit into her narrow view of the world."

"Did she ever say anything to you specifically?" Harry asked.

Sarah sighed. "Last year, she found out that Peter and I were friends with Warren Smith. She accused us of trying to corrupt the flower show by associating with him. It was ridiculous, but she was very adamant about it."

Peter added, "She even tried to get David banned from participating. She claimed his presence was 'inappropriate' and 'offensive' to the traditional values of the show."

Harry and Tom listened intently, noting the deep-seated prejudice that Margaret harboured. "Did you ever hear her make any threats against Roger or Dawn?" Tom asked.

Peter shook his head. "Not directly, but she often spoke about how disappointed she was in Roger. She believed he was straying from their marriage vows, and she blamed Dawn for it."

Sarah added, "Margaret once told me that she would do whatever it took to protect her marriage.

At the time, I thought she meant she would try to work things out with Roger, but now..."

Harry and Tom thanked Peter and Sarah, leaving the nursery with a clearer picture of Margaret's motives. They headed back to the station, their minds racing with the new information.

Back at the station, Harry and Tom sat at their cluttered table in the evidence room, sifting through the documents and files related to the case. The dim light and musty smell of paper and dust filled the room as they worked tirelessly, determined to find the final piece of the puzzle.

"Let's go through these emails and documents again," Harry said, pulling out a stack of papers. "We might have missed something that ties Margaret directly to the murders."

Tom nodded, flipping through the files. "Agreed. Her connection to Roger and Dawn is too significant to ignore."

As they examined the documents, Harry's eyes fell on an old email exchange between Roger and Margaret. She read aloud, "Roger, I know what you've been doing with that woman. You're making a fool of me, and I won't stand for it. If you don't end it, I will."

Tom's eyes widened. "That's pretty clear. She knew about the affair and was angry enough to do something about it."

Harry continued reading, "Margaret's response: 'Don't you dare threaten me, Roger. I have more power over you than you think. End it with her, or I will make sure you regret it.'"

Tom leaned back in his chair, his mind racing. "This is it, Harry. This is the proof we need. She was angry, felt betrayed, and was willing to do anything to protect her marriage."

Harry nodded, her face set with determination. "We need to approach Margaret carefully. We can't let her know we're onto her. If she senses we're closing in, she might try to run or destroy evidence."

Tom agreed. "We should start by questioning her again, but this time, we need to be subtle. We'll ask about her relationship with Roger and Dawn, but we won't show our hand just yet."

Harry thought for a moment. "We could also look into her movements on the nights of the murders again. Maybe there's something we missed, some detail that can place her at the scene."

Tom picked up the phone and dialled the number for the station's tech team. "Let's get a thorough review of any surveillance footage near Margaret's house and the flower show. We need to see if she was anywhere near the crime scenes."

Harry nodded, feeling a surge of determination. "We're getting closer, Tom. We just need to keep pushing. Margaret's jealousy and rage make sense now. We just need concrete evidence to tie her to both murders."

As they waited for the tech team's report, Harry and Tom continued to comb through the emails and documents, their minds sharp despite the fatigue that gnawed at them. The evidence room, with its dim lighting and dusty shelves, seemed to close in around them as they worked tirelessly, the weight of the case pressing down on their shoulders.

Every photograph, every note, every report brought them one step closer to the truth. But until they had irrefutable evidence, the case remained a haunting puzzle, its pieces scattered in the shadows.

Hours passed, and the phone finally rang. Tom answered, listening intently to the report from the tech team. He hung up and turned to Harry, his expression grim but resolute. "They found footage of Margaret near the flower show grounds on the night of Dawn's murder. She was seen driving away from the area shortly after the estimated time of death."

Harry's eyes widened. "That's it, Tom. We've got her. Now we just need to bring her in for questioning without alerting her."

Chapter 30 Justice at Last

Detective Inspector Harry Lambert and Detective Sergeant Tom Reed sat across from Stephen in the small, dimly lit conference room at the Taunton police station. The air was thick with tension, the gravity of the situation hanging heavily between them. Stephen's eyes darted nervously from Harry to Tom, trying to grasp the full extent of what they were asking him to do.

"Stephen," Harry began, her tone gentle but firm, "we need your help to bring Margaret Morgan to justice. We believe she's responsible for Roger's murder, but we need solid evidence. We need her to confess, or at least incriminate herself, and we think you might be the key to making that happen."

Stephen swallowed hard, his mind reeling. "But why me? Why would she come after me?"

Tom leaned forward, his gaze steady and reassuring. "Margaret sees you as a threat. You've been vocal about your suspicions regarding Roger's death, and you've had public disagreements with her in the past. She's aware that you're not convinced by the story she's been spinning. If she believes you're working on something that could expose her, she might make a move."

Harry nodded. "We want to use that to our advantage. We need you to lure her out, get her to reveal her true intentions. We'll equip you with a hidden microphone and camera, and we'll be monitoring the entire time. If things go wrong, we'll be there to step in."

Stephen's mind raced. The idea of confronting Margaret terrified him, but the thought of letting her get away with murder was even worse. He took a deep breath, trying to steady his nerves. "How exactly do you plan to do this?"

Harry and Tom exchanged a glance, and then Harry spoke. "We'll create a scenario where Margaret believes you have new evidence about Roger's death. You'll invite her to your studio under the pretence of discussing a new photography project, something that would naturally pique her interest given her connections in the community. Once she's there, you need to steer the conversation towards Roger and subtly imply that you have information that could be damaging to her."

Tom added, "It's crucial that you remain calm and collected. Margaret is cunning, and if she senses a trap, she might bolt. But if she believes she has the upper hand, she might let her guard down and say something incriminating."

Stephen felt a cold sweat break out on his forehead. The plan was risky, and the thought of facing Margaret sent chills down his spine. But he knew he couldn't back down. Roger had been a friend, and he deserved justice. "Alright," he said, his voice steady despite his fear. "I'll do it."

Harry gave him a reassuring smile. "Thank you, Stephen. We'll be with you every step of the way. Let's go over the details once more, make sure everything is in place."

As they discussed the plan, the reality of what lay ahead began to sink in. Stephen would be the bait, drawing Margaret into a carefully constructed trap. The fear gnawed at him, but so did a fierce determination. This was his chance to bring the truth to light, to ensure that Roger's killer faced justice. He would face the darkness, not just for Roger, but for himself and the community that had been overshadowed by Margaret's malevolence.

The following evening, Stephen sat in his studio, preparing for the confrontation. He carefully positioned the hidden microphone and camera, ensuring they were well concealed yet effective. The studio, usually a place of creativity and solace, now felt like a stage set for a perilous performance.

He rehearsed his lines, practicing how to steer the conversation, how to draw Margaret in without raising suspicion. The fear lingered, but it was tempered by a growing resolve. He knew what he had to do.

As the appointed time drew near, he felt his anxiety spike. He took a deep breath, recalling Harry's and Tom's reassurances. They were nearby, monitoring everything, ready to step in if needed.

The atmosphere outside was eerily calm, the silence broken only by the occasional rustle of leaves. The seclusion of the studio, once a source of inspiration, now felt oppressive, amplifying the tension that gripped him.

In a surveillance van parked a safe distance from the studio, Harry and Tom watched the live feed from Stephen's hidden camera. The van was filled with equipment, screens displaying various angles of the studio and its surroundings. Harry's eyes were glued to the monitors, every muscle in her body tense with anticipation.

"Stephen's doing great so far," Tom remarked, his voice low and steady. "We just need to keep our eyes peeled for any sign of trouble."

Harry nodded, her focus unbroken. "He's braver than he knows. Let's just hope Margaret takes the bait."

They watched as Stephen paced the studio, his nervous energy palpable even through the screens. Every second felt like an eternity, the tension building as they awaited Margaret's arrival. The plan was in motion, and now all they could do was wait and hope that their trap would spring shut, bringing an end to the dark chapter that had overshadowed their community.

Stephen's photography studio is a blend of modernity and vintage charm, reflecting his artistic vision. The spacious room is filled with natural light pouring in through large, industrial-style windows, casting long shadows on the polished wooden floors. The walls are adorned with a mix of Stephen's works—black and white portraits, vibrant landscapes, and candid shots of everyday life—each framed meticulously and hung with care.

In one corner of the studio stands a large, antique mahogany desk cluttered with photography equipment: lenses, cameras, and stacks of glossy prints. A plush leather couch and a few comfortable chairs are arranged near the windows, creating a cozy area for clients to sit and admire Stephen's work.

Stephen paces nervously around the studio, occasionally glancing at the clock on the wall. Harry and Tom are hidden in a back room, their presence kept secret to spring the trap on Margaret.

Stephen has arranged to meet Margaret under the guise of discussing a photography project, aware that this meeting is a dangerous gambit to draw her out.

The studio was dimly lit, the only light coming from the large windows that framed the sunset, casting a warm glow over the room. Margaret Morgan stepped inside, her heels clicking on the wooden floor, the sound echoing in the otherwise silent space. She was dressed impeccably, a stark contrast to the turmoil inside her.

Stephen was sitting at his desk, a pile of photographs spread out in front of him. He looked up as Margaret entered, his eyes narrowing slightly. He stood up, his movements deliberate and measured.

"Margaret," he greeted, his voice calm but with an undercurrent of something she couldn't quite place. "Thank you for coming."

"You said you had something important to discuss," Margaret replied, her tone equally measured. She took a step closer, her eyes flicking to the photographs on the desk.

"Yes," Stephen said, a faint smile playing on his lips. "I found something that might shed some light on Roger's death."

Margaret's heart skipped a beat. "What do you mean?" she asked, her voice barely above a whisper.

Stephen picked up a photograph and held it out to her. "This was taken the night before Roger died. Look closely."

Margaret took the photograph, her hands trembling slightly. It showed Roger in a heated argument with someone whose face was partially obscured. Her breath caught in her throat.

"I think you know who that is," Stephen said softly.

Margaret's eyes widened. "You think...?" she trailed off, unable to finish the sentence.

"I think it's time we stop pretending, Margaret," Stephen said, his voice hardening. "I know about Dawn's affair with Roger. And I know how you felt about his...lifestyle."

Margaret's face paled. "What are you implying?"

Stephen stepped closer, his gaze piercing. "I'm implying that you had a very strong motive to kill Roger, Dawn, and David."

Margaret's facade cracked, her expression twisting with anger and fear. "You don't know anything," she hissed.

"Oh, but I do," Stephen replied, his voice low and dangerous. "You see, Margaret, I have my own secrets. And I've been watching you very closely."

Margaret's eyes darted around the room, looking for an escape. "You disgust me," she spat. "Your kind is an abomination before God."

Stephen's expression remained impassive. "Your hatred blinded you, Margaret. It drove you to do terrible things."

Margaret's hands clenched into fists. "Roger was going to leave me," she said, her voice breaking. "For that...that tramp. And you...you're no better. You corrupt everything you touch."

Stephen took another step closer, his voice barely above a whisper. "And so you killed them all. To protect your precious reputation. But it didn't work, did it? Because now everyone knows what you really are."

Margaret's composure shattered. "Yes," she screamed. "I killed them. Roger, Dawn, David. They all deserved it. Roger for his betrayal, Dawn for seducing him, and David for being a raving homosexual. And you...you're next."

In a sudden, swift motion, Margaret pulls out the knife and lunges at Stephen. He stumbles backward, knocking over a tripod as he tries to evade her attack. The studio is suddenly filled with the chaotic sound of crashing equipment and frantic footsteps.

Just as Margaret raises the knife again, the back room door bursts open with a resounding crash. Harry and Tom rush in, their expressions a mixture of determination and urgency.

"Margaret, drop the knife!" Harry commands, her voice cutting through the tension like a blade.

Margaret's eyes flick to Harry and Tom, but the fury in her gaze remains fixed on Stephen. "He ruined everything," she hisses, the knife trembling in her hand.

"Margaret, it's over," Tom says, his voice calm yet firm. "Put the knife down. We can talk this out."

"Talk?" Margaret laughs, a harsh, brittle sound. "There's nothing left to talk about. You don't understand! He was supposed to be mine!"

"Margaret, listen to me," Harry interjects, stepping forward slightly. "This isn't the way. Think about what you're doing. There's no going back from this."

Stephen, still on the floor, inches away from Margaret, his eyes wide with fear and desperation. "Please, Margaret," he pleads. "You don't have to do this."

Margaret's grip on the knife tightens, her knuckles turning white. "You think you can just destroy my life and walk away?" she shrieks. "No, Stephen. You'll pay for what you've done!"

Margaret hesitates for a fraction of a second, then turns and bolts for the door. Harry and Tom give chase, yelling for her to stop. She races through the streets of Taunton, her breaths coming in ragged gasps as she pushes herself to run faster.

The bustling evening crowd parts in surprise as Margaret sprints past, with Harry and Tom hot on her heels. The detectives weave through the pedestrians, their focus unyielding as they pursue the fleeing woman.

Margaret's eyes dart around, searching for a way to lose her pursuers. She turns sharply into a narrow alleyway, her feet pounding against the cobblestones. The alley is dark and cluttered with trash bins and discarded boxes, but she navigates it with desperate agility.

"Stop, Margaret!" Harry yells, her voice echoing off the brick walls. "You can't get away!"

Margaret ignores the command, her mind racing as fast as her feet. She can hear the footsteps of the detectives growing closer, the adrenaline fuelling her frantic escape. She bursts out of the alley and into a quieter side street, glancing over her shoulder to gauge the distance.

Tom, slightly ahead of Harry, spots her hesitation and quickens his pace. "We're right behind you, Margaret! Don't make this worse!"

Margaret's heart pounds in her chest as she sees a small park up ahead. She makes a beeline for it, hoping the trees and pathways will provide some cover. As she enters the park, the dim light of the street lamps casts long shadows, adding to the eerie atmosphere.

She dashes through the park, weaving between the trees, her breaths coming in ragged gasps. Harry and Tom are relentless, their determination unshaken. They follow her into the park, their eyes locked on her fleeing figure.

Margaret darts down narrow alleyways and across busy roads, her knowledge of the town giving her a slight advantage. She barrels past market stalls, upsetting displays of flowers and produce, creating obstacles in her wake.

Harry and Tom navigate the chaos with practiced ease, their determination driving them forward. The chase takes them through the historic centre of Taunton, past the ancient timber-framed shops and the majestic presence of Taunton Minster church.

Margaret's breath comes in ragged gasps as she pushes herself to keep moving. She ducks into another alley, hoping to lose her pursuers, but Harry and Tom are relentless, their footsteps echoing off the narrow walls.

As she exits the alley, she finds herself in a crowded square, the evening market in full swing. Vendors shout their wares, and the air is filled with the mingled scents of fresh bread and ripe fruit. Margaret ploughs through the throng, knocking over a display of apples that scatter across the cobblestones.

"Stop her!" Tom yells to the crowd, but people are too startled to react quickly.

Margaret's pace falters as she reaches the edge of the square and spots Taunton Minster church looming ahead. The ancient structure, with its towering spire and stained-glass windows, seems to watch over the chase with silent judgment. She darts around the side of the church, heading for the gardens behind it.

Harry and Tom are close behind, their progress unhindered by the chaos Margaret left in her wake. "She's heading for Goodlands Gardens!" Harry shouts, her voice strained but focused.

Margaret's stamina begins to wane as she reaches Goodlands Gardens, a sprawling park known for its manicured lawns and serene atmosphere. She dashes through the entrance, her pace slowing as exhaustion starts to set in.

Harry and Tom are close behind, their breaths heavy but their resolve unbroken. The park's winding paths and dense foliage provide a challenging terrain, but they press on, driven by the need to apprehend her.

Margaret stumbles as she navigates the winding paths, her vision blurring from fatigue. She pushes through a cluster of bushes, emerging onto a picturesque lawn dotted with sculptures and flowerbeds. The serenity of the scene contrasts sharply with the chaos of the chase.

Harry and Tom burst through the same bushes moments later, their eyes scanning the area for any sign of her. Tom spots a flash of movement near a large oak tree and points. "There!"

Margaret, sensing she's been spotted, musters her remaining strength and sprints towards a condemned wooden bridge spanning the river. Her footsteps are heavy and uneven, her breath coming in short, painful gasps.

"Margaret, stop!" Harry calls out, her voice echoing across the park. "You're only making it worse!"

Margaret's foot caught on a loose stone, and she tumbled to the ground, her hands scraping against the rough path. She cries out in pain but forces herself to her feet, limping towards the bridge.

Harry and Tom close the distance rapidly, their eyes locked on Margaret's struggling form. Just as she reaches the middle of the bridge, her legs give out, and she collapses in a heap, unable to go any further.

Harry reaches her first, crouching down and placing a hand on her shoulder. "Margaret, it's over," she says gently. "You need to come with us."

Margaret looks up, her face streaked with tears and dirt. "I... I can't...," she gasps, her voice barely a whisper.

Tom arrives and kneels beside Harry, producing a pair of handcuffs. "We're taking you in, Margaret," he says firmly but kindly. "You need to answer for what you've done."

Margaret doesn't resist as Tom secures her wrists, the fight drained from her body. "I didn't want this," she murmurs. "I just wanted... things to be different."

"We understand," Harry says, helping her to her feet. "But this isn't the way."

As they lead Margaret back across the bridge, the park seems to hold its breath, the tranquillity returning as the chase comes to an end. The sound of sirens grows louder, signalling the arrival of backup.

Margaret walks between Harry and Tom, her steps unsteady but resigned. "What will happen to me?" she asks, her voice small and fearful.

"You'll get a fair trial," Tom replies. "And you'll have the chance to tell your side of the story."

Margaret nods weakly, tears continuing to fall. "I'm sorry," she whispers again, her voice filled with regret.

Harry and Tom guide her towards the waiting police cars, the weight of the evening's events heavy on their minds. As they approach, officers step forward to take Margaret into custody.

"Good work," one of the officers says to Harry and Tom. "We've got it from here."

"Good work, detectives," one of the officers says to Harry and Tom, his tone professional and respectful. "We'll take it from here."

Harry nods, watching as Margaret is carefully helped to her feet by the officers. They guide her, still handcuffed, towards the waiting police cars, ensuring she doesn't stumble or fall. The blue lights of the patrol cars flash intermittently, casting a rhythmic glow over the park.

Margaret's face is a mixture of resignation and exhaustion, her earlier defiance replaced by a weary acceptance. She glances back at Harry and Tom, her eyes filled with a complex mix of emotions – regret, sorrow, and a glimmer of relief that the chase is finally over.

The officers lead Margaret to one of the cars, opening the door and helping her into the back seat with care. They close the door securely, double-checking the locks before stepping back.

As Margaret sits in the car, she leans her head back against the seat, closing her eyes. The weight of the night's events seems to press down on her, her shoulders sagging under the burden.

Harry and Tom exchange a look of weary relief, their expressions reflecting the intensity of the chase and the emotional toll it has taken. "It's finally over," Harry says softly, her voice tinged with exhaustion and a hint of satisfaction.

Tom nods, placing a reassuring hand on her shoulder. "You did great, Harry. We both did."

They stand together for a moment, taking in the calm that has returned to Goodlands Gardens. The tranquillity of the gardens is a stark contrast to the chaos of the chase, and the peaceful surroundings offer a brief respite from the tension.

As they turn to leave, the patrol cars remain parked for a few more moments, the officers ensuring everything is in order and that Margaret is secure. The blue lights continue to flash, a silent signal that justice is being served.

Harry and Tom walk away from the scene, their steps slow and deliberate. The sun sets behind them, casting long shadows that stretch across the manicured lawns. The park, once the scene of a desperate chase, now seems to breathe a sigh of relief along with them, the echoes of the pursuit fading into memory.

Chapter 31 Shadows Lifted

The night was quiet, the chaos of the chase having given way to a still, almost eerie calm. The streets of Taunton were empty, the only sounds the occasional distant bark of a dog and the whispering breeze that rustled the leaves. Harry and Tom drove in silence, their thoughts occupied by the events of the evening and the new case that awaited them.

But first, they needed to check on Stephen. He had been through a lot, and they wanted to ensure he was safe. As they approached the photography studio, the familiar façade came into view, bathed in the soft glow of the streetlights. The building stood silent, the windows dark.

Harry knocked on the door, her knuckles rapping against the wood in a firm but gentle rhythm. "Stephen, it's Harry and Tom. Are you alright?"

There was a brief silence, then the sound of footsteps approaching. The door creaked open, and Stephen's face appeared in the doorway. He looked tired, his eyes shadowed with worry, but he managed a small smile.

"Detectives," he said, stepping aside to let them in. "I wasn't expecting to see you again so soon. Is everything alright?"

Harry nodded, stepping into the studio. The familiar smell of photographic chemicals and the sight of equipment scattered around greeted her. "We just wanted to check on you, make sure you're okay after everything that happened."

Stephen closed the door behind them, locking it with a sense of finality. "I appreciate that," he said, leading them into the main studio area. "It's been a rough night, but I'm holding up."

Tom glanced around the studio, his eyes taking in the various photographs and equipment. "It's understandable. Margaret's actions took everyone by surprise."

Stephen nodded, running a hand through his hair. "I never thought she would go that far. The hatred in her eyes... it was terrifying."

Harry placed a reassuring hand on his shoulder. "You did the right thing, Stephen. You helped us bring her to justice."

Stephen sighed, sinking into a chair. "I just wish it didn't have to end like this. So much pain, so much loss."

Tom leaned against the wall, his expression thoughtful. "Margaret was driven by emotions she couldn't control. It's tragic, but at least now she can't hurt anyone else."

Stephen looked up, his eyes meeting Tom's. "I suppose you're right. Still, it's hard to process."

Harry walked over to a nearby table, picking up a photograph of Roger and Dawn. "They were both talented," she said softly. "It's a shame their lives were cut short."

Stephen's gaze softened as he looked at the photo. "They were. Roger was a mentor to me, and Dawn... she was a bright light in a dark world."

The room fell silent, the weight of their shared grief settling over them. After a moment, Stephen stood up, taking a deep breath. "Thank you for coming to check on me. It means a lot."

Harry nodded, her expression warm. "We're here to help, Stephen. If you need anything, don't hesitate to call."

Tom pushed off the wall, straightening his jacket. "Take care, Stephen. And try to get some rest."

As they made their way to the door, Stephen walked them out, locking the door securely behind them. The night air was cool, a gentle breeze ruffling their hair as they stepped onto the street.

"Think he'll be alright?" Tom asked, his voice low.

Harry glanced back at the studio, the light inside now extinguished. "I think so. He's strong. He'll find a way to move forward."

They walked to their car, the engine purring to life as they drove away from the studio. The night stretched out before them, full of uncertainties and new challenges. But they were ready, their partnership a steady beacon in the darkness.

Chapter 32 The Truth Unveiled

The dimly lit interview room cast long shadows across the sterile walls, a stark contrast to the vibrancy of the Taunton Flower Show. Margaret sat at the metal table, her wrists still bearing the faint red marks from the handcuffs. Her eyes, once filled with a spark of life, now bore the weight of secrets and remorse.

Detective Inspector Harry Lambert and Detective Sergeant Tom Reed entered the room, their footsteps echoing ominously. The air was thick with tension, the kind that only comes when the truth is about to unravel. Harry took a seat directly across from Margaret, her eyes sharp and penetrating, while Tom stood to the side, his presence a silent reminder of the gravity of the situation.

"Margaret," Harry began, her voice steady but not unkind, "we need to understand why. Help us understand why Roger, why Dawn, and why David."

Margaret's gaze faltered, her hands trembling slightly as she clasped them together on the cold metal table. She took a deep breath, the words seeming to fight their way out of her throat. "I didn't want to do it, you know," she whispered, her voice barely audible. "But they left me no choice."

Harry leaned in, her expression softening ever so slightly. "Tell us about it, Margaret. Start from the beginning."

Margaret's eyes glazed over, as if she were seeing the events unfold in front of her. "Roger was obsessed with his photography. It wasn't just a passion; it was his life. He spent every waking moment on it, and I was just...there. An afterthought. Then I found out about his affair with Dawn. It was like a dagger to my heart. He didn't just neglect me; he betrayed me."

Tears welled up in her eyes, and she swiped at them angrily. "But it wasn't just about the affair. It was about the lies, the deceit. He made me feel worthless, like I was nothing without him. And Dawn... Dawn was the embodiment of everything I wasn't. Young, beautiful, confident. She took him away from me."

Harry nodded, encouraging her to continue. "And David?"

"David," Margaret's voice hardened, "David was a parasite. He latched onto Roger's success, tried to take it for himself. He was always there, always whispering in Roger's ear, undermining him. They all did. They all drove him to the edge, and I couldn't stand it anymore."

Tom finally spoke, his voice measured. "So you decided to take matters into your own hands?"

Margaret's eyes met his, a fire of defiance and desperation burning within them. "Yes. I did. I couldn't watch them destroy him. They took everything from us. Our love, our life, our future. I wanted them to feel the pain, the betrayal, the loss."

Harry's voice was gentle but firm. "You know this doesn't justify murder, Margaret. You know that."

Margaret's shoulders sagged, the weight of her actions pressing down on her. "I know. But I couldn't see any other way. I was blinded by rage, by hurt. I wanted them to pay, to suffer as I had suffered."

The room fell silent, the only sound the hum of the overhead light. Harry and Tom exchanged a glance, the enormity of Margaret's confession settling over them like a shroud.

"We're going to need a full statement," Harry said softly. "But for now, Margaret, know that you've done the right thing by telling us the truth."

Margaret nodded numbly, the fight drained from her. As they escorted her from the room, the cold reality of her actions hung heavy in the air, a tragic testament to the darkness that had consumed her.

Margaret was led back to her cell, the weight of her confession settling heavily on her shoulders. Harry and Tom remained in the interview room, the silence between them thick with unspoken thoughts. Harry finally broke the silence, her voice barely above a whisper.

"She snapped, Tom. The betrayal, the constant neglect, the humiliation. It was all too much for her."

Tom nodded, his expression grave. "I understand why she did it, but it doesn't change the fact that she took three lives. We need to piece together exactly how she did it, and why she chose those particular victims."

Harry sighed, rubbing her temples. "Let's start with Roger. We know he was her husband, and he betrayed her with Dawn. But what about Dawn and David? Why did she go after them?"

Tom flipped open his notebook, scanning his notes. "Dawn was the other woman. She was young, beautiful, everything Margaret felt she had lost. And David... he latched onto Roger's success, tried to take it for himself. Margaret saw him as a parasite, someone who was undermining Roger's achievements."

Harry nodded slowly, her mind working through the details. "So she saw them all as threats, as people who were destroying her and Roger's life together. But how did she manage to kill them? She's not exactly physically imposing."

Tom frowned, considering. "She must have planned it carefully, caught them off guard. Maybe she used Roger's photography equipment as weapons. The monopod, for instance. It's long and sturdy enough to be used as a weapon."

Harry's eyes widened slightly. "Of course. The monopod. She could have easily used it to kill Roger. But what about Dawn and David?"

Tom flipped to another page in his notebook. "Dawn was found with a stocking around her neck, strangled. But the coroner's report showed that she was actually killed by a blow to the head, likely from a cricket bat. And David... he was struck from behind and then pushed into the river. She used their own surroundings and their trust against them."

Harry shook her head, a mixture of awe and horror in her eyes. "She turned their passion into their demise. It's twisted, but it makes sense."

Tom closed his notebook, a sense of finality in his movements. "We need to get her full statement, find out exactly how she did it. But I think we have a pretty clear picture of what drove her to this point."

The next day, Harry and Tom returned to the interview room, prepared to get Margaret's full statement. She was brought in, looking even more haggard than before, her eyes haunted by the weight of her actions.

"Margaret," Harry began gently, "we need you to tell us exactly how you did it. We need to understand everything."

Margaret nodded slowly, her hands trembling as she clasped them together on the table. "I... I planned it all. I knew I couldn't overpower them physically, so I had to catch them off guard."

She took a deep breath, her eyes distant as she recounted the events. "I knew Roger would be at the park late, working on his photos. I took his monopod and waited for him. When he was focused on his camera, I... I hit him with it. Hard. He didn't see it coming."

Tears welled up in her eyes, but she pressed on. "Dawn... I knew she often worked late in her studio, alone. I waited for her there. She was so surprised to see me. I pretended I wanted to talk, to understand why she did what she did. She let her guard down. That's when I hit her with the cricket bat. She collapsed, and I... I used her stocking to strangle her, to make it look like that was the cause of death."

Her voice broke as she continued. "And David... I waited until he was alone too. I followed him to the river. He didn't hear me coming. I struck him from behind, hard, and then I pushed him into the river. I wanted them all to feel the pain, the betrayal, the helplessness that I felt."

Harry leaned in closer, her eyes narrowing slightly. "Margaret, there's one more thing we need to understand. Why did you... mutilate Dawn's body? Why did you cut off her breasts?"

Margaret's eyes filled with tears again, but there was a fierce, almost wild look in them now. "Dawn represented everything I had lost. She was young, beautiful, confident. She had Roger's love, his attention. Cutting off her breasts... it was my way of taking back some of that power. Of destroying the symbol of what she had that I no longer did. It was my way of making her suffer, of making her feel the pain and humiliation I felt every single day."

Harry and Tom exchanged a glance, the enormity of Margaret's twisted logic settling over them. Harry finally spoke, her voice gentle but firm. "Margaret, we understand your pain, but what you did was monstrous. You took three lives in your quest for revenge. You need to understand that there will be consequences."

Harry and Tom listened in silence, the gravity of Margaret's confession settling over them. Harry finally spoke, her voice soft but firm. "Margaret, what you did was wrong. You took three lives. But understanding why you did it, and how, helps us. It helps us make sure something like this doesn't happen again."

Margaret nodded, her eyes filled with a mixture of remorse and relief. "I know. I know what I did was wrong. But I couldn't see any other way. I was consumed by my anger, my hurt. I wanted them to pay."

The interview continued for hours, Margaret detailing every aspect of her actions, her motives. By the end, Harry and Tom had a complete picture of the tragic events that had led to the murders of Roger, Dawn, and David.

As Margaret was led back to her cell, Harry and Tom remained in the interview room, the weight of the case settling over them. "It's done," Harry said quietly. "We have her confession. We know why she did it."

Tom nodded, but his expression was troubled. "It's not just about why she did it, Harry. It's about how she got to that point. The isolation, the neglect, the betrayal. It all built up until she snapped."

Harry sighed, rubbing her temples. "I know. It's a reminder of how fragile people can be, how easily they can be pushed over the edge."

Tom looked at his partner, his expression serious. "We did our job, Harry. We got the truth. But this case... it's a reminder that sometimes, the line between victim and perpetrator is a lot thinner than we think."

Harry nodded slowly, the truth of Tom's words settling over her. "You're right. Let's make sure we never forget that."

Epilogue

The fluorescent lights of the police station flickered slightly, casting a sterile glow over the room. Harry and Tom walked in, their footsteps echoing in the nearly empty space. The weight of the night's events pressed down on them, each step feeling heavier as they made their way to the CID office.

Inside, the murder board stood as a grim testament to the case they had just closed. Pictures of Roger, Dawn, and David were pinned alongside notes and timelines, the chaotic puzzle they had finally managed to piece together. Harry and Tom stood before it, their expressions reflecting the exhaustion and relief that only came from solving a difficult case.

Harry sighed, reaching up to remove the photographs. "It's always the same," she said, her voice soft. "Jealousy, betrayal, secrets. Human emotions are so predictable, yet they lead to such unpredictable outcomes."

Tom nodded, helping her take down the notes and sketches. "People get consumed by their emotions, and logic goes out the window. Margaret... she was driven by fear and hatred. It clouded everything else."

Reflecting on their journey, both detectives felt a profound sense of accomplishment. Yet, beyond the professional victory, there was a deeper, more personal triumph. When they first began the investigation, Harry and Tom were as different as night and day. Harry, with her intuitive leaps and emotional investment, often clashed with Tom's methodical and evidence-based approach. Their initial interactions were fraught with frustration and misunderstanding.

Harry thought back to those early days, remembering the heated arguments and the feeling that Tom didn't respect her insights. She had always trusted her gut, using her background in criminal psychology to get inside the minds of suspects. But Tom's insistence on following protocol and relying strictly on hard evidence had made her feel undervalued and isolated.

Tom, too, reflected on the beginning of the case. He remembered feeling exasperated with Harry's seemingly impulsive conclusions. He had prided himself on his meticulous nature, a trait honed through years of experience and an early career mistake that had taught him the importance of leaving no stone unturned. To him, Harry's approach seemed reckless and imprecise.

But as the investigation progressed, something changed. The discovery of Roger Morgan's secret life and the depth of Margaret's vendetta required them to combine their strengths. They found themselves in situations where Harry's psychological insights provided the key to understanding motives, while Tom's detailed evidence-gathering built a solid foundation for their case.

One pivotal moment stood out in Harry's mind. A late-night conversation in the quiet of the office, where she shared her personal reasons for becoming a detective. She spoke of a family tragedy that had driven her to seek justice for those who couldn't find it themselves. Tom, in turn, opened up about his early career, revealing a case that had gone wrong due to a lack of procedure. This exchange of vulnerabilities broke down the walls between them, fostering a new level of mutual respect.

They faced danger together, protecting Stephen and capturing Margaret in a tense showdown that tested their trust and reliance on each other. Harry's instincts and Tom's precision became two halves of a well-oiled machine, each making up for the other's weaknesses. Their partnership was no longer a reluctant compromise but a powerful alliance.

As they cleared down the board, they recounted the twists and turns of the case, each revelation that had brought them closer to the truth. The disjointed puzzle pieces of human emotion and motive slowly fell into place as they talked.

"She loved Roger," Harry said, placing the last photograph on the desk. "But she couldn't handle his infidelity, his disregard for her. And then there was the contempt she felt for his lifestyle, something she couldn't accept."

"Her hatred for Dawn and David was an extension of that," Tom added, folding up the timeline. "They were just collateral damage in her mind. Obstacles to her twisted sense of justice."

The room fell silent for a moment, the gravity of the situation settling in. They had brought justice to the victims, but the cost was high. Lives were shattered, and the echoes of the tragedy would linger for a long time.

Harry took a deep breath, glancing at the now-empty board. "It's hard to understand how someone can go so far. But I guess that's why we're here. To bring light to the darkness, no matter how deep it runs."

Tom placed a reassuring hand on her shoulder. "We did good, Harry. We brought her in. Now it's up to the courts to finish it."

Just as they were about to leave the office, the phone on Tom's desk rang, the shrill sound cutting through the quiet. They exchanged a glance, the familiar signal of another case bringing a mixture of anticipation and weariness.

Tom answered the phone, his expression shifting from curiosity to determination as he listened. He hung up and looked at Harry, his eyes reflecting the readiness they both felt.

"Looks like we've got another one," he said. "Suspicious death over at the caves of Wookey Hole. They need us there ASAP."

Harry nodded, grabbing her coat. "No rest for the wicked," she said with a wry smile. "Let's go see what's waiting for us."

They left the CID office, their minds already shifting gears to the new mystery. As they walked through the station, the familiar buzz of activity surrounded them, the lifeblood of the place that never truly slept.

Outside, the cool night air greeted them, a stark contrast to the warmth of the station. They headed to their car, the sense of closure from the previous case giving way to the anticipation of the next.

"Whatever it is," Harry said as she started the engine, "we'll face it together."

Tom nodded, a determined look in his eyes. "Always."

As they drove off into the night, the weight of their work was ever-present, but so was their resolve. The partnership between them, forged in the fires of countless cases, was their greatest strength. Together, they were ready to dive into the next mystery, knowing that whatever challenges lay ahead, they would face them head-on, side by side.

A Note from the Author

This novel is a work of fiction. While it is set against the backdrop of real locations in the county of Somerset, including but not limited to Taunton and Wookey Hole, all characters, incidents, and dialogue are entirely the product of the author's imagination.

Any resemblance to actual persons, living or deceased, or to real events, past or present, is purely coincidental. The fictional detectives, investigators, and residents portrayed herein are not intended to represent, parody, or impersonate any real individual.

Place names are used for atmospheric effect, and no implication is made about the character or activities of the real communities or individuals associated with them.

Printed in Great Britain
by Amazon